everybody
lies

everybody
lies

emily cavanagh

Bookouture

Published by Bookouture in 2020

An imprint of Storyfire Ltd.
Carmelite House
50 Victoria Embankment
London EC4Y 0DZ

www.bookouture.com

ISBN: 978-1-80019-089-4
eBook ISBN: 978-1-80019-088-7

To Nevah and Oliva—the center of my world.
To those who have lost this battle and to the ones they've left behind.

PROLOGUE

The crossing is slow-going. The beach is packed with snow, a thick crust of it left over from a week of storms. Layla's boots catch as she runs, the heels sinking into the ice. Even as her mind thinks *run*, her body will not cooperate. The snow, the drinks, the bulky winter coat, the cold air chafing at her lungs, all of these conspire against her, and she moves slowly along the water's edge. Her lip throbs, and she tastes the coppery flavor of her own blood.

He's behind her. She can't see him in the dark, but she feels his presence like a dark cloud gathering force. She hears the crunch of his boots, slower than her own crashing footsteps, but more confident, too. He knows this beach, this snowy climate. He's at ease in the icy darkness of Great Rock. She is just an intruder here, a foolish interloper who doesn't belong on a frigid island in the middle of winter. The waves lap at the snowy shoreline. The night is black, a starless sky, the slender scrap of moon hiding behind clouds.

Echoing in her mind is her mother's voice, chastising her. "You're reckless, Layla. You need to think first." Even as a little girl Layla had this problem, jumping head first into the neighborhood pool before she knew how to swim, knocking over someone else's block tower for no reason other than wanting to hear the crash. Then later, quitting jobs in anger, ordering too many sugar-sweet cocktails on a Saturday night, bringing home men that she regretted even before her clothes were off. "You need to think first, Layla," her mother's words echoed.

She will not return home. Even as she tries to run, even as her mind screams *escape*, even as she chokes in cold gulps of air that burn her lungs, she knows the ending. The fear that fills her body is like a trapped bird, flapping wildly into windows and walls in an effort to get free.

"Layla." He yells her name. His voice is absent of the anger she'd assumed. For a moment, she allows herself to hope. "Wait. I just want to talk."

She's tired. Her lungs aren't made for this watery air, each breath sharp with the frozen sea. She pictures her purse, its skinny red strap slung over the back of her chair. Down the road from the bar, he'd looked at her with kind eyes, but panic coursed through her at how close she'd come to getting caught. The nervous laugh had escaped without her consent. It was seeing his eyes after she laughed that frightened her. She should have gone to the hotel, but instead she'd run, away from the safety of downtown and toward the beach, a black no man's land. *Stupid, stupid.*

But his eyes had been kind, she reminds herself. Her legs are heavy and her boots are wet. And she's too tired to keep running.

She stops. The night is silent except for the steady crackle of his boots as he nears. He appears from the blackness, an apparition materializing out of the empty night sky. It's too dark to see his face, but she allows herself to hope his eyes are crinkling at the corners with a flicker of tenderness.

His hands around her neck take her by surprise, the raw strength contained within his fingers. Even as she fights, her heels scrabbling on the beach, hissing sounds escaping from her lips, she hears her mother's voice, the admonition of her whole life. "You need to think first, Layla."

No more thinking now.

PROLOGUE

The crossing is slow-going. The beach is packed with snow, a thick crust of it left over from a week of storms. Layla's boots catch as she runs, the heels sinking into the ice. Even as her mind thinks *run*, her body will not cooperate. The snow, the drinks, the bulky winter coat, the cold air chafing at her lungs, all of these conspire against her, and she moves slowly along the water's edge. Her lip throbs, and she tastes the coppery flavor of her own blood.

He's behind her. She can't see him in the dark, but she feels his presence like a dark cloud gathering force. She hears the crunch of his boots, slower than her own crashing footsteps, but more confident, too. He knows this beach, this snowy climate. He's at ease in the icy darkness of Great Rock. She is just an intruder here, a foolish interloper who doesn't belong on a frigid island in the middle of winter. The waves lap at the snowy shoreline. The night is black, a starless sky, the slender scrap of moon hiding behind clouds.

Echoing in her mind is her mother's voice, chastising her. "You're reckless, Layla. You need to think first." Even as a little girl Layla had this problem, jumping head first into the neighborhood pool before she knew how to swim, knocking over someone else's block tower for no reason other than wanting to hear the crash. Then later, quitting jobs in anger, ordering too many sugar-sweet cocktails on a Saturday night, bringing home men that she regretted even before her clothes were off. "You need to think first, Layla," her mother's words echoed.

She will not return home. Even as she tries to run, even as her mind screams *escape*, even as she chokes in cold gulps of air that burn her lungs, she knows the ending. The fear that fills her body is like a trapped bird, flapping wildly into windows and walls in an effort to get free.

"Layla." He yells her name. His voice is absent of the anger she'd assumed. For a moment, she allows herself to hope. "Wait. I just want to talk."

She's tired. Her lungs aren't made for this watery air, each breath sharp with the frozen sea. She pictures her purse, its skinny red strap slung over the back of her chair. Down the road from the bar, he'd looked at her with kind eyes, but panic coursed through her at how close she'd come to getting caught. The nervous laugh had escaped without her consent. It was seeing his eyes after she laughed that frightened her. She should have gone to the hotel, but instead she'd run, away from the safety of downtown and toward the beach, a black no man's land. *Stupid, stupid.*

But his eyes had been kind, she reminds herself. Her legs are heavy and her boots are wet. And she's too tired to keep running.

She stops. The night is silent except for the steady crackle of his boots as he nears. He appears from the blackness, an apparition materializing out of the empty night sky. It's too dark to see his face, but she allows herself to hope his eyes are crinkling at the corners with a flicker of tenderness.

His hands around her neck take her by surprise, the raw strength contained within his fingers. Even as she fights, her heels scrabbling on the beach, hissing sounds escaping from her lips, she hears her mother's voice, the admonition of her whole life. "You need to think first, Layla."

No more thinking now.

himself to throw out the one he'd had since he started playing in middle school. It's in a beautiful vintage case, leather with tarnished silver buckles and pockets on the back, picked up at a music store in Cambridge on a trip to Harvard Square.

I run my hand along the rough leather of the neck. It's smooth under my palm, the leather cracked and worn with handling and age. For years the case was a part of him, like a security blanket or teddy bear that a toddler takes everywhere. He brought the guitar to school every day, playing in the quadrangle at lunch or sneaking into the music room during study halls for an extra thirty minutes of practice. Even though I know he has his guitar at his new apartment in a new case, I doubt he plays every day, and it's been years since I heard him. But every night from middle school through high school, the twanging chords would drift downstairs, his soft voice barely audible through the closed door of his bedroom. Connor could play on a stage in front of a hundred people, but he was self-conscious to play when it was just me and Jack. Or maybe it was just Jack, because on the nights when his father worked late, Connor was more likely to play in the living room, not minding if I came and sat on the couch to listen.

I leave the catalogs on the bed with a sigh, knowing that they'll still be there a week later, whether Connor comes to do laundry or not. I have a nervous ache in my stomach, a cold damp dread that's been there all day. Before I even think about dinner, I slip into the bathroom to brush my hair and reapply blush and lip gloss. The plain face of a middle-aged woman stares back at me, limp hair, skin pale from another New England winter, dusky shadows under my eyes from restless nights sleeping alone. I add a quick swipe of mascara, for there's only so much I can do.

In the kitchen I survey the sparse pantry and settle on a can of lentil soup. One of the few nice things about this new separation from Jack is there's no need to cook. Jack is the one who likes big meals at the end of the day—a roast beef or chicken, mashed potatoes and green beans, even if it's just an ordinary Tuesday. I'm perfectly content with a salad or can of soup for dinner, and I haven't made much more than toast or grilled cheese in the month and a half he's been gone. Meals are quiet, and I've taken to eating in front of the television with the plate perched on my knees.

I don't eat much, too anxious to manage more than a few spoonfuls of soup. Tonight is the night we agreed to have "the talk." It's a trial separation, though neither of us has uttered those words, too formal and planned for his hasty departure.

If I could divide our marriage into a list of pros and cons, I don't know which side would be longer. Remembering to keep the kitchen tap dripping on these frigid days, shoveling my own car out after another snowstorm—these are the inconveniences of living alone. Focusing on unfamiliar noises in the middle of the night, wondering if I remembered to lock the door, the panic that grips me before I realize it's just the dog's thumping tail—this is the downfall of having depended on someone else for nearly all of my adult life.

Even if I were to tally up the list, how can *not having to cook dinner every night* compare to *I love him*? Because I do. Despite everything, I love him.

Thank God for Champ. His steady presence calms me, though I never gave the dog much attention before, a boxer-husky mix we got when Connor was in middle school. I was surprised how insistent Jack was that Champ stay with me. Though we all took care of him, he was Jack's dog, nosing Jack's palm when he came home from work, settling at his feet at the end of the day. Champ may have been Jack's dog, but he's taken his new role as my protector seriously, and the clicking of his nails on the wood floors follows me from room to room.

I rise from the counter and dump the soup in the trash, placing the bowl in the dishwasher as my phone beeps with an incoming text. It's a message from Jack. *Running late.*

"Of course you are," I mutter under my breath. Champ lets out a whimper, attuned to my mood.

It's the recurring flare of anger that's most confusing. The distance from Osprey to where Jack's staying in Heron is only a few miles, but it might as well be the mainland. From a distance, I can love and miss Jack. Up close, in real life, it's not that simple. My love chafes and burns, too hot to touch, always leaving a mark.

I sigh heavily, even though there's no one but Champ to hear me. I settle on the couch with a stack of new releases I brought home from the library and flip through the pile, finally selecting a vegetarian cookbook by a local author. I'll never make a single recipe in here, but it's the book that requires the least amount of focus. I took it out mostly for Evvy, thinking she might work some of the dishes into the menu for Petunia's, her catering business.

I didn't tell Evvy that Jack was coming over tonight, haven't told her that tonight may be the night when I find out if I'm getting a divorce. It's the type of thing that I imagine most women would share with their best friend, particularly when that friendship is as old as ours. Evvy is the only one I've told about the separation—not Connor, not my sister Shana in D.C., not my co-workers or other friends, only Evvy. Yet even with Evvy, I've told her only the basics, none of the details, in my typical dry-eyed fashion. I haven't fallen apart, haven't cried in front of her, haven't raged in anger. Sometimes I wonder if I've lived for too long with a cop, grown too accustomed to the stony reserve and matter-of-fact approach to life. I don't know if this is a character flaw or strength, this ability to rise up above emotion and get on with what needs to be done. Jack would say it's a strength while Evvy would argue it's a weakness. I suspect it's both.

Twenty-two years is a long time to be married, yet it's not so long that there are no surprises. I've never been more stunned than the night I came home from work to find a note from Jack saying he was subletting the Feldmans' place in Heron for the next few months. I stood in the kitchen and reread the note. It was only a few lines, carefully written in Jack's square print, and I wondered how many times he rewrote it before he got it just right. Or if it only took him one try.

Twenty-two years together, and I never actually believed our marriage might not survive. Until the night I came home to that note and realized it was a possibility. Standing in the kitchen, I was rocked by grief and anger and shock, but something else too, just the palest glimmer of anticipation, so unexpected and unfamiliar that it's easier to ignore.

The dog's ears perk up at the sound of the car, and Champ rises from his bed, body alert. There are footsteps on the front stairs and a heavy knock on the door.

"It's me, Caroline." Jack's voice is steady and familiar. Champ is already wagging his tail. I open the door and there's Jack, though he's in plain-clothes tonight. "You should lock that," he tells me, tipping his head toward the door. For the twenty-two years that we lived together, we only locked the door right before we went to sleep. This is Great Rock, an island of five thousand, where everyone is connected by three degrees of separation. I refuse to let the night-time fear swallow up my days too.

I ignore his comment. "You're late."

"Sorry. I got hung up at work." He stands awkwardly in the doorway, rubbing his knuckles. He glances around the house, our house, *his* house, the one he built with Cyrus the year we bought the land. I haven't changed anything. This is a trial separation after all, though with each day my anger seems to burn brighter, and it's difficult to imagine how we'll ever find our way back after this. Though it's also difficult to imagine the alternative.

"How are you?" I ask.

"Fine." He steps inside and his eyes flit around the kitchen, likely assessing it for damage or change. In the past month and a half, he's barely been to the house, and the few times he has come by, it's been for a quick retrieval of something he's forgotten—a pair of rain boots, or an extra shovel from the basement.

We cross the room. "Do you want a drink or anything?" I ask. There are options—both red and white wine and a half-full bottle of whiskey that Jack left behind.

"Maybe some tea?"

"Peppermint or lemon?"

"Lemon. Please."

I fill the kettle and take out a set of blue-glazed handmade mugs. We bought them on a trip to the Southwest several years ago, one of the few vacations we'd ever taken without Connor. We stayed for a week in March at a beautiful ranch with terracotta floors and a fireplace in the bedroom. When we hiked Bryce Canyon, Jack had been awed by the orange rock formations that exploded from the ground like the ruins of some mythical age. When we drove south to Tucson, I'd never seen him so overwhelmed by a place, the way he kept exclaiming over the architecture, the light, the shops, and restaurants. I'd long ago stopped thinking I could convince Jack to leave Great Rock, but for a few days the possibility seemed to present itself. Until we came home.

I put the mugs back in the cupboard and pull out a set of plain white ones I picked up at the thrift store. We're quiet for a moment, and I'm grateful for the simple act of preparing the tea. Otherwise I would appraise Jack the way he did the house. Already I've noticed he's gained a few pounds, though he's always been so thin it looks good on him. I wonder what he's been eating.

The silence isn't awkward, but it isn't comfortable either. I wonder if this will be a long and drawn-out talk or if Jack has come with a plan in mind. Knowing him, he's already decided what he wants, and it's just a matter of him telling me. I realize that if he says he wants to move back, I'll let him, clearing my books off his nightstand and making room in the closet. If he says he wants a divorce, I'll accept that too, going about the motions of figuring out the rest of my life. My own passivity infuriates me, yet this has been the truth of our entire marriage.

I pour the steaming water into the mugs and hand him his, then sit beside him at the counter, my chair a little further away than usual. Jack winces at the heat as he takes his first sip. I wait, knowing he'll speak when he's ready.

"They found a body on Osprey Beach this morning," he finally says.

These are not the words I expected, and it takes me a moment to process them, my mind still focused on our marriage.

"Who is it?" Jack's family extends across every town. His position as police chief makes him a public figure. There is every likelihood that we're connected to this person, this *body*, in some way.

"It was a woman. Layla Dresser was her name. Not from here, only twenty-two. She was here last summer, working at one of the restaurants on the harbor. She was living in Boston, but she was over for the winter festival."

Great Rock is a seasonal town. In summertime, the smallness of the island evaporates, and it's possible to become anonymous. The population soars to seventy, eighty, ninety thousand on a sunny week in August. In the winter, one of the few tourist draws is the winter festival, a day of chili and chowder cook-offs, ice sculptures, and drinking. The festival takes over all of downtown Osprey. The bars and restaurants set up tents and heating lamps on Main Street, and the whole road becomes a bar. Inside, the restaurants have freebies and specials. It's bigger than the Fourth of July. Though it's run by the restaurants and bars on the island, it's an event for off-islanders, full of twenty-somethings and tourists. I haven't been in years.

"What happened?" I ask him, although I already have a pretty good idea.

Alcohol is a problem on the island. In the winter it can be a lonely place, where work is scarce and entertainment options are slim. Walk down Tunnel Drive on a Sunday morning, and you'll come across more discarded nips bottles and empty beer cans than people. The only businesses that thrive in the off-season are the liquor stores. I'm imagining this girl drank too much and passed out on the beach, froze to death in the cold February night, so I'm unprepared for Jack's response.

"She was strangled." Jack's large hands grip the mug. His face tightens in a grimace.

"My God." Great Rock is a land from another time. A place where people leave their doors unlocked and you know every neighbor on your street. It's a place where the most common crime is public drunkenness and disorderly conduct, shoplifting or check fraud. There hasn't been a murder on Great Rock for as long as I can remember. A few cases of manslaughter or attempted murder—bar fights gone wrong, domestic disputes. But not like this.

"A dog walker found her early this morning." I shudder, thinking about how often I take Champ for early morning walks, sometimes along that very strip of beach.

"The last bar she was seen at was Moby Dick's." Jack meets my eyes. Moby Dick's is the restaurant where Connor works as a sous chef, the same restaurant he's worked at since high school. Scott Lambert is the owner, a local guy who takes good care of his year-round employees.

"Was Connor working last night? Did he see her?"

"He worked last night, but I haven't been able to get ahold of him. Have you talked to him today?"

I shake my head. The last time I talked to Connor was a week ago when he came over to do laundry. He came when he knew I'd be at work, and I only caught him because I left early with a headache.

"I saw him last night when he got off work. The bar was packed."

"You were there?"

"I was working earlier in the evening. Cyrus and I had a drink when I got off." Cyrus is Jack's best friend, also a cop, and he's Evvy's ex-husband. When the kids were little, we used to do everything together—dinner every weekend, beach days in the summer, pizza nights at Papa's. Evvy and Cyrus split up nearly eight years ago, not long after their daughter Serena died, and while we've managed to maintain our friendship, it's been a long time since it was the four of us. Evvy's been with Ian for several years now, but Jack and I don't socialize with him and Evvy the way we did when she was married to Cyrus.

"Do you know what happened?"

"Not yet. We think someone might have followed her out of the bar. Lured her down to the beach." It sounds like something out of a movie or one of the BBC mysteries that Jack and I often watch. I think of how dark Osprey Beach must be at night. There are streetlights on the road, but the beach is down a set of stairs and it's one of the wider beaches on the island, with a broad stretch of sand before you reach the water.

"Do you have any suspects?" He averts his eyes at this last question, for we both know that even if he did, he wouldn't tell me. "Never mind," I add before he can say this, knowing it will just leave me bristling, even though he's doing his job. When he looks up, I see the dark circles beneath his eyes. Perhaps I'm not the only one who's having trouble sleeping.

"If you talk to Connor, tell him to call me," Jack says.

"Why? What does he have to do with any of this?" I ask, another jolt of alarm cutting through me.

"Nothing, I just need to know if he saw anything that night. Just tell him to call me."

I nod because this is how it always is with Jack and Connor: me the middleman trying to help them find some common ground.

"I have to get back to work, but I wanted to come over to tell you why," Jack says, but he doesn't make any move to leave.

Despite the reason, I feel a rush of relief at having been given a reprieve before we decide our fate. It will not be tonight after all. He hasn't shaved today and without touching him, I know the feel of his cheek against my palm, the sandpapery roughness and softness together. I keep my hand firmly on my mug.

Jack and I rarely fought. We'd bicker in the way that married people do, over housework and chores, the daily details of family life. More often, our arguments happened through silence, the distance between us growing larger and colder, until something made it thaw. But over the past year, something's changed between us. Jack's quicker to yell, his frustration bubbling to the surface more quickly. And I'm quicker to fight back, no longer taking the easy route for the sake of peace.

Maybe it's Connor having moved out. In August, he moved into a cramped apartment over a hair salon on Main Street in downtown Osprey. The house was once so full of his presence—his hockey gear thrown carelessly on the floor of the mudroom, his guitar on the couch, music always creeping from his bedroom, friends constantly coming and going. Since he left, there'd been too much space between me and Jack, the two of us bumping around the suddenly oversized house. We'd grown awkward with each other, too, the silence between us suddenly stilted without Connor's voice to fill the quiet.

I like to believe that it's just empty nest syndrome, the two of us figuring out how to be together without Connor, but I also know that it's not just Connor's absence that has taken its toll. It's the role he used to play in our household. Jack never yelled at me, but he yelled at Connor all the time. A daily grind of barked complaints—shoes left on the floor, his hair grown too long, chores left incomplete, a poor play on the ice. Connor is no longer there to take the brunt of it. And then there's me, so quick to jump in and interfere, so ready to smooth things over in the effort of creating harmony between Jack and Connor, finishing the chores, tidying up behind my grown-up son, tending his bruised ego after a slight from his father. Without Connor at home, there is less reason to keep the peace.

On the counter between us my phone rings, and I reach to silence it, seeing Evvy's name light up. A moment later it beeps with a voicemail, followed quickly by the ping of a text. I don't read the message, certain that Jack will leave the moment my attention wavers.

I've heard rumors in the time he's been gone. It's a small island after all, and just because I haven't told people he's moved out doesn't mean they don't know. Deanna Partridge's name has come up, the new administrative assistant at the police station who started in September. Young and cheerful, with bouncy hair, always eager to go out with the guys for a drink after work. Evvy heard through Cyrus that she's been flirting hard with Jack, and last week she was squeezed into the booth at Tanner's beside him, batting her eyes at him as she sipped her glass of wine. There were others at the table too, but according to Evvy, it was pretty clear who Deanna was there to see.

At one point I would have dismissed such a rumor with a roll of my eyes and a laugh. Jack Doherty is the most straight and narrow man I've ever met, honest to a fault, his moral compass rigid and unwavering. These days I'm less certain. While I don't believe he'd sleep with Deanna while we're still in this murky gray in-between place, I bet he's enjoying her attention. The line between flirting and cheating is a solid one, but it becomes a little fuzzier when you don't live with your wife.

Jack takes another sip of tea, steam rising before his face. For years he drank coffee at all hours of the day. It's only in the past year that the caffeine started to affect him, keeping him from sleeping, making his heart race if he had more than a cup or two. One night last spring, I brought him to the hospital because he thought he was having a heart attack, only to find out it was an anxiety attack. *Accumulated stress from the job*, the doctor said. He wrote down the name of a therapist on a slip of paper that Jack threw in the trash on the way out to the parking lot. I was the one who convinced him to cut out caffeine, a Band-Aid on a gaping wound, though it seemed to help some. If Jack had another anxiety attack, he didn't tell me about it, though I also know my husband is the type of man to suffer silently rather than face what he perceives to be a character weakness. I imagine his borrowed kitchen is stocked with an arsenal of flavored fruit teas, the closest to therapy he'll get.

"I should go," Jack says, but neither of us moves. He puts his nearly full mug back down, leaving a ring of water on the counter. Reaching for a paper towel, he carefully wipes the circle till it disappears. "Are you doing okay?"

"Yeah. You?"

Jack nods and I wonder if he's lying too. "We'll talk more soon," he says.

"Okay." I wonder if soon means tomorrow or next month. Either way, I doubt I'll be ready.

Jack rises, pushing himself to standing with effort, the weariness suddenly obvious. We stand facing each other, not touching.

"Thanks for coming by. For letting me know," I say.

Jack nods. I have thought about our relationship more in this past month and a half than I have during our entire marriage, picking apart the patterns and habits we've long fallen into as if I'm unbraiding a rug. I see things more clearly now—the good and the bad—yet I don't know how to remake our entire marriage or if it's even possible.

I feel him wanting to reach for me—to hold my hand or squeeze my shoulder—but he doesn't. It's not until he doesn't make any move to touch me that I realize I want him to. The late nights waiting for him, the silence that stretches between us, born of distance or habit or both, the endless stretch of the rest of our lives on Great Rock, even the closed walls of his heart—I wonder if I'm still willing to make these sacrifices in exchange for his return. I don't know if this is love or fear or simply the desire for something familiar.

I stare down at the tiled floor and the dirty water stains left by his heavy brown boots because I can't bear to look at him any longer, his arms hanging limply by his sides, making no effort at all to hold me, still married, but not quite. At our feet, Champ begins to whine.

EVVY

Chapter Two

When Caroline calls me back, I'm trawling Facebook, scrolling through the islanders' group, looking for news of the murder or talk of possible suspects. I answer on the first ring.

"Did you hear? There was a murder at Osprey Beach." My words tumble out too quickly, matching the racing of my heart.

"I know. Jack just came by." I don't think Jack's been to see Caroline in weeks; I file this information away for later, when I can pay attention to it.

"What did he say?"

She lets out a little laugh. "Not much."

"They've brought Ian in for questioning. Did Jack tell you that?" I hear the accusation in my voice, and I don't know why I'm directing my anger at Caroline.

"What? Why?" I can tell that Jack didn't say anything about it.

"A formality, I guess. I think they're talking to everyone who was at Moby Dick's last night," I say, praying this is true.

"Do you want me to come over?" she asks, and I realize this is why I called her in the first place.

Caroline's house is a five-minute drive from mine. You can walk it in a half-hour, though at this time of year the paths are piled high with snow and the roads too treacherous. In the warmer weather, we go for walks on the weekends, meeting halfway between our two houses and then heading toward the bike path. During the winter, we exercise separately at the local Y, and spring feels very far away.

Caroline gives a quick double knock and then opens the front door without waiting for my answer. I rush into her arms, relieved she's there to buoy me up with her common sense and innate understanding of what needs to be done. Cold air pours in through the open door, and Caroline slams it shut behind her.

She follows me into the living room where I curl up on the couch under a fleece throw. "Are you okay? What happened?" Her calm voice is like a hand on my back.

"I don't know," I say, and it's true. One moment Ian was making lasagna, the next a police officer was at the door to bring him to the station. Carter Davis was the officer they sent, a young man just a few years ahead of Serena in school. "They asked if he could come down to the station so they could ask him some questions. He was at the festival last night."

"Did you go with him?"

"I had to work a party in Heron and then I came home. Were you there?" I ask, already knowing the answer.

Caroline shakes her head. "You know I hate that stuff. Too many drunk tourists. Jack said they were talking to everyone who talked to her last night. Did Ian mention talking to her?" she asks. She's trying to catch my eye, but I focus on her hands. Like Caroline herself, her hands are strong and capable, the nails trimmed sensibly, light blue veins coursing the backs. I notice she's still wearing her wedding ring, a simple brushed silver band. I remind myself to ask her about this later. I squeeze my own hands into fists and stare at my ringless fingers. I have the pale freckled hands of a girl.

"We didn't even know there had been a murder."

"When did Ian get home last night?" Caroline asks. Her careful questioning makes her sounds so much like Jack—always the cop's wife, even when she isn't sure she wants to be his wife anymore.

"I came home and I crashed. I don't know what time he got in." I meet her eyes and then look away.

It's true I was in bed. But I did feel Ian climb in beside me and in my fuzzy state, I glanced at the clock and saw it was just past one. I could tell right away that he was drunk, by the distillery smell he brought into the room with him and the dead weight of his inert body beside me. All of this means nothing though, and there's no reason to share it with anyone, even Caroline.

She reaches over and pats my hand. "I'm sure he'll be home soon. They're probably calling in as many people as they can find who were at the bar last night. You know Ian. He likes to talk to everyone." She doesn't look at me when she says this, and I know she's only trying to make me feel better. Ian and I have been together for six years, not married but almost. Caroline has never liked him much, but she's careful not to tell me. "Have you spoken to Cyrus?"

I shake my head. Cyrus and I still talk, because of Daisy, less frequently now that she's older. Daisy is twenty, though she still lives with Ian and me. Cyrus hasn't remarried either, but he's been with Gina Lerner for several years now. I remember Gina as a shy girl on the freshman soccer team when I was a senior, too timid to get close to the ball. Now, she's assistant principal at the high school. Like many of the people I grew up with who left Great Rock and then came back, it's hard for me to reconcile these two versions of her.

"He'll be home soon. Don't worry," Caroline assures me.

I nod and sigh. "Let's have a drink."

In the kitchen I pour us two tall glasses of red wine and bring them back to the couch.

"So Jack called to tell you?" I ask.

"He came by. Wanted to tell me in person."

I raise my eyebrows. "That was nice, I guess."

"We were supposed to have *the talk*," she says. Her voice is light, trying to minimize the significance of her words.

"And did you?"

"He had to go back to work. Another time, I guess."

"How was it seeing him?" Despite our closeness, Caroline hasn't said much about Jack. She doesn't need to, though. The anger emanates from her like waves of heat whenever his name is mentioned. I don't know what he did to make her so angry, but Caroline isn't the wallowing type. She doesn't cry or throw things or fall apart. She wears her grief like a suit of armor, an impenetrable force that keeps both pain and comfort at bay.

"Fine," she answers. After a moment she relents, likely because otherwise the conversation will go back to Ian and his whereabouts. "He scolded me about not locking my door. Who does he think he is?"

"The chief of police," I say with a smile.

"Always." She bows her head toward the glass.

I want to ask what she thinks about their marriage—if Jack is going to come home, if she *wants* him to come home—but she'll cut me off with a quick word. I know things about Jack, and Caroline could ask me, but she won't. In a place like Great Rock, it's not difficult to find gossip if you're looking for it. Caroline won't go looking, and she refuses to admit she's curious.

I know, for example, that Jack is eating most of his meals at the Salty Whale. I know he's been getting to the station early and staying late, and that he's been buying British mysteries and history books from the local bookstore, probably because he doesn't want to get them from the library where Caroline works. I know that Cyrus went over for drinks a few weeks ago and the place looked barely lived in, not a dish in the sink, not an article of clothing misplaced. I know that Deanna has been pulling out all the stops, wearing low-cut tops to work and skirts that are far too short for both her chubby legs and her professional position. But Caroline doesn't want to hear these things. If she did, she'd ask.

"How's Connor?" It's a blatant attempt to change the subject, but we're running out of topics. Pretty soon we'll be talking about the weather.

"Okay." Caroline takes a sip of wine. "I don't know really. He's doesn't come around much, and he hardly ever answers his phone. What is it with guys and phones? What's the point of having one if you're not going to even answer it?"

I force a laugh. "Ian's terrible. Half the time his phone is on silent and he doesn't even realize it. Or so he claims."

"Has Daisy seen much of Connor?" Caroline asks.

"I'm not sure. She's so busy with school and work that I hardly see her myself."

"Yeah, Connor's busy too, I guess," Caroline says. She meets my eyes then looks back down at her lap.

I sense there is something more, but she won't say it. Keith Dunphey, Connor's current roommate, is a small-time drug dealer on the island. I know this from Cyrus, and I suspect that Caroline knows it too, or maybe she really doesn't. Jack has always protected her from things like this, and despite how long Caroline has lived here, there are things about the island that she still doesn't understand. The Dunpheys are an island family with a long history of trouble. Their last name appears frequently in the police blotter, and the cycle of abuse and neglect, poverty and survival, has been going on for years. Caroline comes from a place where people don't dismiss you just because of your last name, but on Great Rock, you can utter the words, "He's a Dunphey, a Seymour, a Kelly," and people will raise their eyebrows and say, "*Oh*," the names carrying the weight of history and understanding.

I'm not sure what it means that Connor is now living with Keith, but it doesn't take much to recognize that no good will come of it.

"All of his friends are gone," Caroline continues. "All those guys he went to high school with. They're at college now. They'll be graduating soon. The only one of his old friends he still sees is Daisy."

I try to catch her eye, but she's focused on the fringe of the blanket, her fingers working furiously to undo a knot. It scares me that Daisy is the only one left from Connor's old life. I wouldn't want Daisy hanging out with his new crowd.

"Want to watch something on TV?" I ask.

"Sure." She drops the fringe and pulls the blanket to cover her own lap.

Caroline is my best friend, but there are things she won't ask and things I won't tell. Easier to sit together and watch TV, drink a glass of wine, and gather comfort from each other's presence rather than strip away the layers of protection we've built over the years.

There are lies we need to tell ourselves in order to survive.

DAISY
Chapter Three

It's been three days since I've seen Connor, and he's not answering my calls or returning my texts. It's unusual for us to go more than a few hours without exchanging at least a text. He's my best friend and my boyfriend all rolled into one dysfunctional relationship.

Today I swing by his apartment and, after some persuading, his roommate Keith lets me into his room. The place smells of weed and dirty laundry. The spindly wooden chair in the corner is piled high with clothes. The rosemary plant I gave him for his birthday last summer is on the windowsill, miraculously still alive despite living in this fog of smoke and sweat. Connor's guitar is propped in the corner of the room; I can't remember the last time I heard him play. The bed is unmade and I lie down in the twist of sheets and blankets. The pillow smells of him, a musky boy smell that I could fall into. I lie there for a moment, my arms crossed over my chest, breathing him in. Then I force myself out of his room, closing the door behind me.

Keith is standing in the tiny kitchen with a sandwich.

"You don't know where he is?" I ask. The hair salon below the apartment is in charge of the thermostat, and the room is too hot. I unzip my coat, but I don't take it off. Keith is in just a tee shirt and shorts. The chemical smell of hair straightener is faint in the air. I don't know how it doesn't give them headaches.

"I'm not his mother," Keith says through a mouthful of roast beef. I look away so as not to see the brown mush.

"Do you know when he's working this week?" I'm grateful when he swallows before speaking.

"I don't keep track of his schedule." Kevin thrusts his hand into a bag of chips and shovels a handful into his mouth. "What are you worried about anyway? That dead girl on the beach?"

"What?" I've been focusing on the crunch of potato chips. "What girl?"

"You didn't hear?" Keith grins, pleased to be the bearer of bad news. "They found some girl on the town beach yesterday morning. She was murdered. Strangled." His hand comes up to his own neck and he sticks out his tongue and makes a choking sound. "She was over for the festival. You haven't heard about this?"

"I worked all day yesterday." An ashtray sits on the kitchen table, just inches from the food Keith inhales, and there is the sweet reek of garbage coming from the overflowing bin.

When Connor told me he'd gotten an apartment with Keith Dunphey, I tried to talk him out of it. Keith is bad news. A loser who dropped out of high school our junior year and has been working at the gas station ever since. Likely will be working there his whole life, if he doesn't get fired for showing up to work drunk or high. Connor was desperate to get his own place, and I guess he figured the price was worth it. I wonder if he still thinks so now.

"Heard they brought Ian into the station yesterday too." Keith sucks salt from his fingers, sticks his grimy hand back into the bag for more.

"Ian? Why?" The skin on the back of my neck prickles.

He shrugs, clearly enjoying all of this. "He talked to the girl at Moby Dick's that night. I saw them together." He cracks open a can of Coke and takes a noisy slug.

"You were there too?"

Keith nods. "Everyone was there. Connor too."

I pretend the news about Ian doesn't rattle me, because I don't want to give Keith the satisfaction. But it does. I *am* rattled. I wonder what my mother knows.

I zip up my coat. "If you see Connor, tell him to call me."

Keith cocks an eyebrow. "Relax, I'm sure he had nothing to do with it."

I'm not sure which "he" Keith means, Ian or Connor. Or how it's possible I could doubt them both so quickly.

CAROLINE
Chapter Four

I'm grateful when Monday arrives. Sunday used to be my favorite day; the chores done, the *Boston Globe* spread across the table, the house warm with a full pot of coffee. Nothing to do but lie on the couch and read—a librarian's dream, as Jack would say.

These days I'm glad of the routine of work and the structure of having a place to go each morning, returning home tired and ready for bed. Sundays now loom emptily, and I fill the day with chores so as not to face free time alone. Grocery shopping, cleaning, walking Champ. When Monday rolls around again, it's a relief to plunge head first into the mundane tasks at work that need attention.

Though the library doesn't open till nine, I get there at eight. The air is freezing as I cut across the parking lot, a sharp wind making the bare branches sway. I enter through the back door and spend a few minutes turning on lights. I start up the computers and photocopier, and crank up the heat until the building comes to life after the quiet of the weekend. I unpack the morning newspapers and unroll them to hang on the wooden racks. By nine-fifteen there will be a small group of retired men reading the papers, thermal mugs of coffee on the tables that I'll politely ignore, despite the *no food or drink* sign at the entrance.

The *Great Rock Gazette* comes out on Mondays, and the story is on the front page. "Body Found on Osprey Beach. Police

Investigate Murder." Below the headline is a photo of several officers huddled on the shores of the town beach. Jack is at the center of the group.

I pause to scan the article and takes in the basics. Layla Dresser was twenty-two, originally from Tampa, Florida. She'd spent the previous summer waitressing on the island and was now living in Boston, working at a bar. She'd come to Great Rock for the festival and had been spotted at several of the bars in Osprey over the course of the night. Just as Jack told me, a dog walker found her body early Sunday morning. "Police are asking that anyone who spoke with or saw Ms. Dresser on Saturday night come forward," the article closes. There is no mention of any possible suspects.

"Caroline? Should I open up?" Marina, the children's librarian, is standing above me, keys in hand. I glance at the clock and see it's already five past nine. The retired contingent is likely already at the door, mugs in hand. I'm surprised they haven't started banging on the glass yet.

"Yeah, sorry." I fold the paper back in place and hang it up on the news rack with the others.

Marina tilts her head at the paper. "I heard about that. Terrible."

"It is." I wait for the question about what Jack knows.

"They'll catch him," is all Marina says, and then walks toward the door, keys dangling from her hand, ready to begin the day.

Later, when the rest of the staff and volunteers have arrived to man the desks and re-shelve books, I go into the children's room. It's the hour in between the morning mothers that come with their toddlers and the older children who will arrive after school. Marina has only worked here for a year, but she's transformed this area of the library. Each week there's a new theme and display coupled with reading suggestions, crafts, and an event.

This week the theme is fairy tales, a common and overdone genre, but Marina has selected modernized versions of the classics. The teen group that meets each week has created a display of papier-mâché heroines. There is Cinderella in plastic-wrap shoes, Little Red Riding Hood in a velvet cape, and the Little Mermaid lying on a rock, her iridescent tail glinting under the fluorescent lights.

Marina is propping up DVDs to go with the display, and I pause to glance at her choices. I know she will have selected more interesting titles than just Disney's *Beauty and the Beast*. I pick up a Polish animation of *Peter and the Wolf*. The background is a close-up of a wolf's face, his blue eyes icy and empty. In front of the wolf is a drawing of a boy, arms and legs splayed out in a posture of self-defense. At the bottom is the caption, "Boys like Peter are not afraid of wolves."

When Connor was in first grade, I took him to see the show in Boston. It was a high-end production with a large orchestra and elaborate puppets. At the intermission I bought him a pack of Twizzlers, which he ate quietly, tracking the other members of the audience with his eyes. By the end of the show, I was already thinking ahead to where we'd have lunch and how much traffic we'd hit on the way back to the Cape, but when I turned to take Connor's hand, there were tears in his eyes.

"Honey, what's wrong? Are you okay?" I crouched down beside him. A single tear had spilled over his lashes and was sliding down his cheek. He wiped it away with the back of his hand.

"He ate the duck?" Connor asked. It took me a moment to understand his question. I'd forgotten all about the duck still quacking in the wolf's belly. I nodded. "Will he die? Is he dead already?" Connor's face was wrinkled in worry.

"I guess he is." Around us other parents were ushering children toward the exits, but Connor and I hovered above our seats.

"But that's so sad." Another tear fell.

"It is sad, sweetheart. You're right." I reached out and held his hand and we stood like that for another moment. At lunch, I let him order a soda with his meal because I felt so bad about the duck, quacking and flying around inside the wolf's belly until its slow and inevitable death.

As a child he'd been so sensitive. The kind of kid who would cry on Halloween when he saw himself in the mirror dressed like a lion. It could be exasperating at times, the way he'd fall apart with a stern glance or harsh word from Jack. Yet watching him harden was even worse. One day when Connor was in middle school, I realized I couldn't remember the last time I'd seen him cry. By then it had been *years*.

These days, the face that Connor shows Jack and me is a mask. A stony mask or a painted smile. For a long time, the face he showed Daisy was the most real thing in the world, but I suspect these days she doesn't get much more than us.

I put the movie back down on the display. I feel Marina watching me as I hurry toward the bathroom. In the privacy of the stall, I close my eyes and breathe slowly to keep control. The last thing I need is to return to the children's section with my face all swollen and blotchy from crying. Who knows who I might run into? And what am I crying about really? Connor's tender heart that calcified over time, till he's just another boy unafraid of wolves.

I have a hair appointment scheduled for the afternoon. My hair is straight and light brown, though I've been coloring it for the past few years to hide the strands of gray. Usually I let it air-dry or wear it in a ponytail. It isn't something I think about often.

Until this afternoon at work, when Deanna comes in to pick up a book she has on hold. She sees me standing behind the counter, and for a moment I think she's going to turn around and walk out. But she's already been spotted and knows it. She comes up to the desk with a fake smile. Sympathy, guilt, embarrassment—there's so much that could be hiding behind her tight lips.

"Caroline, hi," Deanna says, drawing out the words. She's wearing a tight pink sweater that shows off the perky breasts of a cheerleader. Her blond hair clearly comes from a bottle, but her skin is smooth and unlined, her smile easy and bright. She must be at least ten years younger than me.

"Hi, Deanna," I say, an equally fake smile on my face.

"I think I have something on hold." Her words rise up like a question at the end.

"Okay." I look behind me at the row of books on the hold shelf. "What is it?"

Her face turns pink. "Um." She lets out a nervous laugh. She leans in a little closer and then lowers her voice, naming a trashy bestseller known for its graphic sex scenes.

I open my mouth slightly and then swallow down any comment. "Do you have your card?" is all I ask, waiting for the disclaimer. Everyone seems to need a disclaimer when ordering this book. This isn't the type of book you order through the library system and pick up from your local librarian, I want to tell her. Especially when people are whispering that you're sleeping with the librarian's husband. Order it on Amazon, for God's sake, if only to spare us all the embarrassment of this interaction. Then again, Deanna probably isn't the type to actually spend money on books.

She fumbles in her purse and hands the card across the desk, and I scan it. "One of my girlfriends really wants to see the movie, but she says I need to read it first." I nod politely. "Have you read it?" When I shake my head, Deanna looks dismayed.

I hand back her card. "You're all set."

"Thanks." She scoops up the book and slips it into her bag. "I'll tell you how it is," she says, and I want to throw something at her, a heavy encyclopedia or the DVD box set of *Game of Thrones*.

*

After work I head to Waves, the salon below Connor's apartment. Main Street is empty, save for a few cars parked in front of the grocery store, people stopping on their way home from work to pick up items for dinner. I hate this time of year, when the sun sets by five, most of the island business is closed for the season, and the gray hours of daylight are lost to the workday. The lights in Connor's apartment are off, but I'm not here to see him anyway. In Waves, Leslie, the hairstylist I've had forever, drapes a plastic smock across my body.

"So," Leslie says after she's washed my hair. "Clean it up a little? How many inches?"

"Actually…" I reach up and wind a wet lock around my finger. "I was thinking of something different. Maybe a few more inches."

"Great. Just below your shoulders?"

"No." I withdraw the folded picture I tore from a magazine this afternoon at work. "Chin-length. Layered in the back."

"Seriously?" Leslie asks in excitement. "You've never done this before."

"Why? Do you think it will look bad?" I ask.

"No, it will look great. You've just never gone so short." Leslie picks up a section and runs the comb through it. "You're going to love it."

I flip through a magazine while Leslie works. I'm not sure why the interaction with Deanna unnerved me so much. It's not as if I imagine Jack and Deanna cozy in bed reading through passages of her book together. That's hardly Jack's style. The idea of him tying anyone to the bedpost or getting spanked is absurd. Jack likes sex slow and steady. A few standard positions, his hands and mouth always confident, always sure of what to do. Nothing fancy, and that's what I like about sex with Jack. I know every inch of his body and while some would find that boring, I've always found it reassuring.

It's not that I think Jack and Deanna are sleeping together. In fact, seeing her today made me realize there's nothing going on between them, except possibly a little crush on her part. What bothered me about Deanna today, I recognize now, is that it reminded me of sex with Jack, and for the first time since he left I realize how much I miss it.

Leslie has finished, and I glance up from the tabloid I've been staring at. "What do you think?" she asks.

The hair curves along the edge of my jaw in a sleek crop, elongating my neck. I look different. Younger, lighter, as if the hair has been weighing me down all this time. I run a hand through it. It feels soft and clean. Healthy.

"I love it," I tell her. Only for a moment do I wonder if Jack will too.

When I leave the salon, I glance up at Connor's apartment; the windows are still dark. Nearly everything in town is closing soon, the street nearly deserted. I feel an unexpected shiver of unease run through me, the realization that someone on this island has committed murder and may still be here, hidden in the shadows. I hope when they do find out who did it, it's someone from off-island. It won't make any difference to the poor girl who's dead, but none of us likes to imagine that a murderer could be living here. Great Rock may be desolate and depressing at times, it may be suffocating in its smallness before it bursts into a chaotic carnival when summer comes, but the one thing we've always counted on is its safety.

At home I make myself a grilled cheese sandwich and settle on the couch. I scan Facebook on my phone while I eat this spare dinner. Jack hates social media, but the Great Rock Police Department has a page, so an alert comes up in my feed. The police are asking that anyone who talked with Layla Dresser the night of the festival come forward to speak with them. There's a photo of Layla, the first one I've seen of her. She has shiny light brown hair and a big smile, but it looks like she's hamming for the camera, like she might stick out her tongue or give the finger any moment. She looks like one of the summer girls whose parents come to Great Rock for July and August, or the college kids who come to make money. The summer girls are fresh-faced and fit, with long hair and slender legs, tanned from days at the beach. They get jobs waitressing or working at the yacht club and sometimes, like me, these girls stay on Great Rock, settle down and make a year-round life here. She looks like the type of girl I imagine Connor would meet one day. The post goes on to list the places she'd gone that night, first to Pete's Porter House, then the Blue Crab, and finally to Moby Dick's. She left alone, but never returned to her hotel.

I wonder if Layla was as aimless as Connor, idling away at a dead-end job, never thinking further ahead than the following weekend, or if she was in college or at the start of a career. Either way, it's clear from the picture that she was still bright with possibility, her life snuffed out before she traveled either road very far. I think back to Connor, my unreturned calls, the one-line responses he's sent to my text messages. He has nothing to do with her, other than both of them being in the same place at the same time, but it unnerves me to know she spent the last minutes of her life in such close proximity to my son. As if her tragedy might rub off on him somehow.

EVVY

Chapter Five

There is comfort in chopping onions. I empty the bag of them onto the stainless-steel table and get out a cutting board. This is always the least favorite job of my staff, a menial and painful task that must be done. Today I'm making an onion soup for a small private dinner in Heron. The winter staff is just me and Daisy, and a small handful of other workers who help with events. It's February, and the weddings, anniversary parties, and family reunions—my moneymaking events of summer—are far away. I must make do with these bits and pieces to carry us through.

With the first slice comes the pungent juice that begins to prickle my eyes. They're yellow onions, far more potent than the milder reds I use in salads and sides. These have bite, and after half an onion, I already have tears streaming down both cheeks.

It's a relief. The tears have been at bay for days now, but it was only a matter of time before they were released. Better this way than any other.

Ian hasn't said much in the past few days. Well, this isn't true. Ian is never quiet. He's always talking. But he hasn't said much about his visit to the police station the other night.

He returned home a few hours later, rumpled and tired-looking. He didn't come into the living room where I was still on the couch watching TV, so I went into the kitchen.

"Are you okay? What happened?" I asked.

"No big deal, love. Nothing to worry about. I stopped for a drink on my way home. Settle my nerves." He gave me his easy grin.

"But what happened? Why did they want you to come in?"

He poured himself a glass of water and stood by the sink, drinking it down in one long swallow. "I saw her that night. Chatted with her for a few minutes at the bar." I raised my eyebrows at him. I don't know why I was surprised. They wouldn't have hauled him into the police station just because they happened to be at the same bar. "It was no big deal," he went on. "She was sitting alone and I just talked to her for a few minutes. Asked her where she was from, what she thought of the island." He came around and planted a kiss on my neck. "You know me. I could make friends with a mailbox." He smiled, because this is our joke, and it's true.

"Did you have dinner?" he asked. I hadn't even cleaned up the lasagna that he was halfway through making. The noodles were sticky in the pot and the counter was still littered with scraps of cheese and dots of tomato sauce.

"No. Sorry." I gestured to the mess. "Caroline came over. I was worried."

"No need to worry, love." He began to tidy the kitchen, dumping out the remnants of the meal and wiping down the counters. All that food wasted. "Are you hungry?"

Though it was nearly nine, I hadn't had anything other than the glass of wine with Caroline and the second one I drank alone. "I guess."

"I'll make us some omelets." And though I wanted to know more, though there were still so many questions to ask, I was quiet. Because as much as Ian likes to talk, often he's not saying much at all.

I turn on the radio as I chop. The music on the local folk station is a peaceful hum in the background, giving some coziness to the industrial kitchen I rent. Despite its stainless-steel sterility, there are few places more comforting to me than the headquarters of Petunia's Pantry, the catering company I started four years ago. I only wish I'd known enough to create this tiny oasis earlier.

After high school I stayed on the island because Cyrus was here, and because I knew he would propose if I did. Then Daisy came along and Serena a few years later, and my days became full of the endless routine of diapers and naps, sticky fingers always reaching for me, needing more and more and more. Cyrus didn't see it. He couldn't understand that it felt like my world was closing in, all doors and windows sealed up tight, just me and the girls trapped inside a tiny airless room.

I was hard on them. I yelled. I cried. Sometimes when I walked into a room, I could feel the air shift, the three of them holding their breath, waiting to see what kind of mood I was in, who I would be today. I hated myself then, but I hated them more for making me feel that way, their love and my love for them leaching me dry of everything else.

And then Serena died, and the whole world fell apart.

I started taking catering jobs when Daisy went to high school. Though I sometimes worked as waitstaff for an event, I was always more comfortable in the kitchen. It never occurred to me I could have my own business, that I was smart enough to even get it off the ground, much less make it successful.

Ian was the one who had the idea, doing research here and there about catering on the island, sending me contacts, pushing me. He was the one who believed in me when no one else did, when Cyrus made jokes about my cooking early on in our marriage, when even Caroline wondered if I knew what I was getting myself into. Ian was the one to give me the money to get started, the one who still throws a little extra at the company every few months, despite his own modest income. Ian saw something inside me that no one else did. I owe him for giving me a second chance—at love, but also at life.

I feel terrible for that girl on the beach, just a little older than Daisy, but I already hate her a little bit too. Her death is like a rain cloud blotting out the sun, dense and gray. I know this is not over for us. We're all connected here on Great Rock, and there's no way this won't touch every one of us somehow, showering us all with its silent and toxic drops.

DAISY

Chapter Six

On Tuesdays and Thursdays I ride the boat to the mainland for classes. I pay the sixty dollars to get a round-trip ticket for my car, but even this monthly cost is cheaper than what I would pay for full-time tuition and board. It's my second semester and I'm taking two classes this term. I can't think too much about how long it will take me to finish my degree this way. It's like drops of water in a paper cup when you're trying to fill a bucket.

On the boat home Tuesday night, I treat myself to a coffee and a chocolate chip cookie and find a booth in the corner to study, hoping I won't bump into anyone I know, understanding that this is impossible.

I've just opened a textbook when my phone buzzes on the table. It's Connor. Finally. I haven't heard from him since his text on Sunday. *You look so studious*, the text says. *You're working too hard.* I look around the half-empty boat and catch him sitting in a single chair on the other side of the snack bar, phone in his hands, eyes on me. He stands and walks over grinning, a black backpack slung over his shoulder. He sits down across from me.

"Okay if I disturb your study session?"

"Where the hell have you been?"

He reaches across and breaks off a piece of my cookie, pops it in his mouth. "I told you, I've been off-island."

"I know, but where? Why?"

"Chill, Daze." He looks terrible, pale and too thin. He has several days' worth of soft blond stubble on his chin. "I went to Boston. Stayed with Pete and Nate. I just needed to get out of here for a few days." Pete and Nate are friends from high school who go to Northeastern. I didn't think he talked to them often.

"You could have told me that," I say.

"Who are you, my mother?" Even though I'm riding him, there's affection in his voice.

"No, but you should call her too." I swat his hand as he breaks off another piece of cookie.

"Yeah, yeah, I will." He digs in his back pocket and pulls out his wallet, opens it and then shoves it back in his jeans. "You have any cash? I'm starving."

I roll my eyes and pull out my purse, fish out a ten, which I pass to him. "Where's your money?"

"Blew it all on booze and babes," he jokes, then gets up and goes to the snack bar. When he comes back, he has a bowl of clam chowder and three bags of oyster crackers. The soup steams between us.

"Did you check out UMass Boston while you were there?" For months I've been begging him to apply. It won't be long before I have my Associate's from Cape Cod Community College, and I plan on transferring to a four-year college to finish my degree. I imagine us leaving the island together, moving to the city and sharing an apartment. This fantasy leaves out so much—Connor's apathy, the money it will cost, not to mention that we're not actually a couple. Yet some days, this dream is the only thing that gets me through.

He blows on the soup. "I wasn't exactly on a college tour." He takes a spoonful. "That's hot," he says, then goes ahead and takes another bite.

"What are you waiting for?"

"The engraved invitation, I guess. The full scholarship that would cover all my expenses. Once that arrives, I promise, I'm out of here," he says bitterly.

"You're so full of it." My tone is more forceful than I intended, surprising us both, but I mean it. It didn't occur to me till midway through my junior year that I might want to go to college, and by then my transcript was a sad record of low Bs and Cs. It wouldn't have mattered anyway, because my father had been stretching his paycheck to cover the house that my mother and I still lived in, as well as his portion of Gina's mortgage. Petunia's was just in its first years and there was nothing left over in the bank. College wasn't an option. But Connor had good grades for most of high school and that was without even trying. He could get into college if he wanted to, and his parents would pay for it. If he'd only make an effort.

"Drop it, Daze. I'm not in the mood." Connor looks down at his soup. He knows I'm disappointed in him. More than that, I'm afraid for him. He doesn't tell me, but I hear things. I know who he's been hanging around with. Keith and the rest of his crew. Guys he wouldn't have dreamt of hanging out with in high school because they had nothing in common. It scares me to think they have something in common now.

"You hear about that girl who got killed?" I ask. I feel like Keith, using this tragedy as a conversation piece. Something flickers across his face, but it's gone before I can get ahold of it.

"Yeah. It's awful." His knee bounces rhythmically under the table. The incessant tapping combined with the rocking motion of the boat makes me dizzy. Connor's eyes dart around as if he's worried someone might overhear our conversation.

"Were you there?" When he doesn't answer, I add, "At the festival?"

"Yeah, everyone was."

"They called Ian into the police station. For questioning."

He squints his eyes in confusion. "Why?"

"I don't know. He must have been talking with her that night. Keith told me."

"Since when do you talk to Keith?" He balls up his napkin and plastic cracker wrappers and stuffs them in the empty paper bowl.

"Since you don't return my calls," I snap.

He ignores this. "Did your mom say anything about it?"

I shake my head. "No, but I didn't ask." Ian and I have a cautious relationship. I don't like him, but I know my mom needs him. She's never been the most stable person, but with Ian around, she's changed. I don't know what would happen to her if he weren't around anymore.

"I wouldn't worry," Connor says. "They probably brought in anyone who saw her that night." His phone beeps, and he removes it from his pocket to read the text.

"Yeah, maybe. Did you see her?"

"Not that I know of." He doesn't look at me, his eyes on his phone.

"Who's that?" I tip my head to the screen.

"Just my mom." He shoves it back in his pocket.

"You should call her."

"Yeah, yeah, I know."

Over the loudspeaker is the announcement that the boat is pulling into Osprey harbor. Connor rises and throws away his trash, and I gather my books together. I didn't even start the chapter I was supposed to read. I'll have to study later tonight.

"Can I grab a ride home?" Connor asks.

"Sure." We head for the stairwell and make our way through the lower level of the boat, weaving between the tightly packed cars. It's cold down here, the icy air skimming off the water mingling with the diesel smell of the boat. I unlock the car, and we sit in the quiet darkness and wait for the boat to port.

Connor puts his hand on the back of my neck. "Sorry I was MIA. I just needed a little time."

"Are you okay?" He's not okay, though I'm not sure he even realizes it.

"Yeah, I'm fine." He gives me a half-smile. There's more I want to ask, but I know "fine" is all I'll get. Before I can press any harder, he leans in and kisses me, and I forgive him for everything. The car behind gives a toot and I pull away from Connor, realizing that it's our turn to exit the boat.

"Want to hang out later?" I ask. His hand has moved from my neck to my knee, and I wish I didn't like it there so much.

"I can't. I've got some stuff I need to do."

"Like what?" I should be studying, but I'd rather be with him.

He squeezes my knee, sending a little ripple of pleasure up my thigh. "Just stuff. Maybe tomorrow, okay?"

"Sure." I love Connor, but I love the idea of getting out of Great Rock at least as much as him. Despite my fantasy of us leaving together, I worry that being with Connor might root me here forever. I drive out of the boat's hold and back onto Great Rock, home again for another night.

CAROLINE

Chapter Seven

When I get home from Tuesday night's Board of Directors meeting at the library, Connor's car is in the driveway.

"Con?" I call as I go inside, surprised that the laundry isn't chugging away with his clothes.

"Yeah," he calls from upstairs.

His bedroom door is closed, and I knock once before going inside. Connor's sitting on his bed, zipping up his old guitar case. He gives me a weak smile when I come in.

"Hi, honey."

"Hey, Mom." He looks tired, and he hasn't shaved in days.

"What are you doing here?" I ask, pleased to see him.

"Nothing, just thought I'd stop by."

I frown at him, as this is so rare. "No laundry?"

"Not tonight. I just came by to say hi," Connor says, and I want to believe him.

"I had a meeting tonight. Second Tuesday of the month, remember?" I remind him.

"Oh, right."

I gesture to the guitar beside him. "It's nice to see you with your guitar. Were you playing?"

"Um, yeah, a little, I guess." He shrugs as if the question is difficult.

"Will you play something for me?" I ask. He used to play for me some nights, shyly trying out songs that he'd spent hours practicing. It was the guitar he loved, but Connor has a beautiful voice too. Listening to him always gave me goosebumps, and not just because he was my son. He really was that good.

"Nah. Not in the mood." He runs his hands along the length of the leather case, smoothing down the pockets.

"Please? Just one? How about 'Have You Ever Seen the Rain'?" I smile, remembering how he used to play this song so frequently that I'd often get it stuck in my head, the lyrics looping through my brain all day long.

"Not tonight, Mom, okay?" He looks so tired and I feel guilty for hounding him.

"Okay, sorry," I relent.

"Where's Dad?" We haven't told Connor that Jack's moved out. I know we'll have to tell him at some point, but this doesn't seem like the right time. I'm probably being paranoid, but it sounds like there's a challenge in his voice.

"Late shift," I answer.

"Right," he says, his eyes narrowed. For a moment, I think he's going to say more, but he doesn't. "I should get going. It's late."

"I thought you came by to say hello." I hate the pleading note in my voice, how desperate I am for him to stay a little longer.

"Yeah, well." He stands up, putting the guitar into the closet and closing the door. "It's getting late."

"Not that late. Come on, I'll make you a sandwich. You look like you haven't had a real meal in weeks. Stay for a little while." I turn and head down the stairs, and he follows me without argument.

In the kitchen I take out ham and cheese, mustard and mayonnaise. I'm glad I bought the wholegrain bread from the bakery in Osprey that Connor likes, and I cut two thick slices for the sandwich, placing a dill pickle on the side of the plate. There's a carton of lemonade in the fridge, and I pour a tall glass, presenting the meal to him. He attacks the food appreciatively, as if he hasn't actually eaten in weeks, though I know he gets a free meal every shift at Moby Dick's. I pour myself a glass of juice and sit down beside him at the counter.

"How are you? I haven't seen you in a while."

"Okay. Just busy." He takes a gulp of lemonade, puts the glass down and picks the sandwich back up. "Work. You know."

"How is work?" I ask. Because Connor works in the kitchen he isn't dependent on tips like the waitstaff, but in the slower months his hours get cut. It's hard to make a living on Great Rock at this time of year.

"It's fine. Pretty slow, but it's February. Hopefully things will pick up in March." February is the cruelest month on the Island. The bright bustle of the holidays is over and most of the shops are closed. The winter weather is raw and unforgiving; the dampness of the sea and ice gets into your bones. It's during February that I most often imagine leaving Great Rock, but then spring finally rolls around, muddy and green and suddenly blooming with possibility, and I forget how much I wanted to leave.

"Have you been playing music much? You'd talked about trying to get some gigs lined up." This was months ago, over the summer actually, at the wedding of one of Jack's cousins. We were at the same table, picking at the vanilla crème cake, watching the couples on the dance floor. Most of the time Jack is too stiff and self-conscious to dance so I've resigned myself to watching other people at events like this. Connor loves to dance, but his arm was still in a sling from a recent surgery. He made a passing comment about looking into doing some event work, and he hasn't mentioned it since, but I've latched onto it.

Something flashes across his face—annoyance, anger, I'm not sure which. This is new, his irritation with me, the way he's quick to snap or bristle. Connor and I have always been easy and gentle with each other, and I'm not sure where this late adolescence is coming from, how I have suddenly become the bad guy. It's a role I'm used to Jack playing, but not one I know well. "I'm not in a band right now. I've got no one to play with. People don't hire just a guitar player," Connor points out.

I pull a paper towel from the rack and hand it to him. He swipes his face with it and then returns to the sandwich. "Have you looked into Berklee anymore? If you were in music school, it would be so easy to find people to play with. Just because you didn't get in the first time doesn't mean you can't reapply." The words come out all in a rush because I know it's just moments before he'll become outwardly annoyed.

"The application deadline passed." He rises from the chair and brings his plate and glass to the dishwasher.

"Why didn't you apply? You said you'd think about it."

"I did think about it." His back is to me as he loads his dishes. "And I decided I didn't want to be in some dumb music school with a bunch of whiny losers all desperate to become the next big thing who will probably just end up teaching band in some crappy high school. No thanks." He slams the dishwasher shut. He sounds so cynical. I get up and stand beside him. It's all I can do not to hold his face in my hands.

"Honey, you know that's not true. You'd love it there. You're so talented." He rolls his eyes. "It's true. And even if you don't want to go to Berklee, that doesn't mean you can't go somewhere else. Maybe not even to study music. There's so much you could do. You just need to put in an application."

"God, Mom, can't you ever just give it a rest?" Here it comes, the anger I knew was brewing. I do reach for him now, holding my hand against the roughness of his cheek. He won't meet my eyes.

"Sweetheart, are you all right?"

"I'm fine." His voice is flat, tired, and devoid of emotion. Sometimes I wish Connor were a girl, an angsty emotional girl who would cry and throw herself dramatically on the bed when she was upset. At least girls aren't impenetrable. Though maybe that isn't true either. Maybe all children reach an age when they become unknowable to their parents, the easy transparency of childhood lost behind the opaque glass of adolescence and adulthood.

"You can talk to me. If you want to. Or your father. You know we're here for you." Though technically, Jack isn't *here* for either of us right now.

"Sure," he says bitterly, and then, softening a little, "I'm okay, Mom. Really." He meets my eyes. Connor is one of those boys blessed with the long lashes that girls wish for, but the skin of his eyelids is oily, purple half-moons beneath his eyes, and he has a musty unwashed smell that makes me step back.

"So Dad's at work?" Connor asks, even though I already told him this.

"Yup. Late shift again."

"Is everything okay? Is Dad all right?" he asks. For a moment, I wonder if maybe he knows about us. We have to tell him soon—it's not fair to keep this from him—but I still don't know what to say. I realize I have no idea how he'll react.

"Of course, he's fine. Why do you ask?"

"I heard about the girl who was killed. The one they found on the beach," Connor says. As if young women are killed all the time on Great Rock and he needs to specify which one he's talking about.

"Oh, that. Yes, it's terrible. It's hard to believe," I say. I suppose everyone who lives in a small town thinks that they're immune from this kind of violence, but it feels even more unlikely in a place like Great Rock where everyone knows each other and is connected in some way. This is what makes it even more frightening to think about, the likelihood that this isn't some random crime, the possibility that someone we know may be responsible.

"Do they have any suspects?" Connor asks.

"As if I would know," I say, and Connor cracks a smile, knowing that Jack would never confide in me about work. I feel guilty making a joke about this, but I need to lighten the mood. "Don't worry about your father. He'll be fine." *He always is*, I want to add but don't. It's true though; Jack is always fine, with or without me, and it's this new awareness that has suddenly become visible, as if someone has shone a flashlight in a dark corner of the room.

"I'm going to go home. Get some sleep," Connor says.

"Why don't you just stay here?"

"No, that's okay."

"Why not?" I'm suddenly desperate for him to spend the night, though I realize this might mean telling him about Jack and why he's still not home by tomorrow. "You can sleep in, and I'll make you breakfast in the morning. There are clean sheets on your bed."

He gives me a half-smile. "Okay, you win. I'm too tired to argue."

I beam at him. "Good. Let's go up."

He follows me up the stairs and says goodnight, heading into his room and closing the door. I get into my own bed and read for a few minutes, knowing I won't be able to fall asleep just yet.

When Connor was a young boy, I remember how tired I was by the end of the day. A full shift at the library and then scooping him up from daycare, struggling through the evening hours of dinner prep and bath time, the endless bedtime rituals, doing much of it on my own, since Jack often didn't get home till later in the evening. Those days, I'd go to bed early, and sleep would come quickly. But I remember mapping out where in the house Connor and Jack were, Jack downstairs watching TV and Connor breathing softly across the hall, the major constellations in my world. I felt such comfort in those moments, knowing that the three of us were safe and warm in our home, all that love wrapped up tight in such a small sacred space.

I feel the same way tonight, knowing that for the moment Connor is just across the hall, safe, out of harm's way.

*

When I leave for work the next morning, Connor is still sleeping. I had hoped he'd wake up before I left and we could have breakfast together, but at eight forty-five his door is still shut, and I need to get to work. I put on a full pot of coffee and set a loaf of bread and jam on the counter.

When I get home this afternoon, Connor is long gone, though his dirty dishes are still in the sink and the counter is littered with crumbs. I clean up the kitchen and then go upstairs to change so I can take Champ for a walk. This morning I unpacked a new novel that's been in all the book reviews, and I'm eager to finish my chores so I can start it.

At the top of the stairs, I pause. Connor's door is closed, though I usually leave it open, just to keep the air circulating so it doesn't get a stagnant smell. I stand for a moment before knocking, even though I know Connor's been gone for hours. Still, I hesitate before turning the handle.

He moved out six months ago, but I haven't done much to convert it into a guest room. Navy blue drapes block out the light so he could sleep late on weekends without the sun waking him. The summer he was a junior, Connor painted the walls black and the ceiling and floor red. Between the walls and the curtains, the room has the feeling of a cave. There's a lot I'd need to do in order to make it a guest room.

The bed is unmade, and I feel a flicker of annoyance. Connor has always been a slob. When he lived at home, his things were everywhere—socks on the stairs, shoes tossed sideways on the living room floor, a dirty hockey jersey thrown over the back of a chair. It was a constant argument between him and Jack, and a source of friction between Jack and me, as he blamed me for allowing Connor's slovenly ways to persist. The drawers are askew and the unmade bed is piled with clothes. I stand in the doorway and debate going inside.

I've never gone digging through either Connor or Jack's things. I've never checked the search history on the computer or snooped on emails or texts. Then again, it occurs to me now, maybe I've never before felt truly suspicious.

What I haven't told Evvy is that right before Jack moved out, I found a bag of pills in the pocket of Connor's pants. It was one of the rare nights when Connor came by for dinner, though it was a quiet, stilted meal, none of us talking much. Moving in with Keith had felt like Connor's admission that this was all he was ever going to do, and everything that came out of my mouth was dripping with my own disappointment. Connor was sullen and defensive, though he is often like that in Jack's presence. Jack was even quieter than usual, and he seemed to be watching Connor carefully, his eyes tracking every bite of steak, every sip of beer.

After dinner Connor went up to his bedroom to wait for his laundry to finish, and I did the dishes. When his first load of washing was done, I went to put in the second load. Even though he was twenty-one, I couldn't resist mothering him. I emptied the dirty items into the washing machine, checking the pockets as I always do to make sure there's not a stray pen or forgotten dollar bill. My fingers closed around a plastic baggie. When I pulled it out, I saw there were a few pills in it.

"What's that?" Jack asked from the kitchen.

"Some pills," I said. I wasn't alarmed yet. I thought of all the times I'd stuck an extra Advil in my pocket when I had a headache, or an allergy pill in the springtime. Yet I also knew these weren't Advil or Claritin.

"Let me see," Jack said, stepping into the mudroom and plucking the bag from my hand. He cursed under his breath.

"What are they?" I asked, taking a step closer. Jack didn't answer, instead going back into the kitchen.

"Connor!" he yelled, loud enough that Champ scrambled to his feet.

"What is it? What are they?" I asked, but Jack was already at the staircase calling for Connor to get down here.

Connor slouched down the stairs. "What?" His jeans hung from his hips, his sweatshirt swimming on his skinny frame.

Jack held the bag up, inches from Connor's face, his fist nearly trembling in rage. "What is this?"

Connor looked at the bag squeezed in his father's hand and then at me. "What the hell? Now you go digging through my stuff? They're just some stupid pills for my shoulder."

The previous May, Connor had surgery on his shoulder. He'd torn his rotator cuff during a hockey game in high school, and it had never healed properly. The surgery was meant to repair the damage. The recovery was hard. He was laid up in bed for weeks, his arm in a sling. He had trouble sleeping at night because of the pain and it was a while before he could go back to work. The surgery was months ago. I hadn't realized he was still taking medication.

"Where'd you get them?" Jack barked.

"Where do you think? From a doctor." The bravado in his voice didn't match his expression.

"Bullshit. You had that surgery months ago."

"Well, it still hurts, all right? It still really hurts." Connor leaned against the wall and his hand came up to rub his shoulder in a way I suddenly recognized as habit.

Jack shook his head, but the anger was draining away. "Do you know what this stuff can do to you? Do you know how addictive it is?"

"I'm okay, Dad," Connor said. "It just needs to heal. I just need the pills until it gets better."

"You need to go back to the doctor," I said, speaking up for the first time since they started fighting. "Maybe you need more physical therapy."

"Maybe," Connor said, but I knew he was only saying it to placate me.

"You need to stop taking this junk, you hear me?" Jack said, shoving the pills in the pocket of his own pants. "They're dangerous."

Connor nodded. "Yeah, sure. I'll talk to the doctor." He looked down at his stockinged feet and then back up at Jack. "I'm sorry, okay?"

Jack grabbed him then, pulling Connor in for a rare hug. His hand palmed Connor's head, and I blinked back tears at this affection, for I know it doesn't come naturally to Jack.

Connor left soon after, without the pills or any further argument, but as soon as the door closed behind him, Jack turned to me.

"This is serious. Those pills are dangerous," Jack said.

"They're for his shoulder. It's not as if he's a drug addict," I said.

"Do you know how many people start on these pills for pain and then get addicted? At a certain point, the doctor cuts them off and they buy it on the street, but then that gets too expensive. That's when they start doing heroin."

"Heroin?" I practically spat the word at him. "What are you talking about? No one's doing heroin."

He looked at me as if he'd expected me to say something like this.

"Do you have any idea how many kids on this island are doing drugs? How many kids get brought in every week for possession or dealing or overdosing? I'm not talking about marijuana. I'm talking about heroin."

I did know, though not as well as Jack. For the past couple of years he'd been talking about the drugs on Great Rock, the spike in arrests for possession or dealing, the increase in overdoses. It's a problem I recognized on an abstract level, but not one I'd spent much time considering on a personal one.

"This is why he shouldn't be here," I said, an old argument colliding with this new one.

"What was I supposed to do? Kick him out of the house? Force him to leave the island?" Jack said.

"Yes." I felt the frustration of the last three years rising up inside me, a hot bubbling brew ready to spill over. "That's exactly what you should have done. If you'd told him it was important, he would have done it."

"He applied to college. He didn't get in."

"*One school*," I cried. "Who the hell applies to only one school? You should have made him apply to more."

"Why was that my job?"

"Because you're his father, Jack. He does whatever you ask. You should have made him," I said. I heard the unfairness in this, the way I ceded all of the important things to Jack and then resented him when he didn't do what I'd hoped.

"Why do I always have to be the bad guy?" he exploded. "Why is it always my job to come in and be the asshole making him do stuff he doesn't want to do, and then you swoop in and try to protect him?"

I digested the truth in his words, but my instinct was to retaliate. "That's not fair. His whole life you've been trying to make him into something he's not. You want him to be hard and tough, and he's not. He's sensitive and thoughtful, and you want him to be like you, but he isn't. He should have gone to college."

"College isn't the only way to have a good life. There are other ways to be happy." He went to the refrigerator and pulled out a bottle of beer. "Besides, you don't think there are drugs in other parts of the country? They don't have drugs on college campuses?" He cracked the bottle open. "Give me a break, Caroline."

I shook my head in anger. "We wouldn't even be having this conversation if he were away from this place."

"*This place?*" Jack shot back. "This place that's been your home for the last twenty-something years?" He shook his head at me. "You hate it that much, do you? Or is it just me?"

"I hate the idea that this will be all Connor does with his life. It's a trap for kids, you know that as well as I do." I felt my breath catch in my throat. This wasn't the way Jack and I fought. We rarely spoke so honestly or tried to hurt each other so directly. I ran my fingers through my hair and took a deep breath. "Connor should have had more choices."

"Are we talking about Connor or you?" Jack held my gaze before picking up his beer from the counter. "I'm done with this," he said and left the room. I stood for a stunned moment in the kitchen before following him into the living room. Jack was sitting on the couch watching TV.

"What are you doing?" I asked.

"Trying to watch the game." Jack kept his eyes on the screen.

"You can't just say something like that and then leave. We need to talk about this."

"About what?" Jack never yelled at me, only at Connor, and despite the many years I had known my husband, his voice made me feel like a frightened child. "That Connor is doing drugs or that you have no respect for this island or me? That you always think there's something better right around the corner and I'm keeping you from it?"

"That's not true. None of that's true," I protested.

"Why don't you just say it?" When he looked at me, I didn't recognize the bitter expression in his eyes.

"Say what?"

"That you wish you'd never come here. You wish you didn't stay, that we didn't get married. That you were free."

"That's not true. None of that's true." It wasn't true, but it wasn't untrue either. It was more complex than that.

He finally looked at me. His face was flat and empty. "Caroline, go to bed. I don't want to fight with you."

"Jack, we're talking."

"Caroline!" His voice was so loud that I flinched. The anger pulsed through his body, and I wanted to reach for him, to press a hand to his chest to still the pounding of his heart, but I thought he might push me away. "Just go to bed!"

I stared at him for another moment, my own heart fluttering in my chest. I couldn't remember Jack ever yelling at me like that before, and I wasn't sure what exactly it was that had gotten us here so quickly. Without another word, I climbed the stairs to our bedroom. Jack slept on the couch for the first time that night.

I'm thinking about this now, as I stand in Connor's doorway, thinking about going through his things, about the last time Jack did this and what it unleashed. I linger for another moment before stepping back onto the landing and retreating downstairs.

EVVY

Chapter Eight

Ian and I are getting ready to go for breakfast when Jack calls. His voice is businesslike when I answer.

"Evvy, it's Jack. Is Ian there?"

"He is. Why?" I look to Ian who's searching for his keys. I point to where they lie on the kitchen counter.

"I need to speak with him." Jack's voice is polite and formal. He doesn't ask how I am, and I don't ask what the hell he's doing sleeping at the Feldmans'.

"We were just going out," I say instead.

"I need to speak to him. Why don't you just put him on the phone." His voice is firm. I want to hang up the phone, but though I've known him my whole life, he's still the chief of police. I hand the phone to Ian. He's only on for a minute, just a series of okays, yeahs, and all rights.

"What now?" I ask when he hangs up.

"They want me to come back down to the station." He squeezes the keys in his fist. His face has gone pale, and I realize he's nervous.

"Why? You had nothing to do with this."

"Relax, Ev, it's okay." He pulls on his coat, the heavy brown barn jacket I bought him for Christmas last year. "I'll be back soon. I'll pick up some croissants on the way home." He kisses my cheek. "Put on another pot of coffee. I'm sure it won't be long."

*

He's gone for two hours, and when he returns, there are no crois-sants. He's empty-handed, his face dark.

"What did you tell them?" he asks, before he's even closed the front door.

"What? What do you mean?" Cold air pours in from outside. It's supposed to snow later today.

"They knew." He looks at me meaningfully. Even before he says it, I already know. My whole body goes cold.

"About what?" I ask anyway.

"About the night we went to Joe and Christine's. You told Caroline, didn't you? You promised you wouldn't." He's staring at me with an expression of profound hurt, and I feel terrible, though I also know I'm not the one who should be feeling guilty.

"Ian, she dragged it out of me. It was a long time ago. I'm so sorry." I go to him and reach for his hands. He pulls them away, slamming the front door shut.

"They think I had something to do with it, Evvy. They're trying to make me out to be violent. Some witness saw me leave at the same time as that girl." His eyes are wild and I can see he's worried.

"Did you?" I ask.

"I might have left around the same time, but I didn't leave with her. I told you. I talked with her for a few minutes at the bar. That's all."

"What were you talking about?" I ask.

"Nothing!" he explodes. He pushes past me and into the kitchen. "She was a pretty girl, she ordered a drink at the same time as I did, I made small talk with her for a minute at the bar. We talked about the weather." Ian's face is red, his whole body tense. If I were to reach for him, he'd be rigid as a statue. "Come on, Evvy, what is this? Are you questioning me now too?" He throws his coat over a chair and opens a bottle of beer, even though it's not yet noon.

"No, of course not. I'm sorry. You have nothing to worry about." I go to him then, stand right in front of him where he has to look at me. "You didn't do anything wrong. They'll find out who did it. No one really thinks you could have done this." These are the words he needs to hear, even if they're not all true. I wait for him to open his arms and let me fall inside.

"Why did you tell Caroline?" he asks, and he looks wounded, not angry.

"I'm sorry, I didn't mean to," I say, and it's true.

"I need to get out of here for a little while," Ian says, turning from me. He drains the last of his beer and picks up his coat and keys. "I'll be back later."

"Where are you going?"

"Just out, Evvy, okay? I need some time to think." He stops to grab me around the waist and gives me a quick kiss on the mouth, a reassurance, a half-forgiveness. "Don't worry," he says, and then he's gone. The wind slams the door shut behind him, and I stand in the empty kitchen, thinking about that night at Joe and Christine's almost five years ago.

There were a lot of people there, some I knew well but hadn't seen much of lately. Before Cyrus and I divorced, we saw this group a lot, at dinner parties with Caroline and Jack and a few other couples. Ian and I had been together for a year, and I still imagined that maybe he'd be able to slide into some of my old friendships as easily as Cyrus had. When I'd asked Ian if he wanted to go to dinner there that night, I hadn't thought too much about whether Cyrus would be there. I'd long since learned I couldn't spend my whole life trying to avoid him. We lived on an island; our lives were bound to intersect.

Cyrus was there, without Gina, and somehow we ended up in the living room sitting on opposite couches. We talked. About

Daisy and work, the business I had only just begun to consider. We weren't flirting, though there was an easiness between us. I'd known Cyrus my whole life. Nearly half of it had been spent in a relationship with him.

Ian had never been married, and he had no children of his own. He couldn't understand the intimacy and history Cyrus and I shared, even now. I saw Ian in the kitchen, watching me with a scowl on his face. I should have gone to him then, should have left Cyrus and gotten myself another plate of food or a drink. But I didn't. I stayed on the couch and kept talking to Cyrus.

By the end of the evening, Ian was staggering drunk, not in any shape to drive home, and I'd already had too many glasses myself. I asked Cyrus if he could give us a lift. I should have known better.

Ian didn't talk the whole way home, seething in the front seat of the car beside Cyrus. I kept up a steady prattle in an attempt to avoid the awkwardness of the moment. Cyrus dropped us back at our house; his old house, the one we'd lived in together and raised our family.

I was in the bathroom brushing my teeth when Ian threw open the door.

"What was that, Evvy?" His face was pinched tight. "You ask *him* to drive us home?"

I spat the toothpaste into the basin, too stunned to be frightened. "It's fine. You couldn't drive home. There were at least four cops at that party. Did you want to pay for a cab?"

"You're supposed to be with me now. Not him." His words were slurred.

"You're drunk," I said, turning away.

I wasn't prepared for his hand. It leapt out of nowhere, the strength of it foreign and surprising us both. I stumbled backward and fell into the shower, crashing through the curtain, my legs buckling under the side of the tub. My head slammed against the blue tile that Cyrus and I picked out years earlier when we redid the bathroom. I lay with my body in the tub, my legs still hanging over the side. My head throbbed and my cheek was on fire. The water left over from the last shower soaked through the seat of my pants.

"Oh God," Ian said. Suddenly he was on the floor beside me, pulling me up, carrying me out of the tub and propping me up on the bath rug. "I'm so sorry, love. I didn't mean to. I didn't… I didn't realize. I'm sorry, I'm drunk. I'm so sorry. Oh God, you're bleeding. Are you okay? Does it hurt? I didn't mean to do that. It just happened. Please. I'm sorry. Do you need some ice? Let's get you some ice. Your head. Oh, there's blood. Just stay there. Stay there and I'll get some ice." His words poured forth, an endless string of shock and apologies.

I lay on the nubby bathroom mat, too stunned to do anything other than wait for him. He came back with an ice pack wrapped in a dishtowel and then helped me to the couch. I rested my head in his lap while he held the ice to my cheek.

I told Daisy and anyone else who asked that I'd fallen on a patch of ice in the driveway. Caroline was the only one who openly doubted the story. So desperate was I to hide it, but I needed to tell someone too. I downplayed it as much as possible and made her promise not to tell Jack. In the weeks after it happened, she tried to get me to talk, but I shut her down every time. He was drunk. It was an accident. It would never happen again.

DAISY

Chapter Nine

No one ever actually says *heroin*.

It isn't a word that Connor would use in a conversation with me. It would be like yelling *fire* in the middle of a crowded auditorium. Or staring directly at the sun. If you say it aloud, it suddenly becomes real. Look away and you can pretend you don't know.

But that doesn't mean I don't know.

It's nearly eleven and I'm just getting ready for bed when he sends me a text.

Quick drink?

Okay, I write back. *Where?*

A bar's not an option, not for me at least. Connor turned twenty-one last summer, but my birthday's not till the end of next week. A fake ID might work for the summer kids but not for us locals. And no one wants to get busted for serving a cop's kid.

My place, he replies. *Pick me up at work in ten.*

We haven't hung out in a while, just the two of us. He saves the nights for his friends, tucking me into the clean hours of daylight—a cup of coffee here, a ride there. My mother and Ian are already in bed, so I'm quiet when I leave the house, backing my car up slowly to avoid the dirty banks of snow that line the driveway.

Connor is already waiting outside of Moby Dick's, holding a bottle of something in a brown paper bag.

"Hey," he says after he's jumped in the car. He blows on his hands to warm them.

"Busy night?"

"Nah, slow as hell. February, man," he says, shaking his head.

I drive the few minutes to his apartment, hoping Keith won't be there. When I park on Main Street, I'm relieved to see that the lights are all off. Keith is either out or asleep. We walk single-file up the narrow steps of the building and Connor unlocks the door. The place is a mess, dirty glasses and dishes littering every surface of the living room. He grabs two cups from the kitchen, and I follow him into his bedroom.

The room still has the same stale smell as when I was here the other day, but somehow with Connor, it doesn't seem as bad. We sit on the rumpled bed, our backs against the wall, and Connor withdraws a bottle from the bag.

"Whiskey?" I ask, annoyed. "You couldn't have bought me something else?"

He laughs and pulls out two nips of Baileys. "For you. You big baby."

I elbow him and pour one of the bottles into my cup. Though I'm looking forward to turning twenty-one, I don't drink that often. When I do, I like my drinks sweet and easy going down.

We talk, about nothing in particular. Connor makes me laugh with tales from the kitchen at Moby Dick's, and I complain about working for my mother. Nothing much, just ordinary conversation, but it's nice. I've missed him.

"Have you heard anything more about the girl they found on the beach?" I ask. It's all anyone can talk about. Great Rock isn't a place where people get murdered. It's horrible, but somehow people want to talk about it too.

Connor shifts on the bed and his face darkens. "No. It's messed up, though."

"I know, she was over for the winter festival, but do you think someone from the island could have done it?" I ask. I realize I've been assuming all along that it was someone from off-island, and it only occurs to me now that I may be wrong.

"I don't know, I doubt it. It was probably some drunk tourist. That's what people are saying online," Connor says. I've heard this too, but I think it's mostly what people want to believe rather than based on any actual information. Easier to think that a murderer came to the island for a night rather than that one was already living here.

"Has your dad said anything?"

Connor drains the last of his whiskey and then pours some more. "You know he doesn't talk about stuff like that with me. I haven't seen him in a while. He and my mother are both pretending they're still living together."

"Wait, what?" I twist the top off the second bottle of Baileys and pour it in the glass, feeling the slow slipping effects of the alcohol. "Your parents aren't living together? Since when?"

"A month? Maybe more?" He lets out a brusque laugh. "Not that either of them have actually told me."

"God, I'm sorry, Con. I didn't know." I sip my sweet drink and wait for him to say more. He just stares into the bottom of his glass.

I lived with Caroline, Jack and Connor for several months when I was eleven, the year that my little sister Serena died in a car crash, the year my mother went crazy. For six months I slept in their spare bedroom, and though Connor and I had been close before having grown up together, our relationship changed during that time. All those nights I snuck into his bedroom and he held me while I cried, all those afternoons he listened to me rail against my mother for falling apart when I most needed her. It changed us. We grew up during those months, and by the time I returned home, our relationship would never be the same.

"I never would have expected your parents to split up. Do you think they'll get back together?"

"How the hell should I know?" I flinch, stung by the harshness of his tone. "Sorry," he says more softly. "It's just messed up. The whole thing." He reaches for my hand and runs his thumb slowly along the top of each finger, outlining my entire hand. Then he leans in and kisses me.

Kissing Connor is like breathing. It's somehow essential to my survival. I pull him closer and want to bury my body inside his, so relieved to finally have him here.

It isn't a good idea. We've known each other too long. Over the years we've tried it all—friendship, sex, the whole boyfriend-girlfriend thing. We can't seem to get it right, but we can't seem to stop either. I wish I had the willpower to end it, because I know how it will go—awkwardness, followed by me feeling hurt, a few days of not talking, and then back to friends. Until the cycle starts all over again.

It doesn't matter though. Between the alcohol and Connor's mouth on my skin, I'm powerless, and there's nothing to do but give in to him.

Until he takes off his shirt, and I finally open my eyes.

His arms are freckled with red-gray sores, a few healed, others fresh. There aren't that many of them, probably three or four on each arm. But my body goes cold, and my stomach drops to the floor like a runaway elevator. Connor doesn't notice, and he keeps kissing me as his hand works its way under my bra.

"Connor," I whisper, pushing him away. "My God."

"What?" His eyes are blurry, still locked in the moment before. He sees where my gaze is directed. "It's nothing. Come here. Relax." He reaches for me again, his hand on my hip, mouth inches from mine, but I pull back, catching hold of his arm. He yanks it from my grasp and sits up. He must see something in my face, that I'm not going to drop this, because he finds his shirt on the bed and pulls it back on.

"Connor, what are you doing?" I want to cry. I want to bang on his chest and slap his face and tell him to stop. I want us to be eight years old again, eating popcorn and hot dogs for dinner, watching movies on a floor full of pillows while our parents laugh in the other room.

"What? It's not a big deal. Stop freaking out about nothing."

I reach for his arm, my fingers grabbing hold of the fabric of his shirt, sliding it up his forearm so the marks are visible. "This is nothing? How can you tell me that?"

He jerks his arm away. "Get off my back, okay? God, Daisy. Just forget it." He gets up from the bed and stares out the window.

A girl we graduated with died of an overdose at Christmas. Another guy a few years older last summer. Yet I don't know this world that Connor has entered. Not the street names or the landmarks or the terrain. This is a different Great Rock than the one I inhabit, though I know this version exists alongside the one where we grew up, just like the summertime Great Rock exists. This Great Rock isn't featured in the postcards or mentioned at back-to-school night at the high school. This Great Rock is quiet and slippery, understood through euphemism and what isn't spoken aloud. *Died unexpectedly* is what the obituary reads after an overdose.

I know all this, even if I don't understand it. But not Connor.

"What are you doing?" I ask again. I go to where he stands by the window and rest my head against his back. I'm surprised when he doesn't pull away. "Please," I say. I don't know what I'm asking for. I might not know this world, but I know enough to understand that me asking nicely won't make him stop. "Please," I say again, a breath into his tee shirt that smells of sweat and laundry detergent. A plea, a prayer, to this boy I've loved my whole life. "Please," I beg, and finally he turns around, holding me in his arms, stroking my hair, as if I'm the one who needs saving.

CAROLINE
Chapter Ten

Thursday is my night out with Evvy. We've done a Thursday night out nearly every week since the kids were little. Some weeks we go to yoga; occasionally we do some activity put on by Adult Ed at the high school—a cooking class or a book group, sometimes with a few other friends. But usually it's just the two of us for appetizers and drinks at one of the restaurants in town.

Tonight, we meet at Sam's Tavern. I like Sam's because it's cozy in the winter with a fireplace and lots of big wooden booths. If you sit in the back, it's possible to have a whole meal without bumping into someone you know.

Our drinks haven't even arrived before Evvy starts talking about the murder. "They called Ian in for questioning again yesterday." Evvy takes off her coat and drapes it along the booth.

"What happened?" People always assume I know more about police activity because of Jack. Even before he moved out, this wasn't true. Jack is one of the most closed-mouthed cops I know.

"They brought up the night a few years ago." Evvy's face is tight.

"What night?" I ask, though I'm pretty sure I already know.

"The night Cyrus drove us home from Christine's." The waitress comes and brings our wine. Evvy doesn't speak again till she's gone. "I told you not to tell Jack about that." Evvy's small, pretty features are wrinkled up in anger.

"He already knew. He saw you with your face all banged up, and he knew as well as I did that you didn't get it from slipping on some ice." I roll the stem of the wine glass between my thumb and forefinger. "It was serious, Evvy. You had a black eye for a week. I was worried."

"It was an accident. I told you that. Now they think he's some kind of violent criminal. It only happened once." Evvy directs these words into her own drink as she takes a large sip, and I'm not certain she's telling the truth. It's still hard for me to believe that Ian is capable of hurting her because it seems so at odds with his easygoing personality. When we see each other, he is charming and friendly, the type of guy that flirts with elderly women to make them feel young. At one point, I had thought we could all be friends, but after the night he hurt her, I realized that all I could hope for was that it was a one-time thing that would never happen again. Yet last spring she had a bruise the size of a baseball on her upper arm. I only saw it when the sleeve of her tee shirt rode up, but when I asked her about it, she said she banged it on the car door. No amount of probing could get her to say anything more.

"I'm sorry," I tell her again. "I really am."

We're quiet for a few minutes, and I'm relieved when the food arrives. It's more difficult to be upset when you're eating. I reach for a triangle of quesadilla.

"Have you heard if they have any suspects?" I don't ask if they have any *other* suspects. No one has officially called Ian a suspect, though we both know he's a person of interest.

Evvy shakes her head, leans across the table, lowering her voice. "No, but I heard they think the girl was bringing in drugs. She had connections on the island."

Her words catch me by surprise and my stomach flips, fingers of anxiety poking and prodding. I don't know what I was imagining as the reason for Layla Dresser's murder—as if anything could explain away such an act—but I realize I'd been hoping it was something random. I think of the photo I saw online the other day of the smiling, bright-eyed young woman. She had the fresh-faced good looks of someone who'd play the girl next door in a movie or advertised toothpaste in a commercial. I don't know what I imagine a drug dealer looks like, but this is not the image I had in my head.

I know there are drugs on Great Rock—an island like this, with little to do in the off-season and limited opportunities for employment. While I wish Connor would go to college and find the desire to dream and plan again, as he did not so long ago, it is the drugs and alcoholism on this island that loom large in my mind, even if I can't say it aloud.

"Where did you hear that?" I ask.

"Jan Bard, who heard it from Nancy Bunker."

Chad Bunker, Nancy's husband, is a cop in Egret. If Jack is known for being overly discreet, Chad has the opposite problem. Island secrets run like a leaky faucet from Chad's mouth, and Nancy is even worse. However, the rumors the Bunkers spread tend to be true.

"I guess she worked here last summer. At the Blue Crab and Moby Dick's. Connor must have known her. Did he say anything?" Evvy asks.

My whole body goes cold and there's a ringing in my ears. I focus on my paper napkin, squeezing it until it's a ball in my lap, trying to control my trembling hands. I can't believe he spent the night and didn't even tell me he knew the woman who was killed. We didn't talk about it for long, but surely he must have been shaken by it, even if they hadn't known each other well.

"We haven't talked in a few days," I lie. "But the summer crew is so big that they don't know each other as well, and the kitchen staff doesn't usually spend much time with the servers. There's so many of them." Evvy's worked in the food industry long enough to know this isn't true. Restaurants are hugely social places in the summertime, cocktail hour at the bar spilling over into late-night parties. "What kind of drugs was she bringing?" I ask.

"Heroin. And pills. People are saying that's why someone killed her," Evvy adds.

The whole thing makes me sick—that Connor hasn't told me he knew Layla, that the pills Jack found in his laundry might have come from her. I think back to Connor's unexpected appearance at the house the other night, the way he was so eager to leave even though he claimed he'd come by to see me. A wave of dizziness washes over me, and I wipe a hand across my forehead and down my temples.

Evvy narrows her eyes and peers more closely at me. "Are you okay? You look a little green."

"I think I might be coming down with something." I reach for my water glass and am grateful that my hand doesn't tremble, though I feel as if I could crack into a million pieces any second. I force myself to eat a bite of food. I don't want to talk about the dead girl anymore, and I know Evvy doesn't want to talk about Ian. Jack is the next logical topic, but this is also something I don't feel like discussing. There are suddenly too many things that seem off-limits. I sigh and sip my wine.

"You okay?" Evvy asks again.

"Yeah. Winter blues, I guess."

"God, tell me about it. It's been awful. Worst I can remember it being in years." Evvy brings her hand up to ruffle her own hair. "I really do love your haircut."

"Thanks." I run my fingers through it. "Though I probably should have waited till it was warmer to cut it. My neck's going to be freezing till spring." Evvy waves to someone across the restaurant. I turn to see Cyrus coming toward us.

"Hey, you," Evvy says shyly, and Cyrus bends down to kiss her cheek. He turns to me and does the same.

"Evening, ladies."

He slides into the booth beside Evvy as if it's the most natural thing in the world. Evvy and Cyrus were high-school sweethearts, both of them born and raised on Great Rock. It was Serena's death that ultimately tore them apart, but they fought even before she died. I imagine Evvy was the force behind those fights, her loneliness and boredom being home all day with the girls boiling over into a frenzy when Cyrus came home late from work yet again. When Serena died, things just fell apart at the seams. Now Evvy is flushed and doe-eyed, listening to Cyrus talk about a patch of ice his car skidded on. For a moment, I understand Ian's anger the night he hit her; it's clear she's still in love with Cyrus.

"You want to join us for a drink?" Evvy asks. If Jack and I divorce, I doubt this will be the kind of relationship we'll have. Daisy was barely a teenager when Evvy and Cyrus split up. They needed to figure out a way to be together without being married. Jack and I won't have that issue. In fact, I wonder if I'll even stay on Great Rock if Jack and I divorce. What would keep me here? Yet despite dreaming about leaving for so long, I have no idea where I'd go.

"Nah, I'm just ordering some takeout." He holds up the paper menu. "Gina loves Sam's chicken pot pie."

Evvy smiles politely. *There it is*, I think. The same jealousy I would have if Jack ever mentioned another woman so affectionately.

"How are you doing?" he asks me. *How are you doing without Jack*, is what he means.

"Fine. Just fine," I answer vaguely. He holds my eye for a moment as if assessing whether I'm telling the truth.

"Okay then. Better put in my order. Nice to see you both." He stands and turns to Evvy. "I might stop by sometime this week. Daisy asked me to look at her car. She thinks the brakes are going."

"Evenings are good this week," Evvy says. Code for *that's when Ian won't be home*.

"Great. I'll see you soon then." Cyrus tips his head at us and returns to the bar.

"Do you want anything else?" Evvy asks. We still have food between us and we haven't even finished our first drink. "You don't feel well, and I'm kind of tired. Do you mind if we head out?"

"Oh, sure," I say, both surprised and relieved that we won't have to pick our way through the minefield of our lives tonight. I gesture to the leftovers. "We can pack this up."

We're walking toward the exit when Evvy turns to me. Her face is flushed, her blue eyes shining. She tips her head to where Cyrus is sitting at the bar. "I just need to talk to him for another minute. About Daisy's car. You go on." The pink flush that spreads across her cheeks quickly confirms the lie.

I hesitate. It's not a good idea, leaving the two of them together. Someone will see them. It will eventually make its way back to Ian, and this scares me. I want to like Ian. He's funny and charming, and Evvy's been happier with him than she was with Cyrus, though this probably has more to do with the antidepressants she takes now than anything about Cyrus or Ian. Yet, much as I want to like Ian, I don't trust him. Not after what happened a few years ago. And I don't trust Evvy around Cyrus.

"I can wait," I say.

"No, really, go on," Evvy urges. "It might take a few minutes. I think we need to lend her some money for a new one. I'm pretty sure this car is on its last legs."

"I don't mind waiting," I try again.

"I'm fine. Really," Evvy says meaningfully.

"Okay. Be safe." I lean in and give her a quick hug.

"Always," Evvy answers with a grin, but it isn't true. Unlike me, Evvy likes to court danger.

EVVY

Chapter Eleven

Cyrus is paying for his food when I slide up to him.

"You leaving already? Where's Caroline?" he asks.

"She didn't feel well." This is partly true. "I was hoping to catch you for a minute before I left."

"I'll walk you back to your car."

Cyrus thanks the teenager at the register, a girl a few classes below Daisy. On the way out of Sam's we wave to a few people. Though I know that Caroline craves the anonymity of another place, I've never known anything else. If it somehow gets back to Ian that we left together, I'll explain why I needed to speak to Cyrus. And then hope he understands.

Cyrus holds the front door open for me, and I wait until we're outside to speak. A light snow is starting to fall. I turn to him once we're in the dim glow of the streetlight.

"Is Ian a suspect?" I blurt out. It's the question I've been wondering since Ian first went into the station, the one he won't answer directly.

Cyrus lets out a sigh. "You know I can't tell you anything, Ev."

"Just tell me if he's a suspect." He catches my elbow to steady me on a patch of ice. He stops walking and looks at me, really looks at me, but he doesn't answer. "It's not going to go away, is it?" I ask.

He shakes his head. "No. It's not. You should get a lawyer."

"He didn't do it," I burst out. "He would never. *Ever.*" Ian's rages are born of jealousy and impulse. He's not calculating or premeditated. He'd never stalk some girl down a desolate beach in the middle of winter.

"You don't know that."

"Yes, I do," I say. "He told me he talked with her at the bar and that they left at the same time. That doesn't mean he killed her." I shiver in my winter coat. The street is empty, the road crusted with a thick gray snow.

"Did he tell you they got into a fight down the road from the bar? That he split her lip?" Cyrus asks. My stomach flips, like someone's jumped out from behind a closed door and yelled *boo*. I don't want to believe it, but somehow I can picture the scene so clearly: a few too many drinks, Ian's temper, the bloody lip. Cyrus's breath is a puff of white that evaporates in the cold air.

I shake my head. "No. No, he wouldn't."

"He did, Evvy. Jack saw them. Jack went to make sure she was okay."

"Then why didn't he arrest him right then? If Ian hit her, why did Jack just let him go?" I ask.

"She told Jack she was fine. Said she slipped and fell."

"So she probably did! You know what the sidewalks are like around here. None of the business owners bother to shovel and salt unless they're threatened with a fine."

The excuse sounds flimsy even to me, but I can't believe that what he's saying could be true. It doesn't make sense—why Ian would fight with some girl he doesn't even know, why he'd smack her in the mouth. She must have fallen on the ice, like she told Jack.

"They found her number on his phone. There are records of phone calls between them. Going back months," Cyrus says, his voice gentler now.

I want to protest, to call Cyrus a liar, but I know he'd never lie to me. Not about anything, and certainly not about this. I bring my hand up to my mouth, feel my ragged breathing stuck in my chest. I feel so stupid. Ian is many things, but it didn't occur to me that he might be cheating on me. There were no obvious signs, no vague excuses or unexpected nights out. No texts messages or mysterious phone calls, no credit card receipts for flowers or hotel rooms. I know I have no right to be so hurt. I've done things I'm not proud of in the years that Ian and I have been together, but that girl couldn't have been much older than Daisy. I feel weak, like my legs might give out any moment. I reach for Cyrus, and he puts his arm around my back, supporting me.

"I'm sorry." He looks remorseful, though he's not the one who's done anything wrong. "I thought you knew. I figured Jack or Caroline would have told you by now."

"No one told me anything." Later, in the privacy of my own home, I'll think about how Jack, a man I've known my whole life, a man who cared for my own daughter like a father, managed to withhold this bit of information from me. I wonder if he told Caroline or if he didn't even bother. For now, I can't get hung up on this, too shaken by what Cyrus has told me to be hurt by Jack or Caroline.

"Between Jack seeing them together outside the bar, the possible assault, and the phone records, it's enough to charge him. Plus, he's got a history." Cyrus's jaw is set hard, and he's still holding on to my elbow, his grip a little tighter.

I'm silent for a moment, embarrassed that he knows, pleased that he cares. "It was once. It was a mistake, and it's never happened since." This isn't entirely true, but it's almost true. It's not a regular thing. I could count on one hand the number of times Ian has hurt me, and none of them has been as bad as the night that Cyrus knows about. Contrary to what Caroline may think, I'm not *afraid* of Ian. I've just learned to manage him over the years.

"You better be telling me the truth," Cyrus says. He's standing so close I taste the faint smell of the beer he had back at Sam's.

"Because I swear to God, Evvy, I will kill him if he ever lays a hand on you again."

I can't help it, but I feel a thrill of pleasure at his protection that rises above my confusion and hurt over whatever Ian has done. "He hasn't. He wouldn't," I breathe. And then I lean in and kiss him, because even now I still miss him so much, and somehow knowing that Ian might have been cheating on me all this time gives me permission. Cyrus kisses me back, hard, before he pushes me away.

"What the hell, Evvy?" We're standing on the sidewalk near the beach, the cold air tearing off the water, and though it's dark, anyone could see.

"Sorry." I look down and pretend to be remorseful, but I'm not. I'm only full of regret. If I could have a chance to do it all over and be a better wife, I would.

"Just don't, okay?" He shakes his head in frustration and starts to walk. I follow him. "Where's your car?"

"Further down." I let him lead the way. The smell of the ocean is rich despite the cold, and the air is icier here. It must be freezing right beside the water. I look down at the beach where Layla Dresser died just a few nights earlier. *Was murdered*, I remind myself, because despite what Cyrus has told me, I still don't believe Ian did it. No one saw Ian hit her, no one saw him follow her down to the beach and kill her. The only link between them is the phone records, which prove that Ian is just a weak man, like so many others.

"Right here." I gesture to my car.

He stands beside me while I dig for my keys, and I slide into the driver's seat.

"I'm sorry," I repeat.

Cyrus just shakes his head and lets out a puff of white breath. "I'll come check out Daisy's car sometime soon."

"I think she'll need a new one. Maybe we can offer her a loan."

He smiles, thinking of his girl. "She's been working really hard. She deserves it." He pushes my door closed and taps the roof of my car. "Drive safe."

I back out slowly and my headlights illuminate the staircase leading down to the beach. Cyrus watches me drive off, his hands pushed deep into the pockets of his coat.

DAISY

Chapter Twelve

After the night in his bedroom, when I saw the evidence of what he's doing written on his body, Connor doesn't call or text, and for once neither do I. I know we'll talk again soon. One of us will break in the next day, but I need to think before I see him again. The marks on his arms scared me. More than once I've seen him remove a tablet from a plastic baggie in his pocket. When I'd ask him what they were, he'd brush me off and tell me he had a headache. As if I couldn't tell Tylenol from something else.

On Friday night I work an engagement party in Egret. The party is for Molly Rankin and Benny Slade, a couple who graduated a few years ahead of Connor and me. Benny is a well-known chef on the island, and it's a big deal that Petunia's got the event. The party is small, just twenty-five people, so it's only me, my mother, and Paul Floyd working it—the winter skeleton crew at Petunia's. It's mostly an island crowd here tonight, and a handful of restaurant people. The whole locally grown thing is popular now, especially with this crowd, and I'm glad my mother spent the extra money on the local purple potatoes and squash we're serving tonight.

Molly graduated from Great Rock High School, but she isn't an island girl in the same way that I am. She moved here as a teenager and then returned after college. She teaches yoga classes at the place my mom goes, which is how Petunia's got this job. Her brother, Bret, was a year ahead of me and Connor in school, and I know he and Connor still hang out, but I don't see him here tonight. Her parents have rented the Egret Town Barn and filled the place with tons of space heaters. There are white tablecloths on the picnic tables and bottles of champagne in galvanized pails filled with ice. Tea candles in jam jars flicker everywhere, and instead of the traditional black-and-white catering outfit, I'm wearing jeans and a black button-down.

I circle the room with a tray, pausing to offer stuffed quahogs. Despite the casual atmosphere and coziness of the room, it's one of those parties I hate to work. Most of the guests are just a few years older than me, and I've crossed paths with almost all of them in some way or another—through school or friends or summer jobs. But the people here are from yet another Great Rock. This is the trust fund crowd. These are the twenty-somethings who spent summers on Great Rock as children and then moved here after college to work part-time on a dairy farm or teach yoga or make jewelry. They're the ones whose parents own property on the island, and they live here for half the year while spending the rest of the year in St. John's or St. Thomas. On the surface they don't look all that different from the rest of us. But if I look a little closer, I might notice that all their sweaters are cashmere, or that they own four pairs of three-hundred-dollar Frye boots. They drive Mini Coopers or old Saabs and live for free in the houses that their parents own.

With this crowd, I feel like the hired help more than anything. I'm pretty sure no one here spent years commuting off-island to community college. They all went to private colleges and graduated after four years without a single dollar in student loans. It's a different life. We might share the same swath of land, but we live a million miles apart.

"Daisy, right? Can I grab one of those?" I look up to see a sandy-haired guy eyeing the tray I'm carrying. I lower the tray, and he takes a napkin and two clams. I peer closer at him, trying to figure out how he knows me. He puts a hand to his chest. "Todd Rankin. I catered for your mom a few summers ago."

"Oh, sure." I remember him now. I was still in high school the summer he worked at Petunia's. He'd been in college—Dartmouth, I think. Not UMass Dartmouth. The *real* Dartmouth. We worked a few dinners together, but not many. "I didn't realize you lived here."

"I don't. I'm just here for a few days. I'll head back to Boston soon."

I glance around the room. My mother hates it when I talk too long to guests without circulating. I gesture to the near empty tray. "I think I need to refresh these."

"Come find me later. We'll have a drink when you finish serving." He has a nice smile, I notice. There's something relaxed about his demeanor that makes me feel as if we know each other well already.

My mother also hates it when I hang out after events. Unprofessional, she says. And a liability, since I'm not twenty-one. I don't say yes to Todd's offer, but I don't say no either, and I'm not sure why. This isn't my crowd; these people alternately annoy me or make me nervous, with their money and pretend jobs. But I'm tired of the world I'm living in right now, with the slow-paced progress toward something better elsewhere. I'm tired of waiting for Connor and his haunted eyes and the secrets he's started keeping from me. Maybe for tonight I can be someone else.

We finish serving by ten, and my mom heads out, leaving me and Paul to clean up. Usually my mother stays to do this with us, but she's been even more on edge than usual the past few days, though she hasn't said a thing about Ian getting brought into the police station. My feet and back hurt after hours carrying trays, but I don't argue. My mother pays me well, and winter work isn't easy to come by.

Paul is out on the floor refilling drinks, and I'm in the kitchen washing the last few dishes when Todd comes in carrying a bottle of champagne. "Ready for that drink?" he asks.

I roll my eyes, though I'm pleased he didn't forget his offer. "I'm still working."

He puts the bottle down on the counter and rolls up the sleeves of his blue dress shirt. "Right. So what do we need to do? Remind me how this goes."

I raise my eyebrows at him, trying to gauge if he's serious or kidding. I decide to take him at his word. "The dishes need to be dried. And then they can get packed in the carrier cases right here." I point to the padded bags on the floor.

"Great." He gets to work quickly, drying the plates. I finish washing and he helps me pack them neatly in the cases. The dishes are heavy and my back aches as I gently load each stack. "Anything else?" he asks, once they've all been washed and packed.

"Trash." I look to the bag in the corner of the kitchen. "But you don't need to do that." My mother would freak out if she knew I let a guest take out the garbage. I pull the bag from the trashcan and have to tug to get it loose. It's nearly overflowing, and the middle of the bag is stuck tight inside the metal bin. I pull, holding it in place with my feet and tugging the plastic handles at the same time. I give the bag a hard jerk and the contents scatter everywhere—clam shells, coffee grounds, hundreds of squashed-up dirty napkins—all over the kitchen floor that I just finished sweeping.

"Shit." It's close to eleven and I'm near tears. Forget the drink, I just want to go home. I put my hands up to my eyes, trying to keep from crying. I'm so tired of this. I'm too young to feel this old. It's a Friday night, and I should be getting drunk at a college party with friends, not cleaning up trash from the floor of a barn kitchen.

"Hey, you okay?" Todd puts an arm around my shoulder, and when I lower my hands he's watching me with concern.

"Yeah, I'm just tired. It's been a long night."

"Let's get this cleaned up and then we can get you home. Here. Sit." He pulls a chair out from the table and pushes me into it. He finds a new trash bag and the broom in the corner of the room and sweeps the mess into a big pile, which he proceeds to scoop with his hands into the open bag. I hope Molly or her mother don't come in and see the scene, as they're the ones employing Petunia's, but I'm too tired to care. He fills the trash bag, brings it to the dumpster out back, and then comes back to sweep the floor again.

At last he gestures to the clean kitchen. "Are we good?"

His eyes are dark blue and a sprinkling of freckles dusts his nose. Definitely has that rich-kid look to him, with the designer jeans and expensive shoes, and the solid build of someone who's played sports his whole life. There's something healthy and bright about him, or maybe it's just in contrast to seeing Connor the other night. Todd is like feeling sun after a long winter.

"Thank you."

"So? What do you think?" He picks up the bottle of champagne. "We deserve a drink."

I hesitate. "I need to drive home." Egret is nearly a half-hour from Osprey.

"I can drop you."

I shake my head. Once a cop's kid, always a cop's kid. Now more than ever, with an unsolved murder on the island, my father would be furious with me if I were to go home with a stranger. Todd's cute and he seems nice, but I know better than to go home with him. Not tonight, at least.

"Just one tiny drink then?" He holds his thumb and forefinger an inch apart, indicating the size of the tiny drink.

The clock on the wall says ten past eleven. Paul hasn't come into the kitchen, which means that people are still drinking and hanging out. I'll need to stay until the party's over and we can collect all of the glasses anyway. "Okay. Just one."

He flashes a smile at me and reaches for the champagne. He removes the cork slowly and it makes a deep thump in the bottle as the pressure is released. He pours us each a glass and then holds his up to mine.

"Cheers. To the end of a long night."

I clink my glass against his and take a sip. The bubbles sting the back of my throat, but in a good way. "How long are you on the island?"

"I got here last weekend. I'll stay for a few more days then I need to get back to work."

"What do you do in Boston?"

"I work in a restaurant." I expected him to have a job in an office somewhere, making a lot of money. My surprise must show on my face, because he lets out a laugh. "Is that so shocking?"

"No, it's just… didn't you go to Dartmouth?" It comes out more bluntly than I intended.

He laughs, unoffended. "I dropped out junior year."

I look at him like he's lost his mind. I don't understand people like this.

"I know it sounds crazy, but I was a business major and I hated it. My dad was the one who wanted me to go there in the first place. It just wasn't what I wanted." He finishes the champagne and pours himself another glass. He refills my glass as well, and I don't stop him. "I'll finish the degree at some point. Just not now."

"And your parents were paying for it?" He nods. "That was dumb."

He lets out a short laugh, though his face has grown dark. "Trust me, nothing's free, but my father would certainly agree with you. Sometimes I think about moving here though."

"God, why?" I frown at him in disbelief.

He laughs, the anger clearing from his face. "Do you always say what's on your mind?" he asks.

I shrug. "I just don't see why anyone would want to move here. I mean, maybe when you're ready to start a family or retire or something, but not now. I can't wait to get out of here."

"Molly likes it. She's done pretty well here."

"What about your brother? I didn't see him here tonight. What's Bret up to these days?" Bret was a year ahead of me and Connor.

His face closes again. "Nothing good." I wait for him to elaborate, but he doesn't. A moment later, Paul comes into the kitchen carrying a stack of glasses.

"Well, aren't you comfy?" he says with a smirk. Paul is an island kid, a few years older than me, and he's been with my mother since she started Petunia's. He's an easy guy to work with, quick to laugh or tell a joke, ready to cover a shift at a moment's notice. I smile guiltily and put down my nearly empty glass. When I rise to help him with the glasses, I realize I'm slightly unsteady on my feet. I hardly had any dinner, just a few bites while I was in the kitchen, and the champagne combined with the late hour has hit me harder than I expected. I consider asking Paul to drive me home but am too embarrassed to ask in front of Todd.

Todd nods his head at Paul. "Hey, Paul, long time no see."

"Hey, man, how's it going?"

"Not bad. Just helping out a little."

Paul nods and then turns to me. "There's not much left to do. You can get out of here."

"Are you sure?"

"Don't worry about it." He tilts his head toward Todd, whose back is to us. I go to gather my things. Todd finishes the last sip of champagne and drops the empty bottle in with the recyclables. "You going to give her a ride home?" Paul asks Todd.

Todd looks over at me. "Do you need one?"

I flush, embarrassed to have my drunkenness be so obvious to Paul. "No, I'm fine."

"She needs one," Paul says. He turns to me. "Don't worry about Todd here. He's a good guy. Used to drive me and Bret home shit-faced all the time."

I find my coat hanging in the kitchen hall. "Thanks, Paul. Goodnight." Todd follows me outside.

The night air is bracing. There's nearly a full moon and the sky is lit in a blue-black glow. We cross the empty field of the barn toward the parking lot. My feet sink into the snow and as we walk, I consider my options. I could drive home and risk getting pulled over. I'm probably not even over the limit, except I'm underage, which would make the whole thing worse. Or I could get a ride with Todd. *Never drink and drive. Never go home with a stranger.* My father's words echo in my ears, and I know the option he'd want me to choose is waiting for Paul to get off work or calling a friend to pick me up. But none of my friends live in Egret. I could call Ian and he'd pick me up. He's offered plenty of times, and I've even taken him up on it occasionally. But I know it will get back to my mother that I was drinking at work, and I'll never hear the end of it. A cab would be a fortune. And waiting for Paul would mean another hour. And technically, Todd isn't a stranger. I've known him for years, though not well, and Paul obviously knows his family. I think back to the woman who was murdered. Did Layla weigh her options and pick the wrong one? But there's something about Todd that makes me trust him—the way he jumped in to help me with the cleanup, the ease with which he left the comfort of the party for the mess of the kitchen. I like talking with him, and I'm not ready to say goodnight.

Todd's Audi is parked a few cars over from my own beat-up Chevy. He opens the passenger side door. "So. You coming?"

I hesitate. Back at the barn the party is slowly winding down. The glittering lights from the candles twinkle inside. Thin peals of laughter echo across the field. Todd's holding the door open for me, an expectant look on his face. I step inside.

CAROLINE
Chapter Thirteen

When I get home from dinner with Evvy, I go straight up to Connor's room. This time I don't hesitate at the door, but go inside. I sit down on the rumpled bed and survey the room, wondering where to begin, terrified of what Connor's got himself mixed up in.

I start with the drawers, pulling them out one at a time, letting my hand roam under the soft pile of tee shirts and worn jeans. I slide each drawer out and search, but the most incriminating thing I find is a roll of condoms. Though it's not what I'm looking for, the condoms make me pause for a moment. Who is he having sex with? Daisy? Some other girl I've never met? Or are they just a precaution, the type of thing every young man keeps in his underwear drawer? I put them back where I found them and circle the room slowly.

I go to his nightstand next and drop to my knees beside it. Inside is an odd collection of junk—an old phone charger, a double A battery, a set of keys, pens, sticky coins, a dark blue bottle of cologne, though I can't recall Connor ever wearing a scent stronger than deodorant. I close the drawer with a sigh and sit back down on the bed.

I want to leave it at that. Maybe I *should* leave it at that. My half-hearted search turned up nothing, so maybe there's nothing to find. But I'm not convinced. The franticness of Connor's late-night visit, his worn-down appearance—it's hard to believe there's no significance to it.

I scan the room. There aren't that many belongings left in here anymore. Most of them Connor took with him when he moved out. His closet door is partly open, and on the top of the closet I see his old guitar case. I think about how happy I was to see him with it just the other night, how I'd asked him to play for me, and even though he'd declined, I'd been encouraged that he'd been playing on his own. I sit on the old blue carpet with the case across my lap. When I open it, the musky scent of leather is released. Inside there's Connor's old guitar. Tucked into the lining is a red handkerchief neatly folded in a square. Connor used to polish his guitar with this, lovingly rubbing the wood in circles as if he were bathing an infant. I carefully unfold the rag and find it empty, smelling sweetly of the citrus-scented oil he used on the guitar. I refold the rag and put it back where it was, sick of this whole mission. I shut the case and redo the latches.

I'm just about to put it away when I notice the bulging pockets on the back. With shaking fingers I undo the buckle of one, only to reveal a small red bottle of instrument cleaner. I'm filled with relief yet go on to the second one. The buckle on this pocket is older, slightly rusted, and it takes longer to open. When I'm able to undo the clasp, I slide my hand into the worn leather pocket, my heart beating heavily as my fingers grasp something soft and moveable, like a bag of marbles. I pull out the object to find another handkerchief, this one purple. I peel back the cloth.

I'm unprepared for the quantity. I'd known all along what I was looking for, but I'd expected to find a baggie with five or ten pills, like the one Jack found in Connor's pants. But this Ziploc is different. It's packed with hundreds of the little white pills. This isn't for recreational use. This belongs to someone who's selling the pills. This is the stash of a drug dealer.

I drop the bag to the floor. My breath comes in shallow pants, like Champ's after a long walk on a hot day. I stare at the bag and try to piece together what it means. Clearly Connor was here the other night to hide this or retrieve something from it. He's either doing drugs or dealing drugs, or he stole them from someone. There are only so many possible scenarios. I think of all the college catalogs I've been collecting and leaving on his bed like presents, my own hopes for the future, a future I realize is slipping further and further away, if it hasn't disappeared entirely. It's not too late. It can't be.

I reach for the bag where it lies on the floor, bringing it closer to examine. The pills are white, like the Great Rock skyline on a winter's day. Except for the plastic baggie, they look innocuous, like something I'd pick up at the drugstore for a headache. It's bad enough to imagine Connor using drugs, but to think he's also supplying drugs to the island is even more terrifying. Not only could he die, but other mothers, mothers that I *know*, may also lose their children because of Connor.

I rise from the floor, clutching the baggie in my hand. My thoughts are murky as I try to focus on what to do next. I could call Connor, demand that he tell me what's going on. But he'd only lie to me, like he did so easily when he was last here. I could call Jack. But Jack is a police officer, *always* a police officer, even when it comes to Connor. Much as Jack loves his son, he wouldn't expect special treatment. In fact, it's entirely possible that if I call Jack, he'll have someone go to Connor's apartment and arrest him. I wish I could call Evvy and ask her what to do, but I know this isn't information I can share with anyone. Other than Connor, I'm the only one who knows this bag is in the house.

I need the pills gone. I realize this suddenly, how their existence underscores a reality that I'm still not willing to accept. The image of a drug dealer doesn't match the pale-haired boy who cried at *Peter and the Wolf*, a boy who was afraid to swim in the deep end till he was eight, who wouldn't hold a sparkler on the Fourth of July because he was worried about singeing his fingers. This can't be my son.

If I throw out the pills, Connor cannot use or sell them. If he can't sell them, no one can take them. It's as simple as that. I know this isn't logical. I know enough about drugs and addiction to realize that there are always more drugs, and that if Connor wants them enough, he'll find them. The only thing that I can control is what will happen to *these* drugs.

My heart flutters rapidly in my chest as I bring the baggie into the bathroom. The artificial heat in the house suddenly feels oppressive, and I'm sweating, my work clothes sticking to my skin. A fine mist of perspiration beads my brow. I squeeze the bag in my hand and the pills click together like castanets.

I could drop the contents of the whole bag down the toilet and just flush it all away. Isn't that what they do in the movies when the cops come? But the septic systems on Great Rock are old. I'm not even sure that the pills will go down the toilet as opposed to just sitting at the bottom of the bowl. Or I imagine the toilet clogging and overflowing, having to call Jack or a plumber or septic repairman and somehow explaining the hundreds of pills stuck deep in the pipes of my toilet. I could flush them a few at a time, but there are hundreds of pills. It will take hours and could also cause the toilet to back up.

I could put the little baggie into another plastic bag, take it out and bury it in the bottom of a garbage pail. But trash pickup isn't till next Thursday, and though it's unlikely that anyone will go digging in my trashcans, I know I won't be calm until the pills are gone.

I take the bag into my bedroom and though I'm suddenly feverish, I find a gray sweater that I wear around the house. It's long and soft with deep pockets, and I drop the baggie into one, unreasonably fearful of walking around my own house clutching this supply of little white pills. I walk back downstairs and into the kitchen. I stand for a moment in front of the closed cabinets, trying to figure out what I'll need. After a moment I find the meat mallet, a cutting board, a small wooden bowl, and a dishtowel. I bring these back up into my bedroom and kneel on the floor, laying the materials out before me. I pour a handful of twenty pills or so onto the cutting board and then spread the dishtowel on top of them. The towel is pale yellow decorated with bright blue birds, a souvenir Evvy brought back from a trip to Maine. When I bring the mallet down on the towel, gently at first and then harder, the birds jerk and jump beneath each metal blow like they're alive. After a moment I peel back the towel to reveal a chunky white powder, which I pour into the wooden bowl. I bring the bowl into the bathroom and pour the powder into the toilet. I flush and watch the powder wash down the drain.

I let out a long breath, feeling a little calmer already. This will work. I can erase all evidence. I return to the bedroom and sink back down to my knees, adding more pills to the cutting board, banging the mallet harder, more forcefully now, more determined to have this over and done with.

It takes eight rounds of hammering and eight trips to the bathroom before the drugs are gone. When I'm finished, my arms and neck ache. I bring the dishes down to the sink and wash them in steaming hot water and soap, then put them in the dishwasher. I turn it on, though there are barely any other dishes in there. I bring the vacuum upstairs and do the carpet in the bedroom, sucking up any fine fragments of pills that have been left behind in the wool. Finally, I take the empty baggie and soiled towel and put them into the trash basket in my room, then take the whole bag out to the car. Tomorrow morning I'll drive straight to the dump and pay five dollars to throw the small bag into a huge trash receptacle filled with other people's garbage. When I come back inside, I take a long hot shower and scrub my skin till it's tender and pink.

By the time I emerge from the shower, I'm exhausted, physically and emotionally depleted. I pull on pajamas and get in bed and try to sleep. But every time I close my eyes, my mind circles back to Connor. What has he done? And what else am I willing to do to protect him? I stare at the ceiling for a long time, afraid of the answer to both questions.

EVVY

Chapter Fourteen

When I get home from the small private function I catered tonight, Ian is still at work, and for this I'm relieved. I don't hear him crawl into bed, yet I wake up Saturday morning to his hands circling my hips and sliding up to my breasts. I let him pull off my thin cotton nightgown, and I wriggle out of my underwear. All week he's watched me warily, since he got back from the police station, armed with the knowledge of my betrayal. His hands on my skin are proof of his forgiveness.

We haven't talked about it. He has told me the bare minimum—that he spoke with Layla at the bar, they talked about winter on Great Rock, she told him she was visiting for the weekend. There is so much that I haven't pushed him on—if they argued outside the bar, why he'd been talking to her for months, how long he's been cheating on me. Everything unsaid fills the space between us, and I wonder if things have always been like this with us, avoiding what's real in favor of what's easy.

I wonder when and where he had sex with Layla. Already she's changing in my mind from *that girl who got murdered* to *Layla*. Did Ian sing that Eric Clapton song to her, crooning *Layla* in her ear? Did they do it in the bathroom of the Great Rock Ferry where Ian works, or in the back seat of his car when he got off work? Has she been in my house? It's terrifying to think about her being here, in my bed, my sheets. Even though I don't think

Ian would actually bring her to our home, it's almost as if she's here anyway, her presence haunting the house even while dead. I wish her murder made me think of her more sympathetically, but I can't help but feel a dirty satisfaction that she got what was coming to her.

Ian is a morning person, and he likes early morning sex, but Cyrus preferred sex at night, the bedroom a black cave where we found each other with our mouths. Ian's eyes on me in the pale morning light are greedy, hungry for more than I can ever offer. With Ian, I sometimes feel as if he sees me like no one else ever has. He knows me better than Cyrus and loves me anyway, cracked edges, sharp angles and all. This is something that Cyrus and Caroline will never understand. There's something else. Ian only knows me as I am since Serena's death, and though I'm only half the person I was before, I'm also somehow stronger and more capable, maybe because the worst has happened and I've managed to go on. When Cyrus and I were together, before Serena died, it felt like I was always a disappointment; to him, to the girls, to myself. I know now that it was the depression and my desire to be more than a stay-at-home mom, and a poor one at that. It was easy for Cyrus and me to drift apart. Serena's death tore us in half, but we were already broken.

With Ian, there are no little children to worry about. There's more time to spend together, more ways to be attentive than Cyrus or I ever thought to do. Ian and I go for walks together every weekend, long routes around the island even on the coldest days. We have favorite shows that we watch together, ridiculous reality shows where we heckle the participants from the couch, laughing till my stomach muscles hurt. He takes me to dinner or to the movies, date nights for no particular reason. Ian loves to buy presents, and he'll often come home with some small gift just because he knows I'll like it—a pair of wampum earrings in the shape of hearts, the banana nut loaf from my favorite bakery still hot from the oven, a bouquet of daffodils that he bought for a fundraiser. Ian makes time for me in a way that Cyrus never could.

Beside me in bed, Ian rolls over and goes back to sleep. He looks calm and peaceful, his mind untroubled. I lie beside him for a few minutes, wondering when he will tell me the truth, wondering if I'll forgive him or if maybe I already have.

I push myself from bed and get up to make coffee. The clock on the stove says it's not even nine. Daisy's bedroom door is closed, but that doesn't actually mean she's sleeping. I crack it open just enough to see that her bed is empty. I close the door with a sigh.

Daisy is twenty, old enough to live on her own if we lived in a place where rent was affordable. Housing on Great Rock is difficult. Homeowners want to rent at top dollar for the summer months, leaving limited options available for people who live here year-round. Each spring, hundreds of families on Great Rock are forced to leave their homes to make room for the summer people and scramble for overpriced summer housing. The summer shuffle, we call it. I'm glad that I can let Daisy live at home while she works her way through school. However, the rules for parenting a twenty-year-old are unclear. I can't give her a curfew, but that doesn't mean I don't worry when she stays out late. I worry when she's out of my sight for more than a few hours. Daisy doesn't have a boyfriend, not now, at least not one that she's told me about. No one except Connor, and her relationship with him is even more dysfunctional than my relationship with Cyrus. Daisy and Connor don't have the relationship of typical twenty-year-olds. What they have is grown-up love. The kind that leads to marriage. Or divorce.

Connor was a child full of light. His smile was mischievous and inviting, like he was willing to share the joke if you'd only ask. Fair-haired and freckled with twinkly blue eyes, his face was open to the whole world. But the last few times I've seen Connor, he doesn't smile. His freckles have all but washed away, taking with them the last remnants of childhood. Now he looks angry and tired, his eyes flat and hooded. The only time he seems to smile is when he looks at Daisy. And I wish that made me happy, but instead it makes me want to scrape together enough money to get her the hell away from this island and him.

I bring my coffee into the living room and take out my phone. There's a new message from Cyrus with "cars" as the subject. When I click on it, there are photos of two possible used cars for Daisy along with the details for each. *What do you think?* is the only thing Cyrus has written in the message. *They both look good,* I write back. *Let's talk later.*

The message isn't about the cars. Like Ian's hands on me just a few minutes earlier was forgiveness for telling Caroline about the time he hit me, the email is Cyrus's forgiveness for the kiss the other night. It's always been this way with us. A push and pull. A give and take. Arguments and then apologies.

Later that night, it's just me and a full bottle of merlot. The Great Rock Ferry is the large steamship that drives back and forth from the island to Cape Cod. He works the evening shift on Saturdays, and I don't have a party or other event to work tonight. The last boat to the island arrives at ten, but Ian usually goes out with some of the guys on a Saturday. I try calling Caroline to see if she wants to go for a movie or grab a bite, but she doesn't answer, so I settle in for an evening alone.

I've just poured myself a glass of wine when there's a knock on the door. I pull back the curtain and see Cyrus standing on my front steps, hatless, in just a thin fleece that's no match for the February wind. I'm glad I haven't put on my pajamas yet and at least still have on a nice sweater and jeans. I open the door wide. The cold air rushes in.

"Hey." Cyrus peers past me, likely looking for Ian, though his car isn't in the driveway. "I was just driving by and thought I'd check in to see about Daisy's car."

I give him a small smile. Daisy's car isn't in the driveway either. In fairness, we do have a garage, but Cyrus used to live here. He knows all we use it for is storage. "She hasn't been home all day. Come on in, though. Ian's at work. You must be freezing." He hesitates for a moment before stepping inside.

"It's not too bad." Across the road I see Mary Porter, my nosy neighbor, watching from her living room. She doesn't even make an effort to pretend she's not spying. I give her an exaggerated wave and she lets the curtain drop, though I can still see her shape by the window. Cyrus follows me inside and then stands awkwardly by the counter, glancing around the cluttered kitchen.

I lift my wine glass from the counter. "You want a glass?"

He wrinkles his nose in displeasure. "You know me. Never been much of a wine drinker."

"I've got beer too." I cross the kitchen and open the fridge without waiting for him to answer. In the inside door is half a six-pack of Sierra Nevada. *Yuppie beer*, Cyrus would say. Far in the back are a few cans of Coors Light, and I pull one of these out and offer it to him. Again, he hesitates for a moment. I know what it is that stops him. It's the part of him that tries to be good—the good husband, good father, good cop. And then there's me, always keeping him from all that goodness. It's why our marriage failed. It's also why he keeps coming back. Because as much as Cyrus wants to be good, there are times he wants to be with me more.

After a moment, he reaches for the beer, and it's then that I know why he's really come by tonight. As he pops the tab, we both know it's only a matter of time before our clothes are heaped on the floor. In the years since our divorce, Cyrus and I have found ourselves here before. Not often, but I'd probably need more fingers to count than I have on one hand. Somehow, miraculously, no one has ever found out—not Daisy or Ian or Gina, or anyone else from the island. I've never told anyone about these one-night affairs, and as far as I know, neither has Cyrus. It's why I can't hate Ian for sleeping with Layla when what I've done is so much worse. I *do* love Ian, and I think Cyrus loves Gina. Each time it happens, I know we both wonder why we've risked so much. We avoid each other for months, hoping we've really gotten away with it, swearing that was the last time, it won't happen ever again. And then slowly, inevitably, it does. And the cycle goes on.

It's Serena that keeps bringing us back here. Her death was the wedge that ultimately drove us apart, but it also binds us. Each time we find each other again, it's like coming home after a long time away. It's fresh air after being underwater. It's sadness and memory and love all wrapped up in an unrelenting grief.

I click my wine glass against the lip of Cyrus's can, and we lock eyes for a moment. "How's her car doing?" Cyrus asks, settling in on one of the stools by the counter bar.

For a moment I forget the pretense of why he's here. "Oh, I'm not sure," I say after a beat. I sit down beside him and rest my feet on the bottom rungs of his chair. "She didn't come home last night, and she's been out all day. Sent me a text this afternoon that she was out with some friends."

Cyrus raises an eyebrow. "Friends?"

I shrug. "I'm not sure."

"Is she seeing anyone?"

"Not that I know of. She hasn't mentioned anyone. Other than Connor." I roll my eyes.

"What? What's wrong with Connor?"

"Nothing. Nothing's wrong with Connor." I drain my wine glass and get up to pour some more. I get another beer for Cyrus though he hasn't even finished his first.

Cyrus narrows his eyes at me. "Come on, Ev. What's that look mean?"

I put my hand on my hip and let out a sigh. "Are you a cop now?"

His face softens, and he shakes head. It's our code. Unlike Jack, Cyrus realizes that life is not always black and white. Cyrus is able to turn off the part of his brain that is a cop in order to let the other part function. "No."

I come and sit back down beside him. "Connor's doing drugs." He doesn't answer, draining his beer in one long swallow and cracking open the second one.

"How do you know?"

"Have you seen him lately? He looks awful. You know he's living with Keith Dunphey?"

"Yeah, I know, but that's not exactly proof."

"It's not just that. Caroline said he was taking pain medication. That she found some a few months back, months after the doctor stopped prescribing it."

"Jesus. Not Connor." He's quiet, mulling over this new information, what it means for Jack and Connor and Caroline, what it means for Daisy. "Oxy, probably. There's a lot of that on the island right now. Heroin too. It's cheaper. When people can't afford Oxy anymore, they start doing heroin." He takes another long pull on his beer.

"Jack didn't say anything?" I ask. I shouldn't be surprised, since Caroline barely told me, glossing over the details and making her own excuses.

Cyrus raises his eyebrows. "You know Jack. He doesn't say much."

"Have you seen Jack lately? I mean, outside of work?"

"We went out for beers last Saturday." He avoids my eyes when he tells me this.

"The night of the festival? Did you see that girl? The one who was murdered?" *Layla*, I think to myself, but I won't use her name, won't bring her into this house anymore than she's already here.

Cyrus nods soberly. "Yeah, I saw her."

I frown at him. "Why didn't you tell me that? Did you see Ian too?"

"He was there." He avoids my eyes.

"Were you going to mention this?" I ask.

"I don't know what you want me to say, Evvy," he says defensively. "I saw him. He was talking to her. I didn't see them arguing, but they were sitting at the bar talking."

"There were hundreds of people out that night. I'm sure she talked to more people than just Ian," I say.

"Yeah." Cyrus looks down at his hands. "Yeah, she did."

"So, are you questioning all of those people too?" I ask.

"Most of them." Cyrus still won't meet my eyes.

"What aren't you telling me?" I know him, and I can tell when he's holding something back.

"Nothing," he mumbles into his beer.

"Cyrus, what is it?" I ask, my voice gentler.

He finally looks up. "I saw her talking to Connor too."

"Connor?" I blink, taking in this information. I think about Caroline, denying that Connor knew Layla despite having worked together over the summer.

"Just briefly. He didn't get there till late. He came and sat with Jack and me for a while before we left. But when he went to order a drink, I saw him talk to her."

"Has *he* been questioned?" I ask, already knowing the answer.

He shakes his head. "I wanted to keep him out of it, so I didn't mention it to Jack. You know Jack—he'd haul Connor in just to prove a point. I didn't think anything of it at the time. Even after, I didn't think it was a big deal. He was standing right next

to her when he ordered a drink, he could have just said hello."
He frowned. "Except…"

"Except what?"

"We know she worked at Moby Dick's for a little while over
the summer, so Connor must have known her. And even though
she stopped working there in September, she'd been coming over
at least once a month since the summer," Cyrus says.

"Why?" I ask, even though I'm pretty sure I already know the
answer. In the summer there are plenty of day-trippers, but not too
many people bother coming in the off-season, not unless they own a
house. It's one thing to come for the winter festival, but there aren't
many other reasons for a visit. Unless you've got a delivery to make.

"We think she was supplying someone on the island," Cyrus
says, and my heart sinks.

"You think Connor might have been dealing?" It will break
Caroline's heart if this is true.

Cyrus runs a hand over his short hair. "I don't know. I don't
want to think that, but I have to wonder now, with what you just
told me. It might explain why Jack's been leaning on Ian so hard."

It takes me a minute to piece together what Cyrus is saying. A
shiver runs up and down my spine, a cold current of air zipping
right through me.

"You think he's setting Ian up?" I ask in disbelief.

"No, not at all," Cyrus says quickly. "I just mean that's probably
even more reason for why he wants to keep Connor out of this."
I sit with his words for a moment, trying to find my bearings in
the conversation. How is it possible that two people I'm close to
may have gotten mixed up in a murder?

"You don't think he did anything to her? God, Cyrus, this is
Connor. You've known him since he was a baby," I finally say.

"I know he didn't. *Of course* he didn't. I'm not saying that." He
rubs his eyes with the heels of his hands. "That's why I didn't say
anything to begin with."

"Connor's a good boy. He'd never hurt anyone." My voice is too loud in the small kitchen. I want him out of Daisy's life, but not like this.

"I know that." Cyrus lets out a long sigh.

"What are you going to do?"

"I don't know."

"Are you going to tell Jack?" I imagine Connor getting hauled into the police station. Poor Caroline.

"I don't know. I think I have to. And then I'll have to explain why I didn't say anything in the first place. I just wanted to keep Connor out of this."

"Jack won't be upset. He'll know you were just looking out for him." Cyrus shakes his head, and his face is dark. Though they're best friends, Jack is still his boss. Not that Jack has ever lorded his position over Cyrus's head, but he makes more money and gets more respect. There have been times when this has been difficult. For all four of us.

I rest my hand on Cyrus's knee. His leg is warm and solid underneath the soft fabric of his jeans. He lets out another sigh, and it's as if the weight of the world is resting on him now. But his face relaxes when he meets my eyes.

I stand and lean into him, and his fingers hook under the belt of my jeans. His mouth finds mine, and his palms move quickly over my hips.

"Come on," I whisper into his lips, glancing at the clock. Ian won't be home for hours. I take his hand and lead him through the living room.

We're at the bottom of the stairs when the front door slams. Cyrus's face freezes in panic, and I know my expression must be the same. I imagine Ian smashing Cyrus's face to a bloody pulp, the force of all that contained rage finally let free. Though it's unlikely he'll release it on Cyrus. He'll wait till it's just me and him.

"Mom?" It's the soft trill of Daisy's voice, and I let out my breath in a harsh puff of air.

"Hi, honey," I call, trying hard to sound normal. Daisy comes into the living room and glances first at me and then at Cyrus, both of us standing awkwardly by the staircase. Her long blond hair spills out from under a pink wool cap and her cheeks are flushed from the cold.

"Hi, Dad." She smiles, though confusion shadows her face. "What are you doing here?"

I look to Cyrus, relieved that we're both still clothed and neither of us looks particularly unkempt. A few minutes later and it would have been a different story.

"I came by to check on that car of yours. Your mom told me the brakes have been acting up. Is it outside?" He cracks an easy grin and lies so smoothly that for a moment I wonder if this was his intention all along. Daisy nods. "I'll go take a look. Got your keys?"

She fumbles in her jacket pocket and hands them to her father. Cyrus slips out the front door, leaving me to deal with Daisy.

"Where's Ian?" she asks.

"Work. I haven't seen you all day. Where have you been?" I say, trying to keep my voice light. I go to straighten the pillows on the couch and then go back into the kitchen. Daisy follows me.

"Out." She stops at the sink and pours herself a glass of water. She drains it in one long swallow and then refills her glass. "So, Dad just stopped by?" There's a hint of accusation in her question, and she eyes the empty beer cans on the counter beside my wine glass.

"Just a few minutes ago. He stayed for a drink."

She folds her arms across her chest and looks at me skeptically, and though I'm the mother and this is my house, I feel like a teenager in trouble.

Through the window over the sink I see Cyrus holding a flashlight up to the wheel of Daisy's car. It's Saturday night and it's been dark for hours. It's only when I see Cyrus splayed on his backside in my driveway that I realize how ridiculous his story is about checking out Daisy's car, and I can't help but be pleased. I take a sip of wine and search for something to talk about.

"Where have you been all day?"

"With some friends." Her face pinkens.

"Who?" I know all of Daisy's friends, since they're the same ones she's had since she was little. So many of them have moved off-island for school that her circle is much smaller now than it once was.

"Nobody." Daisy's always been a terrible liar. She's not even lying now, merely evading, but we both know it.

"A boy?"

"Maybe." A smile lurks at the corners of her mouth.

"Anyone I know?"

She shrugs. "Just someone I met at the party last night."

"At Molly's?" A flicker of annoyance cuts through me. "You were supposed to be working."

"I *was*." She shakes her head in frustration. "God," she says under her breath.

"Honey, I'm just saying, I want to make sure you're focusing on work. I'm still a new name in this business. We need to act professionally at all times. I hope you weren't drinking—that's a liability." I hate that I have to give her this lecture. I'd much rather hear about the boy she spent the day with. But companies on this island collapse every season. Each year that Petunia's survives is a gift.

"I turn twenty-one *next week*. And I had one drink while I was waiting for the party to finish up. There was nothing for us to do anyway. We were just waiting for everyone to leave."

"Well, there's always *something* to do," I can't help but add.

She stands up quickly. "Can you ever give it a rest? Just once?" She puts her cup into the dishwasher too hard, and it rattles against the other dishes.

"Hey." I hold up my hands in defense. "If you don't like the way I'm running things, you're always free to find another job."

I regret the words as soon as they're out of my mouth, but I can't help myself.

"Oh, you'd like that, wouldn't you? Then I'll be home forever. Living in your house, asking for money like I'm twelve years old." She slams the door to the dishwasher with such force that I flinch.

"Daze." I grab her hand as she stalks past me. "I'm sorry. Come on, tell me about the boy."

"There's nothing to tell. I have homework to do." She extricates her hand from mine. "Tell Dad to leave my keys on the counter."

She goes upstairs and I hear the click of her door closing. I bring my wine back into the living room and lie down on the couch.

I hate arguing with Daisy. It always leaves me feeling like a bad mother, no matter what it's about. Part of it is the guilt I still have over how completely I fell apart when Serena died. I wailed and cried in Caroline's arms. For some reason I turned to her instead of Cyrus, and I think that's what finally did us in. I knew full well I wasn't capable of taking care of Daisy, and Cyrus wasn't doing much better. He threw himself into work, and I got in bed. Daisy stayed with Caroline and Jack. Daisy was eleven, at the start of sixth grade, and for six whole months she lived with them. Cyrus would stop by their house every day on his way home from work and stay for dinner, but I barely saw her, too consumed with emptiness and despair to rise from my bed.

I stayed in bed for weeks, rising only to use the bathroom. I felt headachy and nauseous, some flu of my heart worming its way through my body. Caroline came by with chicken soup and buttery loaves of bread, endless cups of tea, and stacks of magazines and novels from the library. She nursed me like I really was sick, and slowly I began to get better. Not heal, because there's no healing after your child dies. Functioning is really the best one can hope for. Finally, Caroline got me to go see a therapist who prescribed the antidepressants. They didn't fix anything. Serena was still dead. But I could get out of bed.

When I was well enough for Daisy to move back, she didn't want to come home. Caroline agreed that Daisy could stay until she was ready. It was a slow process. Coaxing Daisy back, convincing her she was safe, was like trying to nurse a skittish dog back to health after it's been abused. A slow winning over of her affection, baby steps forward as she learned to trust me again. In the afternoon I'd meet Caroline at the dog park. She'd bring Daisy and Champ, and the four of us would slowly walk the wooded trails that circle the perimeter of the park. Those walks took all the energy I had in me, but slowly Daisy returned.

When she finally moved home six months after she'd left, she'd grown two inches and gotten her period. She wore unfamiliar clothes, jeans and shirts that Caroline must have bought for her when she outgrew the things she'd come with. Though I was grateful to Caroline for all she'd done, part of me couldn't help but be jealous of the role she'd played in my daughter's life when I couldn't function enough to shower daily, much less make sure she was fed and clothed. It was almost like I'd lost not only Serena, but Daisy too.

Serena was seven when she died. A beautiful child but tormented. Daisy had always been so easy, but Serena was like a tornado. At an age when Daisy had long outgrown tantrums, Serena was still having them, full-blown meltdowns in which she'd physically lash out at whoever was closest, usually me. She'd gone through a whole slew of appointments where she was tested for everything—autism, ADHD, nonverbal learning disorder, Oppositional Defiant Disorder, and every other label they could find—but so far, none of them had stuck. Her teachers didn't know what to do with her and she'd been referred for special education services, though she was dead before the process had finished.

She wasn't always difficult. Some days she was cheerful and easygoing, coming to sit in my lap and reveal a picture she'd made for me. She loved to help me in the kitchen and we'd bake cookies together often, even though I knew the sugar probably wasn't helping matters. But she looked so delighted to help, her tongue sticking out of her mouth as she focused on whisking the batter in the bowl, sneaking chocolate chips as she poured them in.

Then something would set her off and it was never anything predictable—a missing sock, trouble decoding a word, a stormy day when she wanted sun—there was no saying what might send her into a tailspin. When she got upset, she yelled, high-pitched screams at whoever was nearby, and I'd yell back even though I hated myself for it. I knew full well where she'd learned to act like that. If it was just yelling, it might not have been so bad, but Serena could upend a room when she was upset, scattering papers, knocking over cups, destroying her own toys in the process. It didn't happen every day, but it happened often enough that I'd feel a sickening panic when she started up, knowing how it would likely end—with me having to restrain her and both of us in tears. Cyrus was often at work and would get the recap when he got home, and while he knew things were bad, sometimes I wondered if he knew the extent of it. There were days I wondered if he blamed me. There were days I was certain it was my fault.

She was having one of those fits the day of the accident. Other parents had seen the start of it in the school parking lot, their mouths pinched in judgment. Daisy had gone home with a friend for the afternoon. In the back seat on the way home from school, Serena sobbed because I wouldn't stop at the grocery store to buy potato chips. When Daisy was seven, she would have shrugged her shoulders and moved on, but Serena flailed in her booster seat, her face hot and red with tears.

She kicked at my seat, her little feet digging into my back over and over with a surprising amount of strength for such a small child.

I took my eyes off the road to yell at her. Just for a moment I turned and saw all that pain and sadness on her face, all that uncontrolled emotion spilling out of her. I didn't know where all that anguish came from, and neither I nor Cyrus knew what to do with it. The rest of the afternoon and evening stretched before me, an endless tunnel of Serena's disappointment.

I didn't see the car merging onto the road, a local teenager driving who didn't know enough to yield at the intersection.

The car plowed into Serena's side. In her frenzy she'd managed to dislodge herself from the cross strap of the seat belt, and the only thing keeping her in place was the lap strap, which dug into her internal organs before she was flung through the windshield.

The boy who'd been driving lost his license and was put on probation, and the family moved off-island. I didn't care about pursuing a case. It was my fault. I was angry and I'd taken my eyes from the road.

I never told Cyrus the details of that day, but less than two years after Serena died, Cyrus moved out. My secret shame consumed everything. It prickled around the edge of my consciousness, a constant reminder that Serena would be alive if I'd been a better mother. More patient, more loving, less unhappy. Being with Cyrus just hurt too much. Every time I looked at him, all I could think about was how much we'd lost. All I could feel was my own devastating guilt. Whether or not Cyrus forgave me, I'd never forgive myself.

When he decided to move out, I tried to comfort Daisy, but I was still a zombie, going through the motions of every day. Some mornings I awoke and forgot Serena was gone, and when I remembered, the air disappeared, leaving me gasping and choking in bed. Still, those few seconds of forgetting were the best part of the day.

A few years ago, I tried to go off the antidepressants. I didn't want to be on them forever and I felt steady enough to stop. But within a few days, I felt the dark swirls of depression starting to close in. The world started to take on a flat one-dimensional shape, all color and sparkle gone from it. Panic set in quickly at the thought of falling face first into that despair all over again. My brain, heart, and even the chemicals in my body all changed permanently when Serena died, and there's no going back to who I was before.

By the time Cyrus comes back into the house, I'm half asleep on the couch. He perches on the arm of the sofa, and I push myself to sitting.

"I'm going to head out."

I nod. "How's the car?"

"The brake pads need to be replaced, but I think she might need new brakes too. She'll have to bring it into the shop this week. Tell her I'll call to set up a time for her to drop it off." Cyrus enjoys this small way of taking care of her. "I still think she might be better off just getting a new one. I'll have them call me with an estimate before they do any work on it."

"Okay."

"About earlier," Cyrus starts.

I wave his words away and shake my head. "Forget it."

"We both know it would have been a bad idea." I know he's right, but his words still sting.

"So why do we keep ending up here?" I ask.

Cyrus shrugs and lays his hand upon my head. I close my eyes at how easily he's able to comfort me. "Old habits?"

"Why did you leave?" The argument with Daisy has gotten me thinking about Serena, about how things could have turned out differently for our whole family.

"Evvy." His smile disappears. "Come on. We've been through this before. Let's not do it again. Okay?"

My eyes fill with tears, and I blink them back, unwilling for him to see any fall. "I know I was terrible to live with."

"You weren't. It wasn't that." He rubs his forehead with the heel of his hand. If he wasn't regretting coming by already, he is now. "You weren't happy. *We* weren't happy." He gives me a wry smile and the corners of his eyes crinkle. "Don't you remember? Even before Serena. We fought all the time."

I nod. I do remember. But what I remember more than the fights is making up after them. I want to say this to him, but the mood has shifted between us, from heated to melancholy.

"I should go." He stands and shoves his hands deep in the pockets of his jacket, as if preventing himself from touching me again.

"Okay. Goodnight, Cy." My head aches, a hangover from the half-bottle I've drunk already setting in.

"Night, Ev."

The front door clicks as he lets himself out. I lie back down on the couch, turning my face into the pillow to cry. I've spent the past six years convincing Ian he has no reason to be threatened by Cyrus, but the jealousy he feels is justified. If Ian ever knew how I really feel about Cyrus, he'd kill us both.

DAISY
Chapter Fifteen

I close the door to my room and flop on the bed. The glow I've felt all day has quickly evaporated since arriving home. The argument with my mother has left me coiled tight, all that pent-up frustration and resentment still stewing despite the minor release. I don't know what I interrupted between my parents, or maybe I don't want to imagine it. There are times when my mother is like a teenager, impetuous and irresponsible, letting her emotions override her common sense. And there are other times when I worry that all those loose emotions will land her in hot water.

Now I'm doubly annoyed with her, because I was in such a good mood when I got home. I push the petty fight aside and lie down on my bed, trying to recapture last night with Todd.

When I agreed to let him drive me, I'd been planning on going home. But when we were between Osprey and Egret, he got a phone call. From the moment he looked at the name on the phone, the tension emanated from him.

"It's my brother." He hesitated before answering. "Hey. What," was his greeting. In the dim glow of the streetlight I saw the tightness in his jaw. "I'm headed into Osprey to drop off a friend. I can't. Are you kidding me? You miss Molly's party and now this?" I couldn't hear Bret's response, only the tinny sound of his voice through the phone. "Where are you?" Todd asked, his voice full of resignation. "Fine, I'm on my way. Just wait for me outside."

"Everything all right?" I asked after he'd hung up.

"Look, I'm sorry. That was my brother. He needs me to come get him."

I pulled my coat tighter around me. "Where is he?"

"Heron." Heron is at the far north end of the island. Osprey is at the south end. Egret is on the west coast, about twenty minutes away.

"Okay." I waited to see if he would offer more explanation. "Do you want to drop me first?" I asked, but already he was taking the turn off for Heron. My mind flashed to Layla, the dark beach she died upon. I thought back to my indecision about getting a ride home with Todd, a guy I barely knew, and wondered if I made the wrong call.

"I'm really sorry about this. It's just… he's kind of messed up right now. I need to get him out of there," Todd said. His voice was so full of tired frustration that I relaxed. He was annoyed and preoccupied, not plotting my murder.

"Where is he?" I asked.

"At some party with a bunch of the lowlifes he hangs with. I just need to get him home."

We were quiet until we reached Heron. Todd turned onto a residential road and then down another one and then onto a small dirt road. While most of the houses on the road were dark, there were lights on in a weathered Cape. Two cars were parked in the driveway and a few more on the side of the road. I recognized Connor's beat-up Jeep, and my heart beat a little faster.

"There he is," Todd said. The headlights illuminated a slight figure leaning against the sagging log fence. Bret was hunched over in jeans and just a sweatshirt despite the frigid February temperatures. Todd pulled over and Bret got in the back seat.

"Thanks," he said to Todd.

Todd didn't answer, focusing on making a three-point turn on the snowy dirt lane. The road was slick with patches of ice, small snowbanks piled to the side.

I glanced over my shoulder. "Hi," I said. He nodded, and though we know each other a little, he didn't acknowledge it. He hunched down further in his seat and closed his eyes.

"If I get stuck down this road you're paying for my tow," Todd said.

"You have four-wheel drive. You'll be fine," Bret muttered in a dismissive voice. He was right, and after another moment we were turning onto the main road.

In the back seat there was the flare of a lighter.

"Don't smoke in my car," Todd snapped without turning around.

"I'll open a window."

"Don't smoke in here," Todd ordered.

"God, when did you get to be such an uptight bastard?" Bret asked mildly. Todd slammed on the brakes in the middle of the road. I jerked forward and then back in my seat.

"Do you want a ride or not?" All of the lightness from earlier was gone from Todd's voice. Instead there was only anger and impatience. I felt a flutter of unease and again wondered if I'd been foolish to accept a ride home.

"Relax, I'll put it out," Bret said, and flicked the cigarette out the open window.

Todd pulled back out onto the road and began driving. He glanced at me. "Sorry."

"It's okay," I said quietly.

"I'm going to drop him and then I'll bring you home. I know it's in the opposite direction, but I just want to get him back before he starts throwing up or something," Todd said under his breath.

"I'm fine. I'm not going to throw up," Bret said from the back seat.

"Yeah? So why did you need me to come get you? Right this second?" We'd turned down the coastal road that led back toward Egret. The ocean was a black glimmer out the window, the moon hidden behind a patch of clouds.

I looked at Bret in the back seat. He was huddled low in his seat with the hood up over his head. "It was a bad scene is all. There was shit going on that I'm not into. I just wanted to get out of there."

I imagined syringes on the table, people shooting up in the living room and dozing off on couches, but all I could conjure up was a series of TV and movie scenes. The parties I'm used to are full of beer and cups of vodka and Red Bull, baggies of pot, and the fug of cigarette smoke.

"Bring him home first. It's no problem," I said to Todd instead.

"Thanks." Todd flipped on the radio and no one spoke for the rest of the ride.

Egret and Osprey exist on the same swath of island, but they're different in nearly every way. While Osprey is made up of a mix of extravagant summer houses and modest year-round homes in residential neighborhoods, Egret is rolling hills with gated properties and private beach access. There are working farms, but mostly it's open space. The money in Egret is old—families have owned the same land for generations. There aren't many year-round families in Egret; mostly summer folks, retired people, and a handful of the trust fund singles. Despite the smallness of the island, it's not a place where I spend much time, and I'm always blown away by its beauty and the wealth.

Todd turned onto a series of dirt roads. After several minutes, we stopped in front of a large gray-shingled house on at least an acre of land. A few lights were on inside.

"Wake up," Todd barked.

Bret gave a grunt from the back seat and then opened the door. "Thanks," he muttered as he stumbled from the car.

"You owe Molly an apology. That really sucked," Todd added.

"Yeah, I know," Bret said, and then shuffled toward the house.

Todd let out a sigh once the door closed behind Bret. "Sorry about that." He ran a hand through his hair.

"It's fine. Really." He seemed so different from the guy who'd helped me wash dishes just an hour ago; more fragile, less confident. "Are you all right?"

"I don't know." He held my gaze. "Do you want to come in for a drink?"

Though I'd been exhausted at the party, I suddenly wasn't the slightest bit tired. If anything, I was the opposite, wound up with extra energy. I knew I wouldn't sleep if I went home. "Okay."

"Really?"

"Sure. Here?" I gestured toward the big house.

"No. This is my parents' place. They have a guesthouse down the road. Molly usually lives there, but she let me have it for the week." He shifted the car into drive and continued until we arrived at another house, this one much smaller. Todd parked in the driveway and we stepped into the cold.

It seemed brighter out here, which was strange because there weren't any streetlights or cars. But it was as if the night were alive. The moon cast a pale blue glow over the endless field of snow, and the stars were bright little buttons in the sky. I stopped to look at the magnitude of it, to breathe in the faint scent of imminent snow, the crisp earthy tang of the air.

"It's so beautiful."

He looked up at the moon that shone down on the field. "Yeah, it is. I love it here." He took my hand and squeezed it, then led me into the house. Todd flicked on the lights. Inside it was warm and cozy.

"Is whiskey okay? I think that's all there is."

"Sure."

I sat down on a plush velour couch while Todd went into the other room to fix drinks. White paper lanterns hung from the ceiling and the windows were outlined with strings of Christmas lights. Todd came in carrying two small tumblers of whiskey.

"Nice place."

"Oh, thanks. My parents used to keep it open for guests in the summer, but Molly's been living in it for the past two years." He handed me the glass and then sat down beside me on the couch. "She and Benny will probably buy a place of their own soon. Here you go."

"Thanks." I took a sip, and my eyes and throat burned. I swallowed hard.

Todd laughed. "Not a whiskey fan?"

"No, it's good," I lied.

"I'm surprised you agreed to come back here."

"Why?"

"I don't know. After that, with Bret. I figured you'd want to go home," Todd said.

"Is he okay? Should you have gone in with him?" It hadn't occurred to me till now that maybe someone should have stayed with him at the house.

"He'll be fine. This is pretty much a weekly occurrence," he said darkly.

"What is?" I took another sip and tried not to wince.

"Him getting wasted. At least that's what Molly tells me. I'm not around much, so I don't always see it. But I've seen it this week." His face tightened. "I don't really want to know. Do you think that's terrible?" He pulled a purple wool blanket off the couch and spread it over our laps.

"No." I tapped my ring against the side of the glass tumbler. "My friend Connor hangs out with Bret." The word *friend* sounded empty and hollow, but I suppose that's what Connor is. "It's the same kind of thing. He's changed. I know it's because he's got into drugs, but I don't really want to know either." I met Todd's eyes. "He was there tonight. I saw his car."

Todd nodded. "I know Connor. He used to come around a lot. I haven't seen him in a while though. He's a good guy."

I nodded into my glass. "Yeah. He is."

"Is he your boyfriend?" Todd held my eyes and something in my stomach flipped, like the wings of a butterfly fluttering inside.

"No, not really. It's kind of complicated." I struggled for the right words. "But no. He's not."

"I'm glad." He leaned forward and brought his lips to mine. His mouth was soft and tasted of whiskey. I was growing to like the flavor. His hand came up to my face and cupped my cheek, delicately, as if I were something breakable that needed to be handled carefully. After a moment, he pulled back. "Was that all right?"

I nodded, my breath still caught in my chest. I let out a long exhale, and Todd's face softened into a smile.

"Don't forget to breathe."

"I won't." My words came out in a whisper.

I've never been into one-night stands. On an island like Great Rock, word gets around fast of who you've been with, and I've never wanted to be the one that the rumor mill churns about. And there's always been Connor. The pull between us is something that forever flickers around the periphery of everything else. Even when I've had boyfriends before, Connor was always there, the hot center of my world.

But I know he'll drag me down, if I let him. Not because I'll join him on the ugly path he's traveling, but because I'll follow him and find myself alone in an unknown dirty place, watching him choke on his own breath.

So I put my glass on the table and reached for Todd. I ran my hands up the solid length of his back, my palms moving over the softness of his shirt, breathing in the soapy scent of his skin. I pulled him down to the couch, my head sinking into a striped pillow that smelled of cinnamon and lavender. His weight upon me was a relief, his chest and limbs pressing me deeper into the safety of the couch. I surprised him with my determination, tugging at the soft leather of his belt, unhooking the clasp of my bra. The desire that reared up inside of me was sudden and unexpected, like I'd finally found something good and clean after so long in the mud.

Back in my own bedroom, I let out a sigh at the memory of last night. We spent the rest of the day in bed, watching movies and talking. When he dropped me off at my car, he promised to see me again before he went back to Boston, and while I know it's unlikely he'll call or text, that I probably won't see him for years until we bump into each other someplace on the island and awkwardly say hello, I can't help but hope that he meant it.

CAROLINE
Chapter Sixteen

All that time when it was just me, Jack and Connor, I assumed they would always be there, flesh-and-bone beings within arm's reach. Though I should know better by this stage of life, it's taken Jack leaving for me to realize that nothing is permanent.

It wasn't always easy. There were money concerns and the day-to-day doldrums of family life, and my chafing desire to leave the island. There was the sadness when I wasn't able to have another child, and we had to let that vision of a louder fuller family fade away. But through it all, I'd been naive enough to think that what we had—the three of us together—was ours to keep. And then within a few months, Connor left home, and Jack left, and now it feels like someone up there is laughing at me, shaking his head at all that I've taken for granted these years, foolish enough to think there's anything in this world that's more than just temporary.

I've lived here for over twenty years now, yet I'm still not really an islander. I grew up in a suburb of Maryland, a little outside of Washington D.C. My father worked as a clerk in the House of Representatives, and my mother was a public defender. We lived on a tidy tree-lined street where every house looked the same, except for the varying shades of pastel paint on the siding, or the choice of flowers under the front windows. Like many others in our neighborhood, my brother, sister and I were dropped early at school so our parents could make the commute into the city. A babysitter picked us up and stayed with us till our parents returned, rumpled and weary, sometime after six.

Every summer, we'd rent a house on Great Rock for two weeks. The house we stayed in each year was on a bluff in Egret with a view of the harbor and a sandy path that led to a thin strip of private beach. At home, my sister Shana and I shared a room, but the rental house had five bedrooms with mottled hardwood floors and white wainscoting. For two weeks, I watched the noise of the city fall away for my parents. My mother wore cotton tunics in pink and yellow, and flowy white linen pants that billowed in the evening breeze. My father wore sandals, actual *sandals*, and by the end of the two weeks his bony white feet would be nutmeg brown, freed from the stiff wingtips he wore the rest of the year. The two weeks were full of annual rituals. A trip to the Cone for soft serve sundaes, a sunset on the beach with lobster rolls and paper cups of coleslaw, frozen lemonade from the stand on the harbor, a drive to Heron for a day of fried clams.

There was no TV in the summer house, which only added to the magic of the vacation, two weeks that hung suspended in time. In the evening my parents would sit on the front porch sipping gin and tonics while my sister and I played board games. Great Rock was a magical oasis, a place where my parents weren't tired and laughed often.

They divorced my freshman year in high school. My father moved to an apartment in the city where we'd visit him every other weekend. We never returned to the house on Great Rock for vacation, and instead spent summers working or at our Aunt Helen's house in Pennsylvania.

One of my closest friends at Boston College, a girl named Betsy, had a family house on Great Rock, and the summer after our senior year, she invited me to spend the summer living with her on the island. It was my first summer back since I was a teenager. It was that summer I met Jack.

Jack had recently returned to the island after finishing the police academy. He'd gotten a job as a beat cop for the summer, patrolling downtown Osprey at night after the bars let out and drunk tourists poured onto Main Street. I was working as a waitress at a restaurant on the harbor, and Jack was assigned to patrol the waterfront. During the lull in business, we'd talk. Tall and lanky in his navy police blues, he was different from the men I'd dated in college. He was quieter and more reserved, but more confident too, like he already knew who he was and didn't need to prove anything. I quickly found myself forgoing the bars and parties for evenings at the movies with Jack, or small dinner parties hosted by his friends and large extended family.

When the summer ended, I thought about my options. Betsy was moving to New York City to work in a financial firm, and my other college friends were scattering all over the country. I could return to Boston, but I didn't have a job to support myself. I considered moving back to Maryland, but the idea of unpacking all of my things into the small house my mother had moved into after the divorce was too depressing to contemplate for long. And then there was Jack: steady, patient, handsome, never pushing me to stay but making it clear he didn't want me to go.

In those days it was easy to get a winter rental. I stayed on at my waitressing job until the restaurant closed for the season. Jack knew someone who worked in the library and helped get me a job shelving books and maintaining the database. The next few years were like a series of dominoes stacking in a sequence. Jack and I got married the following summer, surprising and disappointing both of my parents, who expected me to be pursuing a career more rigorously and putting off marriage. Just a little over a year later Connor was born; not an accident since we hadn't been trying very hard not to get pregnant, but not quite planned either. Slowly, over several years, I took the necessary courses to get a job, first as assistant librarian and then director.

For a girl who had grown up in a large suburb right next door to a major city, Great Rock's smallness was shocking at first. I wasn't used to bumping into four people I knew when I needed to run to the grocery store for milk. I was always surprised by the close proximity of everyone, like when I learned that one of Jack's closest friends did the landscaping at Betsy's cottage or that Jack's cousin was the caretaker for the house I'd spent summers in as a child. I'd heard of six degrees of separation, but on the island it was closer to two degrees of separation. One morning at the gym I realized that out of the thirty people in the group exercise room, I was connected to at least fifteen of them—through Jack, Connor, work, or some other relationship. It all felt so close, so suffocating, like living under a magnifying glass.

For a long time, I didn't think of the island as our real home. Even after Jack and I were married, even after Connor was born, I thought of it as just our early years, the jumping off point for the rest of our life. We talked about moving, constantly, to Boston or D.C. or New York, somewhere with more opportunity, a place where you could buy a pizza after eight and go to a museum on the weekend. But I realize now that it was me who talked, who planned alternative realities in my mind, while Jack just nodded patiently. He'd tip his head to the side occasionally and point out that, while you couldn't get takeout here in the winter, didn't I actually enjoy cooking? All the while, he was advancing in the department, first to sergeant, then lieutenant, and then, just a few years ago, to chief.

It wasn't until Connor was in high school that I realized this was it. We had a house and two good jobs. Connor was in school and had friends. Most importantly, I finally admitted that Jack didn't *want* to leave. The island was his home. His mother was here, along with siblings and cousins and aunts and uncles and childhood friends. The only time Jack had ever been away from Great Rock was the time he spent in the police academy. There was no greater plan. This was our life.

It was with this realization that my resentment started to grow, a tiny bud blooming and then taking over everything in sight. My anger was like bittersweet, the invasive weed that runs rampant on the island, strangling every other plant in reach unless yanked out by the roots each season.

I think about this often, now that Jack has left, and I'm alone. What had suddenly seemed so important for the last twenty years feels trivial now. Where did I want to go, after all? What was I looking for? A place to get takeout, an art museum? Hadn't Jack been right all along—I do prefer to cook and how often would I actually go to a museum, even if I lived next door to one? My friends are here, a job I care about, Jack's family, which has become my family. My *life* is here.

I remember a day this past July. It was my birthday, and Jack and I spent the afternoon at Seastar Beach in Heron. It was one of those perfect Great Rock days, the sun high in a cloudless blue sky, a light breeze keeping it from being too hot. The salt from the water was crystallizing on our arms and shoulders as Jack and I sat side by side and read, two new mysteries I'd brought back from the library. Connor came over for dinner that night, and the three of us sat in the backyard around the fire pit. The sky was a milky blue studded with stars that glittered like shards of shattered glass. My skin was still warm from the sun and I wore an old wool sweater of Jack's. We didn't talk about anything in particular. I don't remember what either of them gave me for my birthday, though I know there were presents. What I remember is sitting between Jack and Connor, the bookends of my life, one a man, the other a boy suddenly become a man right before my eyes, and thinking *this is good*. Simple and good.

It was a day when I didn't resent living on Great Rock, too preoccupied with the beauty of the place and my own good fortune. Connor's shoulder surely must have been bothering him, though he didn't complain. Jack didn't ride Connor the way he sometimes does, and no one argued. The day is a snapshot, a memory contained in a jar where it sits preserved and untouchable. And though I can look at it, though I know the lobster was tender and succulent, the corn the sweetest of the season, the sun and water the perfect temperature, though I remember the overwhelming feeling of well-being at the end of the day, I cannot recapture any of it, only press my fingers against the glass.

DAISY

Chapter Seventeen

When I open the *Great Rock Gazette*, there's a picture of Layla Dresser, and I realize I've met her before. In the black-and-white photo, she looked like some sorority girl, smiling shyly into the camera, hair that could have been honey blond falling over her shoulder.

She didn't look like that when I met her on a sticky summer night last August at a party in the woods. The house belonged to a girl Connor and I had gone to school with whose parents were away for the week. A bunch of us were sitting outside on the deck. Someone had built a bonfire and the air held the smoky scent of summer. I was squished on a wicker couch beside Connor, drinking beer, debating how much longer I wanted to stay. Many of the people there were kids I'd grown up with, but there were plenty of people I didn't know too, college kids on Great Rock for the summer.

It was that point of the night where everyone was wasted. The table was covered in empty beer cans, and I had a feeling pass over me, like I'd been to this exact party one too many times before. The same people, the same crappy beer, the same stupid jokes and hookups. And for many of the people here, this party was already a moment of nostalgia before they packed up their duffel bags and headed back to college. But for me, this was all there was. I knew I had to get out of there before I completely sank into depression and self-pity. I was about to tell Connor I was leaving when Layla Dresser came and sat down next to him, half on the arm of the couch and half in his lap.

She wore a silky tank top with jean shorts, and her arms jangled with bracelets. There was a tattoo of a dragonfly on her shoulder, and she smelled sweet, like shampoo and bubblegum, the artificial fragrance of a young girl. She perched beside Connor, looping her leg over his, and his hand came to rest on her smooth tanned knee.

"Hey, you," she said to him. I attempted a smile at the girl, but she was only paying attention to Connor. "Aren't you happy to see me?" She arched her back and leaned down as she said this, so Connor had no choice but to stare at her boobs that were barely contained in her tank. Not that he was trying very hard not to look. I picked up my beer and finished it off in one long swallow.

"I'm going home," I said, half hoping he'd offer to come with me.

"Yeah?" Connor tore his eyes away from the girl's chest just long enough to glance at me.

"I'm done. I need to get out of here," I said.

"You okay?" he asked, but I could tell his attention wasn't really on me.

"I'm fine. I'll talk to you tomorrow." I picked my purse up from the floor. The girl was waiting patiently for me to leave. By the time I'd crossed the room, she'd slid into my spot on the couch. I never learned her name.

I never saw her after that night. Connor didn't mention her, and I just assumed she was a summer girl here for a few months, one of the many who come to Great Rock for July and August before returning to their real lives in September. It wasn't until I saw her picture in the paper this morning that I realized she was the same girl that had hovered around Connor like a bird. Yet he didn't say a thing.

Connor and I haven't spoken since the night I saw his arms. When I text him he doesn't answer. For the second time in a week, I find myself climbing the stairs to the apartment he shares with Keith. When I get to the top, Keith opens the door before I have a chance to knock. He's carrying a backpack and a thermal coffee mug.

"Connor's still in bed, but go on in if you want." He doesn't step out of the doorway, and I have to squeeze past, pressing myself against him in a way that makes my skin crawl. Connor's door is closed and I knock, wait a moment for the sleepy sound of his voice telling me to come in. When I open the door, he's in bed, his shirt off and an arm thrown above his head. I try to avoid looking at his arms, but the marks are still there. He pushes himself to sitting when he sees me.

"Hey. You're here." He pulls me down beside him on the bed, resting my hand on his stomach. His flesh is warm beneath my palm, and he leans closer, his mouth finding mine. He tastes sour, like sleep and a hangover, and I tilt away, though it's not because of his breath. It's because of Todd, how just yesterday I was in his bed, his lips, his arms. I have no idea if I'll see him again, or if he'll even call, but I know that I want him to, and just that is enough. I don't want to start this with Connor. Not now.

"What's wrong?" he asks.

Connor's guitar is propped in the same corner of the room where it was last week. Something tells me that if I were to come back a month from now, it would still be there, and this makes me so sad I want to cry. It's this that makes me know Connor is different. He's not the same boy who saved me when my mother went crazy, who lay in a twin bed with me after his parents were asleep and let me cry till his shirt was wet. He's someone different now. And it doesn't just make me sad—it scares me, because I realize I don't know him anymore.

"You didn't tell me you knew that girl who was murdered." He flinches, like I've raised my hand to him. "Connor, that's messed up. How could you not say anything?"

"I barely did. We hung out a few times, but I didn't know her well."

"Did you sleep with her?" He blinks but doesn't reply, and I realize I already know the answer. "You did, didn't you?"

He sighs and stares at the ceiling. "It wasn't like she was my girlfriend or anything."

A chill settles on my shoulders. "What is wrong with you?"

He looks at me in surprise. "What do you mean?"

"How can you be so callous? You knew that girl. You slept with her." I shake my head in disbelief, that he's hidden this from me. "Someone murdered her and you're acting like it's no big deal."

"Of course it's a big deal. It's terrible. But what can I do?" He rubs his hand on my back to try to calm me down. I shrug him off.

"Is it true she was here to sell drugs?"

His face darkens. "Where'd you hear that?"

"Have you been on social media lately?" I shoot back. I wait for him to answer, but he doesn't. "Is it *true*?" My anger is hot and sudden, a burning little stone I could hold in my palm and throw at him.

"I guess." Connor looks away.

"Did you buy drugs from her? Is that how you knew her?"

Connor gets up and out of bed, pulling on a tee shirt from the floor. "You don't need to get involved in this."

"Involved? Are *you* involved?" My head is spinning.

"No. I mean you don't need to know about this. It just upsets you."

"Yeah, it upsets me that you're screwing up your life. Just tell me. Did she sell you drugs? Is that how you knew her?" I practically spit the words at him and then I hold his eyes till he relents.

"I met her through Keith," he says, which doesn't actually answer my question.

"Were you there that night? Did you hurt her?"

"Jesus, Daisy, of course I didn't." There's a wounded expression in his eyes that makes him look like a little boy. "How can you even ask me that?"

"Do you know who did?" I ask again.

He looks away, his eyes shifting just the slightest bit. "No. I don't know anything about it." He looks back up at me imploringly. "God, Daisy, you've known me my whole life. You don't actually think I could do something like this, do you? Murder someone?"

"No. Of course not. I'm sorry." I don't think he did it, but I also know there's something he's not telling me. Connor sits back down on the bed and pulls me to him. He links his fingers through mine, tugs me in close again. I rest my cheek against his chest, but when his hands start to travel under the fabric of my shirt, I sit up.

"What's wrong?" he asks.

"Nothing," I say, but Connor can see right through me.

"It's Todd, right?"

"How do you know about that?" I want to guard the other night from Connor.

"He's Bret's brother." Of course. It's a small island. I should know better by now. "So what's going on with you guys?"

"I don't know. Nothing." I push myself up to sitting.

"Not nothing. You spent the night there."

"God, how is that any of your business?" My face burns.

He shrugs. "It's not. Rich trust fund guy. That's just what you're looking for, right?" I'm surprised by the bitterness in his voice.

"What do you care?" It's always been me who's wanted something more with Connor. He's never been able to commit, and I've never made him. For a long time I figured it would happen when we got older, but it occurs to me now that it might not, that we could drift apart and eventually just be two people who grew up together. I don't really know why I've come here or what the purpose of my questioning actually is. It only makes it clearer how much further apart Connor and I have grown.

In the pocket of my coat, my phone beeps. I'm glad for the interruption, and I know Connor is relieved not to have to answer my question. It's a text from Todd.

Want to get breakfast?

I've been wondering if I'd hear from him, and my pleasure must show on my face because Connor turns to me with a smirk.

"Lover boy?"

"Shut up."

Connor stretches like a cat, a strip of his pale torso expanding and retracting beneath the ratty tee shirt. I hold my phone in my hand, wanting to write back, wanting to say yes, but not in front of Connor.

"What time is it?" Connor asks. "I need to be at work by eleven."

I pull my phone out again. Todd's text lights up, waiting for my reply. The minutes seem to tick by faster now. How long till he gets breakfast without me? "A little after ten."

Connor groans and pushes himself off the bed. "Want to get some coffee before I go in?"

"I have plans," I say vaguely. Connor cocks an eyebrow but doesn't ask more. "I should go."

He turns to face me. "Todd's a good guy. I'm just being a dick."

I'm not sure what he's saying, if he's giving me permission to see Todd or apologizing for being a jerk. I shouldn't need his permission, but I can't help but be disappointed that Connor's given me up so easily.

"It's okay."

His arms encircle my shoulders, hugging me to him. I rest my head on his chest and smell the musky scent of his tee shirt. "I should have told you. About the girl. About Layla," he says.

Once upon a time, Connor and I told each other everything. He knew the dark corners of my heart like a well-worn map, the seams soft from use. But now it seems we're just smiling and nodding, telling each other what we want to hear.

Connor walks me to the door and I hurry down the steep stairs, grateful for the cold air that washes over me. I cross the street to where I've parked my mother's car, since mine is in the shop. Before I get in, I reply to Todd's text.

Where?

When I look up at Connor's apartment, he's standing at the window, watching me. I clutch the phone guiltily and give him a little wave, getting in the car to avoid his eyes. I'm suddenly in a rush to get away from his desperate gaze. As I drive down Main Street, my phone pings in response and my heart lifts a little higher.

EVVY
Chapter Eighteen

I've made stew for dinner, Ian's favorite, but when his shift ends at five, he calls to tell me he's going for a drink.

He still hasn't told me about what really happened the night of the festival, and what's been happening these past few months. Every time I've asked him about it, he's been evasive. He hasn't mentioned the evidence connecting him to Layla, and I haven't had the courage to ask him, worried that if I ask too many questions, my whole life will come crashing down on me. I realize this is cowardly and eventually I'll need to confront the truth—the cheating, I mean, because I still don't believe Ian had anything to do with the murder. This is a man who once brought home a stray cat with a broken leg that he'd found mewling behind the ferry terminal. He left work early and drove her to the vet himself, then brought the cat home and named her Minny. She lived with us for two years, spending every night curled up in Ian's lap. When Minny died last spring, he buried her in the backyard and put flowers by the stone he'd placed on her grave. He's not a man who could kill someone. I realize that this image of Ian doesn't align with the one the police have—the abuser—and maybe it doesn't make sense, but I know that this version of Ian—the one that is good and kind and gentle—is at least as real as the one that occasionally loses his temper and lashes out.

If someone else is charged with the murder, I wonder if this is one of those things that we'll just pretend never happened. It could sink like a pretty piece of jewelry at the bottom of the sea, slowly drifting to the ocean floor, never again to resurface.

"Everything okay?" I ask.

"Just had a lousy day," he says. In the background I hear the long low bleat of the foghorn. He promises to be home in time for dinner.

He's not home by seven or eight, either. At eight-fifteen, I spoon myself a bowl of stew and sit at the counter to eat alone. The beef is tender with soft potatoes and carrots in a rich dark sauce, but I barely taste it, too preoccupied by Ian's whereabouts and what state he'll be in when he returns. At nine I'm mad but by ten I'm anxious, and I know I should go to sleep, but I don't. I sit on the couch instead, watching a dumb reality show about polygamy.

His car pulls in a little after eleven. He throws the front door open too hard and it knocks against the washing machine. I can tell he's drunk the moment he walks into the living room. Something about the loose movement of his body, limbs akimbo, footsteps clumsy.

"You're home late." I keep my eyes on the TV.

"Sorry. Any dinner left?"

I clench my jaw so I don't snap at him. "There's a bowl for you in the kitchen."

He bangs around in the fridge, and I hear the slam of the microwave door, and then he sinks down on the couch beside me. "It's good," he mumbles through a full mouth. "Oh. I brought you something." He fumbles in the pocket of his vest, pulls out a greasy white bag, and hands it to me. Even before I open it, I smell fried food and sugar. Inside is an apple fritter from Flour and Sugar, the bakery in Osprey that sells pastries late at night while the bakers are prepping for the morning. I tear off a piece and feel myself softening, the sweetness of the dough and the thoughtfulness of the gesture smoothing out my anger.

"What the hell are you watching?" he asks, looking at the screen. There's an argument happening between the husband and the three wives.

"I don't even know," I say, and turn the TV off. The quiet is a relief. I take another bite of fritter, enjoying the sharp rush of sugar, the way it makes my whole mouth ache with pleasure.

"Where have you been?" I ask.

"I went to the Blarney Stone. Had a few beers."

"You said you'd be home by seven."

"Evvy, just don't, okay? I had a bad day. Don't make it worse," Ian says.

"What happened?" I ask, putting the rest of the apple fritter back in the bag. Already I can feel the start of a stomachache, all that flour and sugar sitting in my gut.

"Nothing *happened*." He grabs my sticky hand and squeezes. "Everybody knows I was seen talking to that dead girl the other night. Everyone knows I was brought into the station to talk to the police. People think I *killed* her."

"Who said that? Who thinks that?" His face is red, his eyes glazed. He's had more than just a few beers.

"Everybody! I've got people I've known for years coming into the ticket office and getting in a different line, looking at me sideways when they're talking to me. No one says anything, but I know. They think I did it."

"No one really thinks that. No one that knows you," I say, wondering if this is true.

"It's over a week since they found her and the police haven't said anything. They haven't done a goddamn thing." He puts the stew bowl down on the table, hard, and the spoon clatters against the ceramic.

"Just because they haven't said anything to the public doesn't mean they haven't done anything," I can't help saying.

"You a police spokesperson now too?" His eyes are narrow slits when he turns to me. "I guess I shouldn't have expected any sympathy from you. You were the one who sold me out in the first place." He turns from me, eyes fixed on the blank television.

"Ian." I don't try to argue. "Honey, I'm sorry. What more can I say?" He's more wounded than angry. I slide from my place beside him on the couch and climb into his lap. He doesn't look at me, but I bury my face in his neck and inhale his warm familiar smell.

I met Ian while buying a ticket to get off Great Rock. For a small island, the ferry service is a bureaucratic organization. Trying to get my car off the island in July felt like trying to get tickets to the Super Bowl. But I needed to leave. It was the fourth anniversary of Serena's death. Not a day went by that I didn't think of her, but the anniversary brought it all back, and suddenly it was fresh, as if it had happened yesterday. Cyrus wanted to spend the day at her gravesite, looking through photo albums and talking about her, but I had no desire to mark the day in such a way. The watery walls of Great Rock were closing in on me, and I needed to get the hell away. I wanted to go shopping and rent a room in a hotel where no one knew me, take a swim in a pool and drink alone at the bar, maybe even go home with someone.

Ian laughed when I asked if I could buy a ticket for the next boat. Not in a mean way, more in an incredulous way. He was a few years older than I was, close to forty, with graying sandy hair and an easy smile. He had the ruddy weathered complexion of someone who'd spent much of his life outside.

"Today?" he asked with a chuckle. "Honey, I don't think I can get you off this week." I nearly put my head down on the desk and burst into tears right there. It was brutally hot that day, and though the air conditioner was working overtime, I was still sweating through my thin tank top. The place was full of tourists, screaming children and tour groups of elderly people all wearing the same ridiculous orange tee shirt. There were three other lines going besides mine, about twenty people impatiently waiting for the end of their vacation.

"Please," I said, and he must have heard something in my voice. Maybe he noticed how close to tears I was, that I was teetering on the brink of something, and close to falling in. He held my gaze for a moment and then turned back to his computer.

"Hang on." His fingers tapped the keyboard. "Would the two-thirty work?"

"Really?" I looked at him in disbelief.

He nodded and then bent his head toward me to speak more quietly. "If anyone asks, you're getting gall bladder surgery." My face must have formed a question because he added, "It's a medical emergency ticket." He brought a finger to his lips. He printed out the ticket and handed it to me.

Relief rushed through me. "Thank you so much. You saved my life. You don't know."

"Sure I do. Got to take care of that gall bladder." He winked as I stepped out of line, clutching the ticket.

He was working the next day when I returned to the island. It was a Monday night and the terminal was quiet. I went into the office and saw Ian in the same place as the day before, chatting with an elderly woman at the window. That was what I first noticed about him—how easygoing and friendly he was. Like Cyrus, though I tried to push this thought from my mind.

I already had a ticket, but I got in line anyway.

"Thank you," I said when I arrived at his desk. He squinted his eyes in confusion, before his face opened into a smile.

"How's your gall bladder?" he asked.

"Much better," I said. "Thank you."

I'd spent too much money shopping at the mall and then gotten drunk alone in my hotel room. No matter how much I spent or how much I drank, Serena was always there but not there, her absence sharp and bitter. I was relieved that the day was over for another year.

"No problem. I could tell you needed a break." There was something private about his smile, like it was meant just for me. "Hell, I'd ask for your number, but then you'd think that was the only reason I got you on the boat."

Cyrus had been gone for almost two years. He wasn't coming back. Ian was the first man to show me kindness since, and maybe that was a bad reason to go out with him and later let him move in, but at the time it felt like the most natural thing in the world.

"Do you have a pen?" I asked.

I lean against him, kissing the length of his jawbone and neck. "You're a good man, Ian. No one thinks you did this." He grunts, but doesn't answer, pulling my face roughly toward his and kissing me hard. I can tell he's been drinking more than beer by the sharp taste of whiskey in his mouth. I want to move on from the argument, but there's something that's been worrying me since I saw Cyrus the other day. I hold a hand to his chest. "I think maybe we should call a lawyer."

He pulls back and his face is clouded again.

"Why? You think I need a lawyer?"

I shift in his lap. "That woman is dead. I know it wasn't you, but… I don't think it's just going to go away."

He's silent and I figure this is as good a time as any to ask. "Were you sleeping with her?" His whole face changes, though it's not guilt I see but confusion.

"No. Why the hell would you think that?"

"I just… I thought… There were phone records," I manage to get out. I don't know what I expected him to say, but flat-out denial wasn't it.

He frowns at me, and his eyes narrow. "Is that what Cyrus told you?"

I feel my skin flush pink, the guilt written all over my face. "I saw him the other night when Caroline and I were out. He mentioned it."

"Really?" There's something sinister in his voice that makes the hairs on the back of my neck stand at alert. "You're sure it wasn't the other night when he came by?" I don't answer, trying to figure out how he knew, and then I remember goddamn Mary Porter sitting at the window, watching Cyrus come inside. Mary's at least ten years older than Ian with the wrinkled face of a raisin, but she flirts whenever she sees him. I should have known she'd rat me out.

I swallow, but don't speak. I'm not sure if my voice would work properly even if I tried. I'm still straddled across Ian's lap, his face just inches from mine, so close I can practically taste the Jack Daniel's on his breath. The smell turns my stomach and I twist away slightly, hoping to extricate myself from such close proximity without making him angrier.

The force with which he pushes me to the floor takes me off guard, and my tailbone hits the hardwood with a dull thud. He stands over me, and I instinctively cross my arms over my chest, but he just pushes me with the toe of his boot. "Do you think I'm blind?"

I know from experience that the only thing to do when Ian is like this is wait him out. Within minutes he'll come to his senses. Soon he'll be on his hands and knees beside me, apologizing. I blink back the tears that prick my eyes, and Ian picks up his stew from the table and goes into the kitchen, leaving me cowering on the floor. I hear him drop the bowl in the sink. His stool scrapes the floor and then there is the sound of the football game on in the kitchen. He doesn't come back.

Ian's anger is like a fire, quietly smoldering until the coals are prodded with a stick. Then the flames leap, hot and dangerous. For the first time I wonder if maybe Layla Dresser somehow shifted the coals. It wouldn't take much—an accidental slight, a careless word. Maybe the line between bruises and something far worse isn't as wide as I've always thought.

Slowly I rise from the floor. My body is tender and my tailbone hurts where it hit the floor, a dull ache that will be with me all week, a painful reminder to keep my mouth shut.

DAISY

Chapter Nineteen

Todd and I have breakfast at the Ferry Diner and then we take a walk on Bassett Beach, one of the island's many private beaches. In the off-season, it's open to the public, but in the summer, you need a residential pass. These passes are precious, adding several hundred dollars extra to a vacation rental for the pleasure of daily trips to Bassett. The rest of us go to the few public beaches on the island, which are packed with tourists and townies, barely a foot between each stretch of towels, competing music blasting.

We park in the empty lot and hike down the thin snowy trail that leads to the ocean. Trees line the path and then clear as the faded sea grass comes into sight. We climb up and over the dunes and then the ocean is upon us, a vast expanse of gray. The beach is wide and white, no sign of the yellow and blue of summer. The air coming off the water is like ice, and I zip up my coat and readjust my scarf. Todd breathes in deeply. Despite the cold he looks content.

"Smells good," he says. It's freezing, but it still smells like summer, the unforgettable odor of fish and salt. The beach is empty, just the two of us, and our boots make soft swishing noises in the snowy sand. "This is my favorite place on the island. I come every day in the summer when I'm here."

"I've only been a few times in the summer."

"Really?" His breath comes out in puffs of white. "It's the best beach on the island."

"It's private. I don't have a pass," I point out.

"Oh, right. I forgot." He links his arm through mine. "You'll have to come with me this summer then."

I nod, but don't answer. Summer's a long way away. "When are you leaving?" I've only known him two days, but I'll miss him.

"What's today, Monday?" His eyebrows go up, disappearing under the edge of his wool hat. "Probably Wednesday. Thursday morning at the latest. I need to work Thursday night."

"So what do you do at the restaurant?"

He turns to me, surprised. "I'm a cook," he says, as if I already knew. "At Avenue X. Southern comfort meets California cuisine. Or something like that."

I shake my head at him. "I don't even know what that means."

He laughs. "Fancy yuppy food. It's not really my style, but it's a good job. What I'd really like is to have my own place." We're just a few feet away from the shoreline, and I step sideways to avoid the foam of water as it washes close to our feet. "Molly's fiancé, Benny, he's cheffing at a bistro in Heron, but we've talked about opening our own restaurant in the next few years. A nice place that's open year-round? Great food and a full bar, but reasonable enough that you could go on an ordinary weekday." He shrugs sheepishly. "Someday, maybe. What about you? You're dying to get off this island, what are you going to do when you leave?"

I kick a rock with my toe, embarrassed to have the conversation turn to me and my plans. "I'm studying to be a speech and language pathologist."

"What's that?"

"I'll work with people who have trouble with their speech. Like kids with communication disorders or adults who've had strokes. Help them learn to speak better." My chest is tight from the cold, but something else too. No one ever asks me about what I'm studying in school. None of my friends, not Connor or my parents. I don't think they even know I've declared a major.

"That's cool. How'd you get interested in that?"

I'm not sure if I want to give him the real answer, then decide I will anyway. "When I was a kid, I had a stutter." I wait a moment and then continue. "I had some learning disabilities too, trouble with reading and writing. Between not doing well in school and stuttering, I used to get teased a lot." It can't be more than twenty degrees, yet my face is warm with remembered shame. Connor was the only one who didn't tease me. Once he got suspended for a day for pushing a kid after he sing-songed *D-d-d-d-daisy*; Connor who was always gentle and shy. For some reason, it never occurred to either of us to tell a teacher or one of our parents.

"That sucks. I'm sorry," Todd says softly.

I shrug, not wanting it to be a big deal, though somehow it still is. "I went to speech therapy, and it changed my life. I still struggled in school, but I stopped stuttering. Kids stopped teasing me."

He nods and squeezes my arm, and I'm glad he doesn't say anything more. I feel like I've told him a secret, and I'm glad he doesn't ruin it by saying something stupid or insensitive. I shove my hands deeper into the pockets of my coat, and we walk in silence. The beach stretches out before and behind us, an endless ribbon of white and gray. I think of Layla dying on a cold and empty beach just like this one, and I feel guilty for my own good fortune, for the simple blessing of being alive and able to appreciate the barren beauty of my home, even if just for a moment.

"Can I cook you dinner tonight?" he asks. It's nearly three and we've been together since this morning. I don't have to work tonight, but there's homework I should be doing.

"Yes, please," I say anyway.

When people like me want to cook dinner, we head to the local Stop and Shop. When people like Todd want to make dinner, they head to the farmer's market. In summer the Heron farmer's market is a tourist's dream, bustling with hipsters and yoga moms, their cherubic babies strapped to their bodies as they fill canvas sacks with bundles of kale and heirloom tomatoes. In winter, there aren't as many people. There are stalls set up; middle-aged couples with kids in tow mill around, carrying bags of produce and thermal mugs of coffee, people with jobs flexible enough that they can go buy a bag of beets in the middle of the day. I recognize a handful of people, but no one I really know, and though there's no reason for me to feel uncomfortable, I do. Maybe it's because the amount Todd spends on a few small paper bags of produce is close to my mother's weekly grocery bill. Or maybe it's the ease with which Todd takes out several crisp twenty-dollar bills to pay for one night's dinner. Or maybe I feel guilty that, despite the scorn I feel for most of the people up here, I'm hungry for what they have.

Todd buys us both coffee and then holds my hand casually as we stroll through the barn, pausing to sample homemade jams and herb-infused olive oils. Part of me is already wondering how long it will be before rumors of the two of us spread across all of Great Rock. How long till Connor hears about me parading through the farmer's market with my expensive coffee, bag of arugula, and Todd? But the other part of me, the bigger part of me thinks, *Who cares? Who cares what Connor or anyone else on this small stupid island thinks. Because I won't be here for much longer.*

"Hey, Todd."

I look up to see a girl a few years older than me standing at a booth that's selling local cheese. She's tall and slender with glossy brown hair that hangs over her shoulders. She wears jeans and old boots and an apron over a white wool sweater that probably cost more than what I make in three nights. Her eyes are on Todd, though not before she's seen that he's holding my hand.

"Hey, Zoe."

He releases me to hug the girl, and I get a whiff of her shampoo as she rests her head momentarily on his shoulder, strong enough to cut through the smell of the ripe cheeses she's selling. He steps back and motions to me. "Zoe, this is Daisy."

I try to smile, but I'm sure it comes out crooked. Zoe smiles without actually looking at me. "What are you doing here this time of year?" she asks.

"Molly's engagement party."

"Oh, I heard about that!" Her pretty blue eyes light up. "I was away for the weekend, so I missed it. Meg and I went skiing." I fade into the background while they talk about people I don't know and hobbies I can't afford. I wait for Todd to invite Zoe to join us for dinner, which will mean I'll have to come up with some excuse to leave. Already I'm mourning the end of whatever this was.

"I promised Daisy dinner, so I'll see you later." He takes my hand once again, firmly, and I swear Zoe's eyes are burning into my back as we walk through the crowded barn. He leads us out to the parking lot. In the car, I'm quiet, though I know my cheeks are still ablaze.

"Who was that?" I try to ask casually, but my voice cracks on the last word.

"Zoe?" Todd fiddles with the radio, settling on a bluegrass station. "Old friend."

I raise an eyebrow. "Friend?"

He takes his eyes off the road and gives me a half-smile. "It's complicated. You know what that's like, right?"

I purse my lips in a tight smile. "Right."

He reaches out a hand and places it on my knee. "Let's forget about her, though, okay? Tonight, I'm with you."

The cynical part of me hears the implication that tomorrow he might be with her, and I don't answer. The whole thing seems pointless all of sudden. So what if I like him? He's leaving in a few days. Where can this actually go? Besides the physical distance, the world he lives in is so completely removed from the world I live in. It feels like some cheesy movie from the eighties where the girl from the wrong side of the tracks likes the rich guy.

We drive in silence. I rest my head on the cold window and watch the rolling fields of Heron fly past. The hills are blanketed in untouched snow, endless acres of white interrupted by the occasional house or stone wall. I've zoned out so completely that I don't even notice when we pull up to Todd's house—not the cottage where I spent the other night, but the big house where his parents live. I turn to him questioningly.

He puts the car in park and cuts the engine. "If I'm going to make you a real dinner, I'll need my parents' kitchen. Molly's barely got a frying pan."

"Okay." I suddenly feel awkward about going into his parents' house.

"You're quiet," he observes.

"I'm fine. It's just…" I trail off, unsure what I'm asking him. "What are we doing? What is this?" I gesture to the empty space between us.

His face breaks into an easy smile. "I don't know yet. Can't we just see?"

"I don't know why you'd want to hang out with me." It comes out wrong. My self-confidence isn't so low that I don't realize that guys think I'm pretty in a generic, blond sort of way. I get why he wanted to sleep with me the other night. What I don't understand is why he's bothered to see me again.

Todd turns toward me and tucks a thumb under my chin. "It's pretty simple. I like you." He kisses me gently, and the warm firm feel of his lips is both new and familiar.

"I like you too." My voice is barely above a whisper.

He brushes a stray hair from my face and tucks it behind my ear. "I don't know where this is going to go, and I know I'm only here for a few more days, but Boston's not all that far. It's not like I live in California. Can't we just hang out?"

I nod. "Yeah, sure."

"Cool." He holds my eyes for another moment and then bends to pick up the paper sacks by my feet. "Let's do some cooking."

Todd's kitchen is in the center of the house. Copper pots hang from hooks on the ceiling and the knives are secured to the wall on a magnetic strip. The marble counter runs nearly the whole length of the kitchen and the appliances are artfully hidden to blend in with the drawers. A bowl of lemons rests in the middle of a gnarled farmer's table that could sit fifteen. One of the walls is all windows overlooking the snowy field. I feel like I've stepped into the pages of a magazine.

Todd lays out the ingredients and gets a knife and cutting board. "What can I do?" I ask.

"Just relax. I'm cooking for you tonight, remember?" He gets to work, nimbly chopping the vegetables, slicing onions and garlic with the efficiency of someone who knows his way around a kitchen. I'm sitting at the counter sipping a glass of wine and watching Todd add olive oil and salt to a salad when the front door opens, and I hear voices in the other room.

"My parents." Todd glances in their direction and then they're in the kitchen, still wearing their coats. His mother is tall and thin with ash blond hair cut in a severe bob. His father is shorter than his mother and thick around the middle, with a full head of white hair.

"Todd," his father says formally.

"Hello, dear." His mother smiles expectantly at me as she unwinds a soft purple scarf from around her neck, and I'm not sure if she's talking to Todd or me.

"I thought you guys were going out to dinner," Todd says, clearly caught off guard.

"No one told us that Bread and Butter was closed for the season. I had my heart set on their rack of lamb," his mother pouts.

His father shakes his head. "I told her we could get burgers at Veronica's instead, but she didn't want to."

She wrinkles her nose in displeasure. "I hate their burgers. Much too greasy and they never get the temperature right. Last time I asked for it medium, and I swear the heart was still beating." She smiles at me again and then turns to Todd with her eyebrows raised. "Well? Are you going to introduce us?"

"Sorry. Daisy, this is my mother, Sarah, and my dad, Greg. Mom and Dad, this is Daisy…" He trails off as we both realize he doesn't know my last name.

"Swain," I add quickly.

Sarah extends a slim hand which I shake. "It's nice to meet you, Daisy." Greg's hand is also extended, his palm slightly damp and meaty against mine. I fight the urge to wipe my hands on my jeans.

"Swain. Any relation to Cyrus Swain?" Greg asks.

"He's my dad," I say proudly.

"Good man. I worked with him at a town meeting not that long ago on some crowd control issues that came up over the Christmas parade in Egret."

"Dad's on the board of selectmen," Todd explains.

I nod politely. My father hates town politics and always complains when he's expected to appear at a town meeting.

"What are you making?" Sarah asks, leaning over the cutting board. "It smells delicious."

"Just pork and some vegetables." It's not just pork and vegetables. It's locally grown pork that was humanely slaughtered, with organic butternut squash and island greens from Sunset Hill Farm.

"Have enough for two more?" She reaches into the salad and pulls out a slice of yellow pepper, which she pops into her mouth.

"Oh." Todd looks at me. "Sure, I guess."

Sarah smiles at me. Her cool blue eyes sparkle. "Daisy doesn't mind. Do you, dear?"

I force a smile. "Of course not."

*

Dinner is long and tense. I spend the whole meal on my best behavior, though it doesn't matter because no one says very much. Todd glances an apology across the table several times, but he and his parents don't seem to have much to talk about other than what restaurants are closed for the season.

"This is wonderful, dear." Sarah gestures to her plate.

"I can see why you're a chef," I add.

"Thanks." Todd smiles.

"Should be in business school by now," Greg mutters toward his plate.

"Don't start, Greg," Sarah says quietly.

Greg continues. "Instead he's a college dropout and I'm out over a hundred grand." He picks up his wine glass and takes a sip, then smiles at me tightly. "Kids." He spits the words out but they lack venom, and I get the sense he brings this up fairly regularly in the same offhand and bitter way. Todd's face is a blank mask and he focuses on the piece of pork he's cutting.

"At least I have a job," Todd says quietly.

"Don't bring your brother into this," Greg snaps. "He's younger than you; he's still trying to figure things out."

"Right. That's what he's doing." Todd shakes his head in disgust.

"Enough," Sarah says, placing a hand on Greg's forearm. "Daisy doesn't want to hear all this. So, what do you do, dear?"

I swallow a lump of squash. Though the dinner is delicious, it might as well be oatmeal for all that I'm enjoying it. "I work for my mother's catering company. And I'm taking college classes."

"Oh, you live here? Year-round?" Her question makes me feel ashamed, even though she lives here too. "Where are you going to school then?"

"Four Cs. I commute a few days a week."

"Four Cs?" Her delicate features furrow into a question.

"Cape Cod Community College," I clarify. Everyone on the island knows what Four Cs is, unless they've never known someone to go to state school, much less community college.

"Oh, of course." She looks down at her own plate, either embarrassed for me or herself, I'm not sure.

Greg doesn't respond, having withdrawn from the conversation entirely after his jab about Todd dropping out. His white linen napkin lies beside his empty plate.

"This was delicious, Todd," Sarah says, and Todd gives his mother an appreciative smile. I can already see the dynamic at work between the three of them; Todd and his father at odds, Sarah the peacemaker who travels back and forth between them, trying to smooth things over. It's a rapport I've seen many times with Connor and his parents. Todd begins to clear the table, and I rise to help him. Greg takes his half-full wine glass and retreats to a room deeper in the house, a den I assume. Sarah brings a few items to the counter before saying goodnight. Todd and I load the dishwasher in silence and then start on the pots and pans.

"Sorry about that," Todd says, focusing on the sinkful of dishes.

"It's okay." I rub the towel in circles on the flat bottom of a copper pan.

"My dad and I have a hard time being in the same room without fighting." He lifts the pan out of my arms and hangs it on a hook. He's rolled up the sleeves of his sweater and I see the fine pale hair on his muscled forearms. "I'm sure this isn't what you had in mind when you agreed to have dinner with me."

"My mom and I fight all the time too," I tell him.

"Really? About what?" He hands me the wooden salad bowl.

"I don't know. Everything?" I try to smile. "My mom's kind of crazy, and she's never happy with me. It's like no matter what I do, it's not enough and it's not right. When Ian's around, it's easier. But when it's just the two of us… not so much. So… we fight."

"I always liked working for your mom. She seemed like a pretty cool lady," Todd says. He's not defending her or arguing with me, it's simply an observation.

"She is. She's just…" I search for the right word. "Unreliable."

Everyone always likes my mom. She has a way of making people feel special. Walking into the grocery store, her face bursts into a grin when she bumps into an acquaintance, or she'll grab you in a bear hug and hold on tight. The thing they don't realize is that her attention never stays on one thing for very long.

I fold the dishtowel into a neat square and stare down at the blue-and-white stripes. "My sister died when I was eleven. Serena was seven. When she died, my mom kind of lost it. She sent me to live with Connor's family because she couldn't deal with anything. Then she wanted me to move back home like nothing had ever happened." I swallow a lump in my throat. "My dad's always been the more stable parent, you know?"

"I didn't know about your sister. I'm sorry." His words are sincere, not rushed and awkward the way people sometimes get when I mention Serena. Not that any of us talk about her much.

"We don't talk about her," I tell him now, shaking my head. "My mom can't, so I don't really either. Sometimes with my dad, but it's hard for him too." When Serena died, it was like she became a ghost, her invisible presence controlling everyone, much as she did in life. When Serena was upset, she was wild, sweeping up everything in her path. It's almost possible to forget what she was like when she was happy, how she'd lie down next to me on the couch while we watched TV, thumb tucked in her mouth, soft blond hair spread against my hip. Some nights, she'd sneak into my bedroom in the middle of the night, and I wouldn't even realize she was there until I woke up the next morning. Sleeping, she looked so peaceful, all the fire and sass drained right out of her. It's hard to believe she'd be sixteen now.

"Bret's the baby in our house, so whatever he does is okay. He's just *figuring things out*." Todd shakes his head. "What *I* can't figure out is if they really don't know how fucked-up he is right now or if they're just in denial." He scrubs the sink with a sponge till the silver gleams. "I'm not sure which is worse."

I suddenly feel close to tears, and I'm not sure why. I stand behind Todd and rest my body against the length of his, pressing my cheek into his back. I close my eyes and breathe in the musty wool of his sweater. Todd turns around and pulls me to him. He's taller than me, and my head only comes up to his chest.

"Pretty heavy stuff for a first date, huh?" I nod. "Let's get out of here."

Outside the air is sharp and cold. There's not a single house or major road nearby, and it feels like we're the only people on the island. For once I see why someone would fall in love with Great Rock. We walk down the driveway and the only noise in the stillness of the night is the sound of our shoes in the snow. Todd presses me into the cold metal of his car, and I close my eyes and get lost in his kiss, only air and the night sky and Todd's mouth on mine.

"Stay the night," he murmurs into my ear.

I have a catering job to prep for in the morning, classes tomorrow night and homework due. I should be working on a paper and reading the chapters I've been putting off all week.

"Okay," I say instead, and reach for him again.

CAROLINE
Chapter Twenty

On Monday I work the morning shift. When I come home, I take Champ for a long walk in Osprey's dog park, a large open field surrounded by wooded trails. In the summer, the park is social, a gathering place where I know every golden retriever and black lab by name, and I can count on a walking companion through the hot dry grass. Even in the winter I usually bump into someone I know on a weekend afternoon. Today, the park is empty, not a dog or owner to be seen.

It's the week of school vacation. February is a bleak and desolate month on Great Rock, but never more so than vacation week, when every family that can scrape together a little extra money flees for warmer locations or the bustle of a few days in the city. When Connor was younger, we always tried to get away. Some years we'd go to Washington, D.C. to visit my family. Another year we spent a long weekend in New York City.

My favorite trip was when Connor was ten, and we went to the Everglades. We took a boat ride through the swampy water, and the air was moist and ripe with the murky green smell of the wetlands. The mangroves bloomed into a dark and eerie canopy over our heads, and we saw alligators and river snakes sunning themselves on the rocks. Connor and I peered over the side of the boat, awed that such savage predators could lurk so quietly just a few feet away. Jack sat back in his seat knowingly.

By the time Champ and I finish our walk, the light is fading and the trees are silhouetted against a dusky purple sky. The car is freezing, my fingers like sticks of ice despite my gloves, and I'm grateful I left the heat on in the house before I left. When I pull into the driveway, Connor's car is in my spot, and I park beside him. My first reaction is pleasure, quickly shadowed by my memory of the other day. I haven't told anyone about what I found in the guitar case. I've allowed myself to push the memory aside, as if not talking about it will make the whole thing disappear.

Champ hurries ahead of me into the house and runs straight for his water bowl. I hang up my coat and scarf in the hall closet. Then I head for Connor's room.

"Hi, honey," I call from the landing, but he doesn't answer. I begin to climb. "Connor?" I hear him banging around in there, but he doesn't respond. Pushing open the door of his bedroom, I let out an involuntary gasp.

The room has been turned upside down. The drawers of the dresser gape open and empty, every item of clothing piled on the floor. The sheets on the bed have been stripped bare and the contents of his nightstand table, items I saw myself just a few days ago, are strewn across the rug. Even the bookshelves have been cleared; magazines and paperbacks spill from the mound of clothes. Poking out from the bottom of the heap is the empty guitar case. Connor lies flat on his belly, searching under the bed. He's nearly disappeared under the wooden frame and only his legs stick out.

"What are you doing?" I breathe.

Connor ungracefully wiggles himself from the narrow space and unwinds his body till he's standing. His face is gaunt, his skin is a sickly shade of gray, and he's damp with perspiration. His eyes have a wild frantic look. How long has he looked like this? How long have I turned away? Because I recognize it now. He looks like a drug addict.

"Where is it? I left something here the other day and it's gone. Where is it?" His words come fast, tripping over each other. I open my mouth, but nothing comes out. It's the gruff way he's spoken that catches me off guard. "Did someone come in here? Did you let someone in my room?" I shake my head. "Then someone must have broken in. What the fuck." He rakes his fingers through his pale blond hair and pulls so hard I worry he'll rip the strands from the roots. "*What the fuck*," he says again, his voice louder and more frantic.

Maybe it's the swearing that finally makes me speak. Jack never allowed Connor to swear, and hearing him speak to me so viciously, it's like Jack has finally stepped into the room and pushed me forward, reminding me I'm the parent.

"It was me. I found it. It was me," I say.

Connor's eyes scan my face, taking in my meaning. What I see next breaks my heart even more than what I found. He looks relieved. He's relieved that I'm the one who has the drugs and not someone else.

"Where is it?" He takes a step forward, as if I might be holding the bag in my jeans pocket. His outstretched hand trembles. "Give them to me."

I shake my head. My mind works in slow motion, trying to pin down what I know to be true. Connor is doing drugs. Connor thinks I have them. He believes I'll give them back to him, that I'll let him walk out of this house and into the world with a bulging bag of pills. "I can't." The words catch in my throat.

"Just give them to me." He's standing so close I can see the pores of his skin and smell his stale breath. He grabs me by the shoulders as if he might start to shake me. "Mom, just fucking give them to me." I shake off his grasp and take a step away. For the first time ever, my own son both repulses and scares me.

"I don't have them. I found them the other day and I got rid of them. I don't have them," I repeat, this time louder.

"What did you do with them? Where are they?" He storms out of his bedroom and throws open the door to mine. When I follow him, he's pawing through my trashcan.

"Connor," I yell. "They're not here. I flushed them down the toilet. All of them. They're gone."

I watch his face collapse, the features caving in on themselves, and then he slowly lowers himself to the foot of the bed. He buries his face in his arms, and I sink down beside him on the soft carpet. "Baby, what's happening?" I ask. When he looks up, he is my son again, not this gray stranger inhabiting Connor's body. His eyes are bloodshot and he wipes away tears. My sweet boy. My heart.

"You don't know what you've done." He drops his head back onto his arms. His body shudders as he's overcome by silent sobs. I cling to his forearm, trying to get him to look at me.

"Where did you get them? Whose are they?" He just shakes his head without speaking, a low keening sound suddenly coming from the tent of his arms. "Were they that woman's? The one they found?" A vision comes to me, horrible and sudden, of Connor's trembling fingers around her neck. Fumbling in the pocket of her coat for the bag of pills. Leaving her alone on that cold and desolate beach. The fear has been with me since Evvy told me about the drug connection, but this is the first time I've let the image form. I think about the way he looked at me just a few moments ago, the wild rage in his eyes, like he wanted to hurt me. There's a ringing in my ears, and my head aches. "Honey, did you do something? Did you hurt her?" I whisper.

My words jar him and swiftly he's on his feet, leaving me curled up on the floor. "What the hell?" he yells, and I wince at the force of his anger. His face contorts in a mask of pain and sadness. "What is wrong with all of you? You're all so stupid!"

"I'm sorry," I say automatically, wanting to take the words back, knowing I never can.

I feel like he's punched me in the stomach, but I rise to my feet anyway and try to hold him. He shrugs me off with a force that takes me by surprise, and I stumble against the bed. Connor turns and leaves, his boots crashing down the stairs. I hurry after him, calling his name, repeating apologies through the house and down the front steps, Champ fast on our heels, but Connor is already in his car and reversing hard, the wheels spinning against the gravel. And then he's gone, leaving behind a fog of dust and exhaust in the dusky twilight. Champ whimpers softly, and I stand in the quiet evening. It's not until the car is long gone that I realize that when I asked Connor if he'd hurt Layla, he never actually said no.

EVVY

Chapter Twenty-One

I'm getting ready for work when they come to arrest Ian. I've just taken three Tylenol with my coffee to combat the pain in my lower back from where I fell on the floor. Ian rose early this morning and is already at work. Before he left, he pressed me into our bed and entwined his body with mine. I closed my eyes and let him make me forget the night before. He held me and murmured into my hair, *I'm sorry, I'm sorry*, over and over again until the words lost their meaning.

There's a knock at the door and when I open it, there are two police officers standing on my step and two police cars in front of my house. One of the cars blocks the other one, so I can't see if there's anyone in it.

"Is Ian Blake here?" the younger officer asks. He's a doughy man, a boy really, with a freckled complexion that makes him look about twelve. I'm surprised I don't recognize him.

"He's at work. Why?" Instinctively I turn to the older one, a dark-haired man about my age who I recognize from around the island, though we don't actually know each other.

Fear floods me, oily and cold in the pit of my stomach, though I can't identify what I'm afraid of.

"We'll find him there," the dark-haired one answers. "You just stay here. And don't call him." Then they turn to leave and get back in their car, pulling out onto the road and leaving me standing there open-mouthed. I'm about to go back inside to call Ian—of course I'm going to call him—when Cyrus gets out of the other car. He's in uniform. I'm so happy to see him I nearly run to him.

"Cy, what's going on? Why are they looking for Ian?"

He lets me collapse in his arms for only a moment before he peels me off with gentle but firm hands.

"Let's go inside." He turns me around and pushes me toward the house.

"What's happening?" I ask once we're inside.

Cyrus's face is serious. "They're going to arrest him."

"What? Why?" I find my phone on the counter and swipe at its black face. "I need to call him."

Cyrus catches my arm and gently extracts the phone. "You can't."

"Cyrus, I need to." I imagine the police marching into the ticket office to arrest Ian in front of all of his co-workers and the morning commuters. The humiliation he'll feel. Ian is easygoing and social, but only I know how insecure he is underneath it all. How desperately he craves the acceptance of others. The shame of such a scene will destroy him. Despite last night, I want to protect him.

"Evvy, no." Cyrus shakes his head.

I drop my hand. "But why? He didn't do it."

He sighs. "Ian talked to her at the bar. He left right after she did and possibly assaulted her. There's the fact that they knew each other based on the phone records. And he was seen walking along Beach Road right around the time of the murder."

"He walked home. That's the fastest route," I snap.

"I know. But they also found boot prints by the body." His eyes lock on mine. "Same size as Ian's."

I'm quiet for a moment, absorbing this new information. "That doesn't mean anything. He's a ten and a half. How many men on this island are the same size? *You're* a ten and a half," I point out. Cyrus doesn't answer. "Those prints could belong to anyone."

"Goddammit, Evvy, there are phone records between him and the victim. Don't be blind."

The screen door slams and then Daisy is with us. I inspect her closely. Her hair is tangled and her cheeks are pink. "Where have you been?" My words come out more harshly than I intend.

"Hi, Dad." Daisy ignores my question.

"Hi, honey." Cyrus kisses her on the head.

"What are you doing here?" she asks.

"Ian's been arrested," I say so he doesn't have to.

"What? Why?" Daisy asks.

I can't read what's behind her eyes. Ian and Daisy have always gotten along, although he's never been a father figure to her. He moved in too soon after Cyrus and I split up, into the house that Cyrus had lived in so recently. Suddenly, there he was in Cyrus's place at the dinner table, on the sofa, in my bed. Ian never knew Daisy as a child; he didn't get to see her as a chubby toddler full of devilment or a cheerful seven-year-old bouncing into the house after school, eager for a snack. Ian didn't get to know Daisy till she was fifteen, a surly teenager still reeling from our recent divorce and Serena's death that infiltrated everything.

I don't want to tell her, but I'd rather she heard it from me than Cyrus. "For killing that woman. It's a mistake. He didn't do it," I add quickly.

"Are you okay, Mom?" My eyes fill with tears. It's the tenderness in her words that threatens to undo me. These days she communicates in shoulder shrugs and one-word answers, still a teenager in her relationship with me, despite being almost twenty-one. The gentleness in her voice is a reminder of when she loved me unconditionally.

I purse my lips and nod, avoiding both their eyes. "So, what now?" I ask Cyrus.

"Now you get a lawyer. Do you have one yet?" I shake my head. "Call Mark Keene. I'll send you his contact info right now."

Cyrus pulls out his phone, and a moment later I hear the ping of a new message on my phone, which Cyrus is still holding. "Call him. He's good."

"What happens to Ian?"

"They'll bring him down to the station to be booked. He should be arraigned in the next twenty-four hours, which means he'll go to court with his lawyer and the charges will be read."

"What about bail? Can he come home?"

"I don't know. In cases of murder, sometimes there's no bail set."

I imagine Ian going to prison. Not just the prison on the island, which is a beautiful old colonial that's been fitted with bars and locks, but *real* jail. Visiting him in a big room with other couples, a plastic table between us, guards looking on. Taking the ferry every weekend and then driving hours for just a few minutes together. Do I love him enough? It frightens me that I'm not sure, and then I'm ashamed that already I'm thinking about myself instead of Ian.

"I'll call Mark right now," I tell Cyrus.

"Use mine," he says and holds his phone out, Mark's contact info already loaded. "Tell Mark I gave you his number," he adds.

Cyrus's name opens doors. Just like Jack's. The two most popular boys in their class grew up to be the most popular men on the island. They both have a way of making the people around them feel safe. Cyrus's love is like a warm room in winter, a haven that keeps the outside world at bay. And sometimes I think it's the feeling of that warmth that I miss as much as I miss him. I think of Ian, so different from Cyrus—louder and funnier, more demonstrative in his affection for me, but weaker in other ways. His worry that I'll leave him, his neediness for me that feels like love but maybe is something darker and more complicated. I take the phone and make the call, wondering if the right lawyer is just a small fix for something that may already be broken.

DAISY

Chapter Twenty-Two

It's Connor that I turn to. Of course it is. We haven't talked since yesterday at his apartment—no texts, no calls, nothing. We crossed some unbreachable line, and I'm not sure what's on the other side, yet I can't imagine going to anyone else right now.

My mother still has a dinner to cater tonight, and apparently a party can't be cancelled just because your boyfriend's in jail. I decide to skip my classes for the afternoon and I promise her that I'll head to Petunia's to get things started. I stop at Moby Dick's on my way.

The restaurant smells of brick ovens and roasting meat, comforting winter smells on a bleak afternoon. It's a Tuesday though, vacation week, and only a few of the tables are filled. I don't know why they bother serving lunch in the winter anyway. The place is too upscale for locals to come midweek. It's amazing they've stayed in business for so many years, one of the few restaurants to stay open year-round. The bartender is watching the news on one of the big-screen TVs and there's only one server on duty. Bella Lincoln is at the hostess stand, ready to greet me, her iPhone perched beside the menu. Bella graduated the same year as me, a bland but harmless girl who wears too much eye makeup and constantly chews gum. She smiles when she sees me.

"Hi, Daisy. You here for lunch?" Her eyelids glitter a sparkly purple and a wad of pink gum flashes behind her teeth.

I shake my head. "I'm looking for Connor."

"He's in the back." She tilts her head toward the door that leads to the kitchen then turns back to the tiny screen of her phone, scrolling through pictures of people we both know.

Connor's in the kitchen with Scott Lambert, the head chef, both of them hunched over their cell phones.

"Daze, what are you doing here?" He's in his chef clothes: striped pants and a long-sleeved tee shirt, a bandana tied around his head. I know that if I got close to him, his skin would smell of cooking oil and garlic, a pungent and unpleasant scent, yet I still want to crawl into his arms.

"Ian was arrested. For that girl's murder."

Connor's face twists in confusion.

Scott's head snaps up from his phone. I know he's dying to hear the rest of the conversation, but instead he tells Connor he can take a break. He'll get the details from Connor later.

I follow Connor out the back door, away from the warmth of the kitchen and into the cold bright afternoon. We end up in the alley between Moby Dick's and the souvenir shop next door where the trash collectors load the dumpsters.

"What happened?" Connor asks.

"They came by and told my mom they were going to arrest him. My dad says he probably won't get bail," I say. The whole thing is still so incredible to me. It's unbelievable that anyone could think Ian had something to do with this. Ian is a grounding force in our household, filling it with his loud laugh and the smells of his cooking. The house has an aura of calm when he's around, and my mother absorbs it like a sponge.

Connor's face crinkles in confusion and he shoves his hands into the pockets of his pants. "That doesn't make sense. Ian couldn't have killed her."

"I know!" I say, relieved that Connor is so quick to dismiss the accusations. "I don't know what kind of evidence they have, but it can't hold up." I rub my hands up and down my arms in an effort to stay warm.

"How's your mom?" Connor remembers when my mother fell apart. He remembers how she couldn't get out of bed, just crying and crying all the time, until his mom stepped in and saved us both.

"She's freaking out. She just got him a lawyer." The cold seeps through the weight of my coat.

Connor pulls me into a tight hug. I breathe in the ripe smell of kitchen on his skin and clothes, grateful that we're not arguing or accusing. "I'm sorry about yesterday," I say when he releases me.

He shakes his head and waves away my words. "You're not the only one who thinks I could have done this." His face has gone dark and he looks over his shoulder like someone might be listening, even though it's only us in the narrow space of the alley.

"I don't think that," I say quickly, then wonder who else he's referring to. "What do you mean?" I ask.

"Nothing." I wait for him to elaborate but he doesn't. "I should get back."

I raise my eyebrows. "Why, coz it's so busy?"

He gives a half-smile. "No, because I don't have a coat. I'm freezing my ass off out here." The cold is bitter and unforgiving. I hate February.

"I have to get to work anyway," I say.

"It will be okay," Connor says. But his face is blank and I don't believe him. "It will."

Driving to Petunia's kitchen, I feel disappointed for some reason. I don't know what I expected from Connor, but I'm no more at ease than before I saw him. I'm not sure what I'm most worried about—that Ian is guilty, how my mother will handle this, or that the whole thing is a giant mistake. I'm pulling into the parking lot of Petunia's when I realize I turned to the wrong Doherty for help. I should have gone to Caroline.

*

When I was younger, there were times I wished Caroline was my mother. I think she sometimes wished it too. Their house was so normal. So calm. I was still reeling from Serena's death when I arrived, but after the first few weeks of letting me lie in bed and watch TV, Caroline forced me out the door and to school each morning. She cooked dinner every night, and we all sat around the table and talked. Nothing big. Just boring stuff about the day. At my house, by the time I was in middle school, dinner was a do-it-yourself affair. Occasionally we'd huddle around a pizza, but usually I ended up eating a bowl of cereal or a peanut butter sandwich in front of the TV. My mom was never big on rules and routines, so Serena and I had no real bedtime—when I was bored of TV or when my dad kicked me off to watch the game, I'd go to bed. When my dad was home, things were easier, and he'd impose some order, but he worked a lot and often it was just me, my mom and Serena. In Connor's house, we needed to be upstairs by nine, lights out by ten. Even with the nightmares that would wake me in the early hours of morning, I slept better at the Dohertys' house those few months than I ever slept at home, a black and dreamless sleep.

Connor had chores, and while I was there, I did too. It wasn't that we weren't expected to help out at home, but there was no order to it. Sometimes my room would go uncleaned for weeks, then my mother would explode in a fit of frustration and threaten to throw out all my clothes unless I cleaned up. She didn't mean to, but back then she communicated mostly through yelling. At my dad, at me, at Serena. She was always exasperated with one of us. Her unhappiness was like a force field around her, keeping the rest of us out. If it had been up to me, I would never have gone home. I could have happily lived as Caroline and Jack's daughter till I graduated from high school.

My mother's different now, and I know Ian's part of the reason why. Even though I wish she was still with my dad, Ian brings out something in her that we never could. Without Ian, I don't know what will happen to her.

In the kitchen of Petunia's, I chop vegetables and herbs. Somehow in her work life, my mother has become incredibly organized. It's spilled over into the rest of her life too, and these days the house is mostly tidy, the toilet usually clean, laundry folded and put away each week. My mother's left out recipes and instructions for everything that needs to be done to get ready for tonight's dinner. Even with Ian in jail, I know she'll still come in to finish the cooking and serve the meal herself. When it comes to Petunia's, she's nothing but professional, nurturing the business like it's a baby, her chance at getting parenthood right.

It takes me four hours to prep, and on the way home, I stop by Caroline's. I usually drop in once a week for a chat, but I haven't been over in a few weeks—partly because I'm busy, but mostly because I don't want her to ask about Connor. Caroline's always been able to root out the truth in me.

I knock on the front door and wait. It's a long time before she answers, and when she finally comes to the door, I worry I might have woken her from a nap. Her eyes are puffy and her cheeks flushed. The fine lines on her face are more pronounced; the little curves around her mouth and forehead appear deeper today. She looks older.

"Daisy." She wraps me into a hug. "How are you, sweetheart? I just got off the phone with your mom. You've heard about Ian?" I nod, and she pulls me into the house. She takes the kettle off the stove and fills it with water. "Tea?"

I nod, and Caroline pulls out the boxes and places a selection before me. I reach for a peppermint and tear the sachet from its protective packet, dropping it into the cup. It's a beautiful hand-made mug, sturdy in my palm, smooth and shiny in a deep blue glaze. It looks like the type of mug that Todd's mother would own.

"What did she say?" I ask.

"He's been booked and he'll be arraigned tomorrow. That's when they'll find out if he's made bail."

"How much will that be?"

She sighs. "If they give him bail, it will be a lot. Probably at least a hundred thousand."

"She can't pay that." I don't know what I was expecting but the amount is like a kick in the stomach. My mother has no money. What she makes from Petunia's barely covers our bills. She can't even help me pay for classes.

"She's going to put up the house."

It hits me then how much this could devastate us. Caroline must see something in my face because she puts an arm around my shoulder. "It's going to be okay."

I give a bitter laugh, uncharacteristic of the way I act around Caroline, and she pulls back and frowns at me with concern. "Connor said exactly the same thing. But it doesn't feel like everything's going to be okay."

"When did you see Connor?" she asks as the kettle starts to whistle.

"This morning." Caroline pours water in the mugs. I lower my face to breathe in the minty smell of the steam.

"How did he seem?"

I hesitate. I hate ratting him out to his mom. It feels like such a betrayal. Then I think of his mottled arms and gray skin, the guitar that's sat propped in the corner of his room for God only knows how long, and I realize it's why I've come. Connor needs someone to rat him out.

"Not great." I pause for Caroline's reaction. She takes a sip of tea, waiting for me to say more. "He's doing drugs, Caroline."

In the movie version, these words would be followed by dramatic music and a close-up on one of our faces. In the real-life version, Caroline doesn't say anything. I expected some response—denial or shock or disbelief—but Caroline's expression is as placid as it was a moment ago. She sips her tea without speaking.

"But you already know that, don't you?" My voice is flat, monotone. Somewhere in the back of my mind, Caroline was the one who could fix Connor, prop him up and put him back together, just like she did for me and my mom all those years ago. I want to put my head down on the table and cry.

But it's Caroline who starts to cry, her features pinching into an unfamiliar expression of emotion. Caroline, who's always so composed and predictable, is suddenly weeping, her shoulders shaking up and down. She reaches for my hand and it's warm from the tea.

"I don't know what to do. I'm so afraid for him. I just don't know what to do. What should I do, Daisy? How do I help him?" She grabs me tightly in an uncomfortable hug, her face wet against my cheek. "What do I do?" she whispers in my ear over and over. I don't say anything. I let her cling to me; my second mother, who I hoped would hold the answers.

Connor is alone. He's out on a sinking raft in the middle of the ocean and not one of us can reach him. It's only a matter of time before he runs out of air and disappears below the black surface of the sea.

I hold Caroline as she continues to cry.

CAROLINE
Chapter Twenty-Three

I still have to work. Despite what I've finally forced myself to admit about Connor. Despite Ian being in jail. Despite my crumbling marriage and the young woman who was murdered on the beach, and the increasing likelihood that someone close to me is responsible for it, I still need to be at the library by two.

When I get there it's a relief to have the normalcy of checking in books and sifting through orders to take my mind off everything else. It's the quiet part of the day, after the moms with kids but before the after-school rush, though that will be slow this week too since school's out. There's hardly anyone in the room with me, just a few regulars and one of the volunteers quietly shelving DVDs. I sink into the hush of the fiction section, focusing on taking down last week's Valentine's Day display. Standing on a small stepladder, I remove paper hearts from the corkboard, each one cut and folded to look like an open book. Soon it will be time to set up the Easter display, though it's so dreary this time of year it's hard to believe spring will ever come.

I'm so focused on the simple task of unpinning the red hearts that I don't see Jack until he's right beside me. He's in plain-clothes, a pair of faded jeans and a wool sweater I bought him a few years ago. The sweater is the same green as his eyes, which was why I bought it. He looks handsome, and I realize how rarely I noticed his looks during all those years when I saw him every day. It's taken him moving out for me to see him clearly again.

"What are you doing here?" I ask.

"Nice to see you too."

"Sorry. You just surprised me. Is everything okay?"

"Can you take a break?" He reaches out a hand and helps me down from the ladder. His palm is rough against mine.

After I've called Marina at the upstairs extension, I get my coat from the office and we head outside. There are rocking chairs at the front of the building, and on summer days people sit out here and use the free wifi. It's not even five and the sun is already slipping behind the stretch of trees that line the perimeter of the cemetery across the street, the same cemetery where generations of Jack's family are buried. There's a whole plot for the Dohertys, though last I heard, the graveyard had reached full capacity. We sit in our rockers, and I adjust my scarf to keep the wind at bay.

"You heard about Ian?" Jack asks.

"Yeah. Evvy's hired Mark Keene."

"He's good." Jack gives a nod of approval.

"The arraignment's tomorrow morning?"

Jack nods and taps his fingers along the smooth wood of the armrest. Years ago, Jack smoked cigarettes, a pack-a-day habit that he quit cold turkey after Connor was born. Though he hasn't smoked for years, his twitchy fingers are the tell when he's craving one. I rest my hand upon his to still its movement, before realizing such a wifely privilege has been revoked. I drop my hand back into my lap.

"I didn't actually come to talk about Ian," Jack says.

"Okay." I wait.

"Cyrus saw Connor the night of the festival. We both did." We're sitting side by side, and Jack stares ahead of him as he speaks so I can only see his profile. I wonder if it's easier for him to talk when he doesn't have to look at me directly.

"So? Half the island was there." An elderly couple nod hello at us as they make their way into the library. We both smile politely and Jack waits till the door has closed behind them to continue speaking.

"Cyrus saw him talking to Layla Dresser. They were only talking for a minute, and he didn't leave when she did. Cyrus didn't want to drag Connor into anything."

Something clutches at the back of my throat, a hand squeezing out the air. It's nearly dark now, and I can just make out a faint row of headstones across the road, the even stone rectangles disappearing in the dusk. The old wood of Jack's chair sighs beneath him as he rocks slowly beside me.

"So, what now?" My voice is just above a whisper.

"Ian's being charged with her murder," Jack says evenly. "Cyrus isn't going to mention anything about Connor talking to her." Cyrus is a good cop, but he's a better friend. Still, it's so unlike either of them to go against police procedure. I don't know if I should be grateful or worried.

"So why are you telling me now?" I ask.

"She was bringing drugs to the island. That's why she was over," Jack says. This must be common knowledge by now, otherwise Jack would never tell me. "She worked at Moby Dick's for a few weeks at the end of last summer. Connor must have known her."

I can barely see Jack in the fading light, but his face is unreadable, even to me. I have never trusted Ian, not after the time he hit Evvy, but I still have difficulty imagining him as a murderer. Ian is loud and charming and funny. It's hard to reconcile this image of him with the idea that he killed a woman. Then again, it is still difficult for me to imagine him hurting Evvy, despite the truth of it. The question remains: if Ian didn't do it, who did? If Connor's connection to Layla and his conversation at the bar with her points the finger in his direction, I have no choice but to hope that Ian did kill her.

"Do you really think Ian killed her?" I ask.

"Yes. Absolutely." His certainty is a relief, but already I fear what this will mean for Evvy.

"So, what does any of this have to do with Connor?" I ask.

It takes him a moment to speak. "I know he's having a hard time. I haven't seen him in a few weeks. He doesn't answer his phone and doesn't call me back." He rubs his temples, fingers pressing hard against the skin. "I'm worried about someone coming forward and saying they saw Connor talking to her. He didn't have anything to do with this. I know that… I want to keep him out of this, but there are drugs involved. I'm losing perspective here, Carrie. I thought you could help me think straight." Jack's the only one who calls me Carrie and the casual intimacy of the nickname is like rubbing a healing wound.

The last thing I can do is help Jack think straight, especially when it comes to Connor. I'm certain now that Connor knows something about what happened to Layla or is somehow connected to the drugs that she was bringing over. Yet I can't tell Jack, not when there's a chance he'll use what I know about Connor against him. Even if he wants to keep Connor out of this, if he suspects that Connor is dealing drugs, I don't know that he'll continue to protect him. Because even though he should be a father first, so often being a cop supersedes that.

"He had nothing to do with any drugs. There's no reason to drag him into any of this." I wish my heart matched the certainty in my voice, but I have no choice but to fake it.

Jack nods and even in the darkness I see the relief on his face. "Have you seen him lately?"

"He's come by a few times recently. He stayed over the other night." I don't mention the circumstances, the middle-of-the-night visit or his ransacked bedroom.

"How did he seem?"

"Fine."

"Really?" he presses.

More than anything I want to tell Jack everything. For a moment I consider it. The bulging bag of pills, the way Connor screamed and swore at me, then broke down crying like a child. The broken man our baby has become. Jack's seen this before in his line of work, he knows people who could help. But I don't trust that he won't make things worse, his belief in the law overriding what could happen to Connor. I can see how conflicted he is, wanting to be a good father while also being a good cop, looking out for Connor while also doing what he thinks is right for the island. So what if Connor was at the bar that night? Jack will turn over this scrap of inconsequential information and it will land Connor in criminal trouble on top of everything else. What will happen to him if the police find out about the drugs? How long would he go to prison? A future where he goes to college, pursues his music, meets a nice girl or finally settles down with Daisy, any chance he has of escaping a dead-end job and the emptiness of life on Great Rock would be gone. It would disappear in my own selfish need to unburden my secrets.

"He seemed great. He's going to come for dinner soon." I force a smile.

"Good. That's good." Jack nods, seeming satisfied. It takes so little to convince him that I want to shake him for his stupidity. How blind we've become, unwilling to see what's right in front of us. "Did you say anything about us?"

"No."

"We should talk to him. Before he finds out some other way."

"What are we telling him?" When he doesn't answer, I ask the question I've been wondering since he left. "Are you coming home?" When Jack turns to me, his expression is gentle.

"Do you want me to?"

I think of the empty house that awaits me at the end of my shift. The can of soup I'll have for dinner followed by mindless television, Champ keeping Jack's side of the bed warm. Then I think about how free I am without Jack, how for the first time in as long as I can remember, I have to figure out who I am without him. And while this is terrifying, I'm also interested in what I'll discover. I want him to come home, but not like this. Not when there's still an impenetrable wall between us that neither of us is willing to acknowledge. Since he left, the distance has only gotten wider. There's so much that we haven't found the words to say.

I'm saved from answering by Marina who sticks her head out the door. "Sorry to interrupt, but you have a phone call, Caroline. It's about the order you placed last week. There's a backlog on some of the titles." She turns to Jack and smiles. "Hi, Jack. Haven't seen you in a while. How are you?"

Always the gentleman, Jack smiles. "Fine, thanks, Marina, and you?"

"Good. Do you want to take it?" she asks me.

"I'll be right there," I say. I think about the question Jack asked me, the one I don't have an answer for.

She nods and then ducks back into the warm solace of the library. Jack and I rise from the chairs; my legs are stiff from the cold.

"Tell Connor to call me if you see him," Jack says. He stoops to kiss my cheek and his familiar scent catches me off guard.

I miss you, I want to say, but I don't.

"I will," I say instead. "Goodnight."

I leave him standing in the cold darkness.

EVVY

Chapter Twenty-Four

Despite Cyrus's long career in the police department, I've only been in Great Rock's district court for jury duty a handful of times. The wives of cops don't usually make it on a jury, which means that the majority of my time in the courthouse has been spent in the overheated basement, waiting to be dismissed.

Not today. Today is Ian's arraignment, and I'm sitting in the third row, waiting for them to call his case. I'm tired after last night's catering job, having gotten up earlier than usual to give myself time to get ready. I've dressed up for the occasion, as I figure I'm supposed to, and my black heels pinch my toes. Daisy sits beside me, in sneakers and jeans, and though I know I should be thankful she's here to support me, I can't help but be annoyed by her casual outfit. She still dresses like a teenager, so I suppose I should be glad she's not wearing pajama bottoms and flip-flops.

There are other cases before Ian's, though I don't know anyone who's being arraigned today. Ian is scheduled for nine-thirty, but at only nine-ten his case is called, and I'm glad we arrived early. He enters with two court officers holding him firmly by the elbow. His hands are cuffed in front of him and he hasn't shaved. He's wearing the khakis and button-down I gave to his lawyer last night. Mark Keene is at the table beside him, a broad man with thinning hair in an expensive gray suit and turquoise tie. Before Ian sits down, he glances over his shoulder at Daisy and me. His face relaxes in relief, as if he'd thought maybe I wouldn't come. I wish I could hold his hand or touch his cheek, offer him some small comfort. I can't help but feel this whole thing is my fault, me and my big mouth, blabbing to Caroline about our stupid fight years earlier. I know the evidence against him is bigger than that, but I regret my own part in it.

The judge is an older man I don't recognize, with silver hair and glasses, and he asks Ian how he pleads. Ian's voice is hoarse and he has to clear his throat for the words to come out.

"Not guilty."

I wonder if he slept last night. I imagine him twisting and turning on a hard cot with a scratchy wool blanket, Ian, who needs two pillows to sleep, not too hard and not too soft. *Goodnight, Goldilocks*, I sometimes mumble at him as he tosses and turns and tries to get comfortable, and I can always count on a playful poke in the back that sometimes leads to something more.

Though he could easily turn to catch my eye, Ian keeps his gaze on the judge. I need him to look at me, to assure me that this will all be okay, that it will end well and we can go on as we were before that girl got herself killed. *Look at me*, I think, trying to telepathically relate the words to Ian, *please look at me*. I'm so focused on getting his attention that I nearly miss when the judge denies bail.

"What? They can't do that. He didn't do anything," I say to Daisy who looks at me soberly, but she doesn't say anything. "He didn't do anything," I say again, louder, and now Ian does look at me, his head snapping in my direction. His eyes hold so much—fear and sadness, but I also see his gratitude, the small solace of realizing I believe in his innocence. Mark holds up a hand in my direction but doesn't even make eye contact. He looks at the judge instead.

"Your Honor, my client has strong ties to the community. He lives with his longtime partner. He has a respectable job. He poses no flight risk." I curl my toes together in the tight shoes, focusing all of my tension on this insignificant pain.

The judge peers over the rims of his glasses. "Given the seriousness of the crime, his ties to the victim, and the allegations of domestic abuse that came up during questioning, I'm denying bail."

My face burns with shame and my heart thuds in my ears, all the blood swirling through my head. I avoid Daisy's eyes, afraid to see her turning the judge's phrase over in her mind: *the allegations of domestic abuse.*

It's not true, I want to yell. *You don't understand.* I'm squeezing Daisy's hand so tightly that she gasps beside me, pulling her slender fingers from my grip. Ian is escorted out of the courtroom, and he looks over his shoulder on his way past. He pulls in his lips, not a smile, but an acknowledgment. He looks worn down and defeated, not angry with me, but I wonder how much rage will build in the next few days and weeks, when it will finally be released, and upon whom.

Daisy pushes me toward the door.

DAISY

Chapter Twenty-Five

A few hours after Ian's arraignment, I'm lying in bed beside Todd. It's strange to me that out of all the people I could have turned to at this time, it's Todd I picked. Obviously not my mother, who's barely keeping her head above water, but not Connor or Caroline either, not my father or any of my other friends. It was Todd I wanted to see.

I haven't told him about Ian. We haven't talked about the murder, and I don't want to bring it into whatever this is that's starting between us, to introduce something so ugly and cold in a place that feels so warm and gentle. Part of me wonders if he'll judge me for it, if he'll see something dirty in me simply through my connection to Ian. I know I will have to tell Todd, soon, if things continue between us. But not today.

"You okay?" he asks.

"Mmhmm," I murmur, shifting in the bed. The soft flannel sheets are a safe cocoon I never want to leave.

"Rough day?"

I nod, my mind flashing back to the morning in court. My mother's ashen face when the judge denied Ian bail. The way she looked when the judge mentioned domestic abuse. Ian and I have always gotten along well, but I feel sick at the thought that something could have been going on in our house that I was so oblivious to. Six years they've been together. What kind of damage can a person do in six years?

After the arraignment, she handed me the keys to her car without speaking and I drove us home. She sat down at the counter and laid her head in her arms. I made her toast and tea without speaking, our roles reversing as I watched her begin to unravel. When Serena died, it was a swift and sudden decline, her legs knocked out from under her as she landed swiftly on the hard ground. This is slower, less dramatic, but I wonder if the end result will be the same.

She picked at the toast and took a few sips of the tea, then mumbled that she was going to lie down. When Serena died, my mother had no business to take care of, and she pawned me off on Caroline and Jack. How long until Petunia's buckles under the weight of her despair?

I checked on her a half-hour later, and she was fast asleep thanks to the open bottle of Ambien on the nightstand. I drove straight to Todd's house, not even calling first to see if he was home. When I arrived, I was relieved his car was in the driveway of the guesthouse. He pulled me into the warm house, and suddenly it felt like everything might be okay after all. I've known him a few days, but he's the only one whose presence I knew would bring comfort.

He pulls me in closer and the stubble on his chin brushes my cheek. I don't want to stick around and see what destruction will come next. I want to fly away from this island, rise up on golden wings and into the sky, not looking back until Great Rock is just a spit of land in the middle of the ocean.

"I need to head home tomorrow." Todd interrupts my daydream, and I tumble into reality. "I took a few extra days off, but I need to get back to work." I nod and swallow hard. I can't believe how close I am to crying. I roll over so he can't see my face. "I was thinking, though. Maybe you could come with me. Hang out for a few days."

I sigh. "I wish I could."

"So come." He squeezes my hip lightly.

"I can't."

"Why not?"

"I've got work and classes. And my mother's going to need me."

"Didn't you say it's your birthday this weekend?"

Just a few weeks ago I was excited about turning twenty-one, but now it's just another day, one that will be overshadowed by everyone else's unhappiness.

Todd rolls over so he can see my face. I love the way he looks, his sandy hair and blue eyes, his square jaw that makes him look so certain. "Come up on Friday. You don't want to spend your twenty-first birthday on Great Rock. We'll do the city for the weekend. You can take the bus, and I'll pick you up at South Station." He leans in to kiss me and I feel myself falling, falling, into something that feels so nice. "Come on. You know you want to," he sing-songs.

And I do want to. More than anything. Forget everyone else's problems and all of the obligations that grind away at me. For once, I just want to be free.

"I'll try."

"Try hard," he says.

CAROLINE
Chapter Twenty-Six

When I pull into Evvy's driveway the lights are all off, though her car is there. The front door is unlocked and I let myself in, wondering why Evvy still isn't locking her front door when someone was just murdered. Then I remember that Ian is the murderer, and he's still in jail, and he has a key to the front door anyway. The storm door slams behind me in the wind.

"Evvy?" I call, walking through the empty downstairs. I texted her before I left work, but she didn't respond. "Evvy, it's me." From where I stand at the bottom of the stairs, I see the closed door of her bedroom. I head upstairs.

Climbing the stairs, I'm reminded of the dark and desperate months after Serena died. Though it was obviously the worst time in Evvy's life, I realize it was also the worst of mine. I came to see Evvy every day after work. I stayed for an hour or two, long enough to get her fed or bathed, a spoonful of soup here, a cup of tea there, and while I did it without question or complaint, I dreaded every minute before my arrival and hated every moment I was there. Seeing the agony on Evvy's face, the boundless anguish that had ravaged her, rendering her unrecognizable, was like entering hell every day. It was seeing my deepest fears realized, and then being able to walk away and return to my own life, unscathed.

Connor and Daisy were old enough to stay home alone after school, and I know that those long afternoons together are what forged the twisted strands of their relationship, creating a bond so deeply rooted in who each of them is that they're unsure how to function separately. Those months are also what connect Evvy and me when we might otherwise have drifted apart. There are events that are written upon the body, moments that alter and define us, even if they're not visible to the naked eye.

Sometimes I wonder why we're friends. Evvy and I are different in so many ways, and at times it seems like our friendship continues out of shared history more than anything else. When I first moved to Great Rock, she took me under her wing. I didn't know anyone other than Jack, but Evvy brought me into the fold of her friends. Back then, Evvy was the life of the party, always ready for a good time. A cluster of pretty young women followed her wherever she went, but for some reason, she always wanted me at the center of that group. Then we both had children, Daisy and Connor around the same age, and things just grew from there.

These days it's habit and history that binds us more than anything. She is my family now, like it or not. Beneath the brash selfishness and tendency toward self-destruction, I know at the center of Evvy is a fragile and grieving child. She lashes out at those around her when she's upset.

Standing outside the door, I knock tentatively. When there's no answer, I knock again, a little harder this time, before pushing open the door. Evvy is still, the heavy pink duvet pulled over her body. Her blond hair sticks out from the covers, and she stirs beneath the blankets, rolling over to face me.

"Hey. What are you doing here?" Her voice is blurry with sleep.

"I wanted to check on you. I texted to say I was coming over."

"My phone's downstairs." Evvy pushes herself up in the bed. She runs a hand over her face. "I took a sleeping pill. I forgot how much those things knock me out."

I sit on the edge of the bed, uncomfortably aware that this is where Ian sleeps. "How did things go this morning?"

Her face clouds. "He didn't make bail. Given the 'heinous nature of the crime', bail was denied."

"Well, it was a heinous crime." I don't know why I'm agreeing, but I don't like the way she's so quick to dismiss this girl's murder. Like all she cares about is how it affects her.

"Of course it is, but Ian didn't do it. Just because he talked to her that night doesn't mean he killed her."

I'm not sure if I'm surprised by her belief that Ian's innocent. Evvy, more than anyone, knows what Ian's temper is like, but maybe it's too difficult to face the fact that he's actually a murderer too. To admit to this would be to look too closely at all the ways things with Ian could have gone so much worse.

Evvy keeps talking. "The only reason they even arrested him in the first place is because of his 'history of domestic abuse'." I cringe, but she keeps going. "Yeah, they said that in court. Right in front of Daisy." She reaches for a glass of water from the night-stand and then presses on. "I hear Connor talked to her as well, but he's not on trial." I open my mouth to speak, but no words come out. "Don't worry, we're all going to keep our mouths shut so nothing happens to your precious baby." The bitterness in her words cuts me and the hurt must be evident on my face. "Sorry," she mumbles, taking another swallow of water.

"Connor didn't do anything," I say to her now. "Who told you he was there?"

Evvy pushes herself up in bed. She removes an elastic from her wrist and fixes her hair into a messy ponytail. "Who do you think? Cyrus."

I thought Cyrus knew better than to go blabbing to Evvy, but even now he's blind when it comes to her. "Are you going to say anything?"

"Who would I tell?" she asks.

"I don't know. The police?"

"I don't see how that would help Ian." She doesn't sound convincing, but I let it drop. Jack used to say I was a better friend to Evvy than she was to me, but I wonder if she'd actually betray me on purpose.

"Have you talked to his lawyer?" I ask.

"He says the trial won't be for at least a few weeks. Possibly months." She pulls her knees into her chest and rests her head against her legs. "Did Jack tell you about the phone calls?" Evvy's voice is small, the fight drained from it.

"Jack hasn't told me anything."

"There were records of phone calls between them. I think he was sleeping with her." When she meets my eyes, she looks so fragile.

"Oh, Evvy," I say softly.

"She's practically Daisy's age. I just can't believe it."

"I'm so sorry," I say, because there's nothing else to say. Neither of us has any answers or any cures. She pinches her lips into a semblance of a smile.

"I'm sorry I was such a bitch. I'm just upset about Ian."

"I know."

She sits up and leans in closer. Her pale blue eyes are fixated on me, smudged with leftover mascara. "Before I fell asleep, I was thinking about Serena. Or I was thinking about me and Cyrus before. Do you think we would have divorced if Serena hadn't died?"

I blink silently, unsure what to say. Evvy never talks about Serena's death. It is an unspoken devastation that colors every moment of her life, but one she rarely acknowledges. "I don't know. Probably not. The kids were little and that was hard. You fought a lot, but you loved each other. Anyone could see that."

She nods, as if I've confirmed something she already knew, then lies back down in bed.

"Do you want to get out of here?" I ask. Evvy groans, wrapping the blankets around her more tightly. "Come on. You can't stay in bed all night. Let's go grab some dinner."

"I can't. I don't want to see anyone. I just want to sleep."

"Ev, you can't stay in bed forever. You can't." When she looks at me, I know we're both thinking of the last time Evvy got into bed and didn't come out.

"Fine. I guess. I need to take a shower first. Where do you want to go?"

"I don't know. What's open?"

"Not much." Restaurant choices are slim in February. In the summer there would be fifty places to choose from, but there's only a handful open now. Even the places that stayed open for the holidays are closed.

"Moby Dick's? It's that or the Blue Crab, unless you want to go to Egret."

I hesitate. I'm not sure if I want to see Connor, especially with Evvy, but I know he won't come to me. "Moby Dick's, I guess."

We make a plan for Evvy to pick me up in an hour, and I head home and grab Champ to take him for a quick walk. I hustle him into the back seat, intending to drive toward the dog park, but instead I find myself heading for Osprey Beach. I park the car by the sea rail. It's dusk and the sky is inky and pink, the rocks of the jetty silhouetted against the gray ocean. Champ whimpers at my side and tugs on his leash, itching to run free. In the late fall and early spring I walk here often, before the summer season beach rules banning dogs come into effect. The beach is empty now, the wind by the ocean too sharp for even the most intrepid runners or dog walkers. Champ guides me down the steps that lead to the sand. The metal railing is freezing even through the fleece of my gloves.

At the water I unclip Champ's leash and he bounds down the strip of beach, grateful to be unrestrained after a long afternoon inside. He runs for a bit and then turns around and comes back to me, ears pricked up, mouth open in a wide canine grin. The air is crisper and blows harder down here. It cuts through my heavy coat and snakes its way under the gap of my sweater. As much as I hate winter, there's something that feels good about the shock of it, a bracing reminder that I'm alive. I pull down my hat to cover my ears and trudge on.

Champ comes panting back to me, a piece of driftwood in his mouth. I throw it, and he hurdles down the beach to fetch it. Fetch and throw. Fetch and throw. It requires so little to make him happy.

Sometimes I think I'm too close to Connor to see him clearly. He'll always be a child to me, and even now, when I'm presented with evidence of all the ways he's changed, the self-destructive path he's set himself on, I can only think about the past.

I remember when I found out about Serena. It was Cyrus who called Jack. Jack came into the living room, visibly shaken. I'd never seen such an expression on his face. Connor was off-island at a hockey game, one of the few that neither of us attended. For a moment, I thought it was Connor. Images flashed through my mind. Red blood on the white ice, a broken neck, a fractured spine, the blade of a skate in his eye. When Jack told me that Serena was dead, for just a fraction of a second, I felt relieved. *Not us*, I thought. *We're okay.* It wasn't even a full second, and the very next moment I was struck dumb with my own shock and desolation for Evvy and Cyrus. I've never forgiven myself for that infinitesimal instant thought, and I wonder if Evvy knows that before I grieved for Serena, I rejoiced in my own good luck. I still feel guilty every time I think about it.

When Serena died, Evvy died too. She's resurrected herself from the brink, but her sadness is still bottomless. Yet Evvy had Daisy to survive for. If I lost Connor, I don't think I'd ever rise again.

I've seen the pictures of Layla Dresser. She was young and pretty, still a girl. What's happened to her mother? There's been little about her in the paper. She doesn't live on the island, or even in the state, and none of us has ever had to see the depth of pain in her eyes, but that doesn't make it any less real. Just like Serena, Layla Dresser was someone's daughter. Everyone's forgotten that a young woman is dead, and there were people who loved her. So preoccupied are we with the way her death, *her murder*, has rippled across the island, that we've forgotten what started it.

I think about Ian, his anger finally boiling over, fingers closing around that poor girl's neck. The sky is getting darker, and I suddenly have no desire to be on this beach, so close to the beckoning fingers of evil, some morbid force drawing me down here. All this time I've been convinced Ian wouldn't kill a girl he barely knew. If Ian were to kill someone, it would be Evvy.

Yet this new information, a relationship between them, ignites the possibility again.

If this is true, then Connor's only crime is the baggie full of drugs, and while this isn't nothing, it isn't murder. I don't know how I can feel relief at such a realization, and my guilt at Evvy's loss and what awaits her is close to what it was the day I found out about Serena.

The streetlights flicker on, and the white orbs cast a dim light on the beach. I call for Champ and clip him on the leash, hurrying toward the stairs.

EVVY
Chapter Twenty-Seven

Moby Dick's is nearly empty. Caroline and I find a table in the back, and I'm relieved there's no one here that we need to talk to. Usually it's Caroline who hates the lack of anonymity on the island, but tonight I don't feel like seeing a single person I know.

"Do you ever dream of just getting the hell away from here?" I ask Caroline after our drinks have arrived.

"All the time." Caroline smiles wistfully.

"I'm like the island freak show. I can almost hear the whispers." I don't say what the whispers are, but we both know. *Poor woman. First her daughter, now this. How she manages to get up in the morning is beyond me.* I can hear their clucking tongues, the *tsk-tsk* as they shake their heads, clutching their own loved ones a little closer. Secretly they all think it could never happen to them. Just for a moment, it would be nice to live in a place where no one knows me.

Yet this is my home. Even as a teenager, I knew I'd live on Great Rock as an adult. For some of us who grew up here, we couldn't imagine living in a place where you have to lock your doors, where there's a mall on every corner, where you can't see the stars at night and there are strangers everywhere. Great Rock is like a place that time forgot, which makes some people crazy, but is actually the best part about it. Caroline's always been itching to leave, but that's because Great Rock isn't in her blood. You need to be born here to truly understand the magic of the island. Then again, Daisy's got the island in her blood and she's dying to get out of here.

Caroline sips her red wine and sighs. "How are you holding up?"

"I don't know. The whole thing feels like a bad dream, you know? I just can't believe Ian could do this." Caroline averts her eyes and doesn't respond. I'm not yet willing to entertain the idea that Ian might have done this, even if it's clear that Caroline thinks he's guilty. "I know you hate him."

"I don't hate him. I just… I don't trust him, and I don't like the way he treats you."

"He treats me fine," I say, but now I'm the one avoiding eye contact.

"He *hits* you," Caroline hisses. She's careful not to raise her voice but the frustration comes through.

"That was only once," I start, but Caroline sees right through the lie. "It's not as if it happens all the time."

She lets out a gasp of exasperation. "Can you hear yourself? You sound like a battered wife on some stupid made-for-TV movie. It's not okay. Not just a few times, not even once. *It's not okay.* And now this. He's cheating on you too?"

I gulp down the rest of my drink and signal to the waitress for another. I haven't eaten in hours, and the drink mixed with the sleeping pills I took earlier leaves me with a fuzzy feeling, all my usual filters gone. The waitress brings our burgers and puts the plates down in front of us. We're quiet while she gets things settled and don't talk till she's out of earshot. Neither of us touches our food.

"I can't make you understand," I say quietly.

"What? What don't I understand?" Caroline looks so sad that I wish we were the type of friends who hugged easily or held hands, but Caroline's not a toucher. The new haircut makes her look younger, like when we first met. We were babies back then, practically the same age as Connor and Daisy. Another lifetime. I swallow down the lump in my throat and force myself to answer Caroline.

"Ian saved me. Without him, I would have rolled over and died." Caroline doesn't answer and I try to explain. "After Serena died, I didn't think I'd ever want to do anything again." Even all these years later, it's hard to talk about Serena. Her life. Her death. I think about her all the time, but talking about her is still so raw. Caroline knows this and never tries to bring her up, though I know she sometimes wants to. I know she thinks it's unhealthy to never talk about her, and while she's probably right, talking about Serena makes me feel like I'm staring head first into the black hole of her death. The loss is still so big that it could swallow me up. I feel myself on the brink of that abyss now, but I have to make Caroline understand why I need Ian. "He brought me back to life. He helped me start Petunia's. He gave me a purpose again."

The words are not enough. Ian did give my life a purpose again, but how do I explain that everything is still shadowed by Serena's death? Though I've learned to get up in the morning again, it doesn't mean I always want to. Since Ian came along, I do it anyway.

Caroline is quiet for a moment. "Evvy, I know you think you need him, and maybe you do, but it still doesn't make it okay for him to hurt you." I look down at my plate and nod. Deep down, I know she's right, even if I'm right too.

Our waitress arrives at our table. "How is everything?"

We've only picked at the meal, but we both smile and tell her everything is fine.

"Is Connor in the kitchen tonight?" Caroline asks. The girl nods. I don't recognize her; she's young, probably still in high school.

"I'm going to sneak in to say hello to him," Caroline tells me, and then heads to the doors that lead to the kitchen.

"Another round of drinks?" the waitress asks.

Caroline's just finishing her first glass but I'm nearly done with number two. "Please." I try to force myself to eat the burger, though all I really want is the wine. I pick at the fries instead, knowing that the uneaten leftovers will sit in the fridge till Daisy finds them. Caroline's gone a long time, but eventually she comes back to the table with Connor by her side.

It's been a while since I last saw Connor, a few months at least, and his appearance is startling. He's always been thin, but he's skinnier than usual, all angles and bones. He looks tired, far more tired than a twenty-one-year-old should look. Despite what I've long suspected, I'm unprepared for Connor's transformation. I press my lips tightly together, hoping my shock isn't evident.

"I wanted him to come say hello," Caroline says.

"Hi, Connor," I manage to get out.

"How's your food?" He gestures to the untouched burger.

"Great."

He nods and turns to Caroline. "I've got to get back to the kitchen."

"Okay. Bye, honey. Tomorrow night, okay?" she says hopefully, but he doesn't answer.

When he's gone, Caroline sits down. The waitress brings our drinks. I'm struck silent by what I've just seen and what Caroline is oblivious to. This boy lay on my living room floor in a sleeping bag. He dressed up as Captain Hook for Halloween and held Serena's hand while we went trick or treating. He brought Daisy to both his prom and hers. My chest is tight and breathing is suddenly difficult. Caroline picks up her burger and takes a bite, then turns to look at me.

"Are you okay?" she asks.

"Have you looked at Connor recently?" My voice comes out as a whisper.

Caroline gives a little laugh. "I just saw him now."

"No, I mean, have you *really* looked at him?"

"He's going through a hard time," she starts, but I hold up my hand.

"He's doing drugs, Caroline. Can't you see that?" My voice is too loud in the restaurant, but there are hardly any other customers to overhear.

"He's not, he's fine," Caroline whispers.

"Don't lie. Not to me. Not about this." I hold her gaze until her eyes fill with tears and she looks down at her plate.

"I don't know what to do," Caroline says, and it's by the way her voice cracks like she's about to start crying that I know how upset she is. I wonder how long she's known, how long she's been in denial and holding this inside.

I'm awake suddenly, the last dregs of the sleeping pills finally worn off, my whole body on alert. I want to clutch her by the shoulders and shake her till the blinds fall from her eyes and the cotton drops from her ears. Caroline doesn't yet realize that sometimes there are no second chances. One wrong move and everything in your life can be undone. What I would give for a chance to save Serena. To have back those precious seconds when I took my eyes off the road. How I wish I'd stopped at the store for that stupid bag of chips, and not just any bag—a super-size bag I'd let her eat all in one sitting. What I would give for the opportunity to confide in someone that Serena's rage wasn't normal, that she needed help, that *we* needed help. I should have called the doctor's office earlier, I should have called her teacher, I should have called a therapist, I should have, I should have, I should have. In retrospect it's so simple.

"You fight for him. Before it's too late," I hiss at her.

"How?" Her skin has gone blotchy and her eyes are shiny, but there's something determined there too. She waits for my answer, and though she needs to see the truth, the way forward is unclear, the road crooked and littered with obstacles. And then it unfurls before me.

"You call Jack. You tell him Connor needs help." She blinks in disbelief and doesn't answer. I reach across the table and squeeze her hand. "You need to call Jack."

DAISY
Chapter Twenty-Eight

I stop at my father's house on the way back from Todd's. I haven't spoken to him since the day he came by to supposedly check on my car. I've been driving my mother's car for the past few days and she's been using Ian's. It doesn't look like Ian will be needing it any time soon.

Gina's little white Honda is in the driveway next to my father's pickup truck, and I can't help but be disappointed that she's home. It's not that I don't like Gina, but she's vice principal at the high school, and she acts the same at home as she does at school. *A place for everything and everything in its place*, she's said to me more than once. She's the complete opposite of my own mother, but at least she's stable and nice enough and she seems to make my dad happy, even if I sometimes wonder if she actually needs him for anything. Then again, maybe this is why my dad likes her. Gina's competent and self-sufficient.

I knock on the front door and then go in without waiting for an answer. I've spent almost as much time in this house as I have in my mom's, but it's never felt like home. My dad and Gina are in the kitchen cleaning up from dinner. Actually, Gina's loading the dishwasher while my dad sits at the table and finishes a beer. I know from personal experience that this isn't because my father doesn't try to help, it's because Gina is totally anal about the way the dishwasher is loaded. It's easier just to bring the dishes to the sink and let her do it herself.

My dad's face lights up when he sees me, and Gina pauses in her work. I step out of my wet boots so they don't leave mud and snow on the shiny hardwood floor.

"I was just on my way home, and I thought I'd swing by," I say.

"We just finished dinner. Are you hungry?" Gina asks.

I haven't had anything to eat since breakfast. "Yeah, if there's anything left over."

"Sit down. I'll get you some pasta," my dad says. The pot is still on the stove and he gets up to fill a plate with spaghetti and meatballs. "It should still be warm. Want some garlic bread?"

"Sure, thanks."

He brings me a bowl and I start to eat. My father brings his beer to the table and sits down with me while Gina finishes cleaning off the counter. When the kitchen is gleaming and the air smells faintly of lemon cleaner, she folds the dishtowel and hangs it on the handle of the stove. "I'm going to go up and do some work. You guys okay in here?"

We nod and I'm glad to see her go. I have a hard time relaxing around Gina. Too many years of seeing her strolling the hallways of Great Rock High, always on the lookout for misbehaving teenagers. I feel guilty around her, even when I haven't done anything wrong.

"So. Everything okay?" my dad asks, once we've heard the office door shut behind Gina. "How's your mom?"

"Okay, I guess. I went with her to the arraignment this morning. They're not letting Ian out on bail."

He nods and takes another swig of his beer. "I heard."

I push the empty bowl away. "They talked about his history of domestic abuse. Do you know anything about that?"

His jaw tightens. "Not much."

"He doesn't hit her, Dad. I've never seen anything like that. He's nice to her. I'd know if he was beating her up." I'm not sure if I'm trying to convince him or myself. "I would have told you if something like that was going on."

His face softens and he pats my hand. "I know, sweetheart." He gets up from the table and goes to the fridge, pulling another beer out. He pops the tab on the can and takes a sip before speaking again. "I think it's only happened once or twice. She told Caroline about something that happened years ago, but it doesn't help his case. Establishes a history of violence."

I shake my head, still stunned by this new perception of Ian. "I'm worried about her," I say.

He nods, his face unreadable. "I know. Me too."

I'm overcome with an unexpected wave of longing for the family we once had. I'm being ridiculous, because I remember what it was like before my parents split up. The endless silence between them that filled every corner of the house. The only way our family could be whole again is if Serena were still alive, though even before she died, her presence was like a storm, something swift-moving and unpredictable, knocking over everything in its path. Sometimes I hate her almost as much as I miss her. It's too easy to blame her for the way things fell apart.

"Do you miss her?" I ask. I'm talking about Serena, but he misunderstands, unable to see the cobwebbed strands in my mind. My father glances upstairs before he answers, and when he speaks his voice is soft and careful.

"I care about your mother very much. But I'm with Gina now. You know that."

I look down at my empty dishes. Crumbs of bread litter the plate and the remains of the tomato sauce glisten in the bowl. "I know."

"Where's all this coming from?"

I fold my arms across my chest and feel like a pouting teenager. "I want to go away for the weekend."

"Okay." He draws out the word, waiting for the connection.

"I'm afraid to leave Mom alone."

"Where do you want to go? To visit Casey?"

Casey Adams, my best friend from high school, is a junior at UMass Amherst. I visited her at school during her freshman and sophomore years, but the visits left me jealous and pissed off about everything I was missing. We don't talk as much these days. I shake my head. "No. I want to visit a friend in Boston."

"Todd Rankin?" I look up at him in surprise. "I saw his father while I was a getting coffee this morning. He said you'd been over for dinner." He raises his eyebrows. A smile plays at his lips.

"We've just been hanging out. It's no big deal." I hear the edge of defensiveness in my voice.

"I didn't say it was." He holds his hands up in defense.

"It's my birthday this weekend."

"I know. I was going to ask if you wanted to go for dinner some night."

"That's nice, but I want to get out of here for a few days. Have some fun, you know? I hate this time of year. It's so quiet."

"So what do you want from me?" He takes another sip of beer.

"Can you just check on her? Make sure she's okay? That she's not in bed all the time or totally ignoring Petunia's? She's got a dinner Saturday night."

"Doesn't she need you for that?"

I shake my head. "I already got the weekend off for my birthday. Paul's helping her, but I'm worried she's going to flake on everything. But I really want to get out of here. Just for a few days." He hears the pleading in my voice.

"Okay," he relents. "I'll check on her. And I'll let Caroline know, too. Maybe she can swing by as well."

"Thank you." I throw my arms around his neck, filled with gratitude and excitement at the prospect of a whole weekend with Todd, away from Great Rock.

"You're welcome." He straightens up from my embrace. "But be careful."

A snowstorm is supposed to be coming tomorrow night, and I've already decided I'll leave tomorrow morning to avoid getting stuck. "I will. I'm going to leave before the storm."

"That's not what I meant. He's a bit older than you, isn't he?"

"Just a few years." I realize I don't actually know how old Todd is.

"He's from a different world," my father points out.

"He's nice, Dad. You'd like him."

"I probably would. But you know what I'm saying," he says with a smile.

Do I? Are the two worlds we live in so different? Is it possible I could fit into his world? Is it so wrong to want something more? Neither of my parents understands my desperation to get off Great Rock, and I know it's part of the reason neither of them has done more to help me pay for college. It's some warped allegiance to the island, twisted with the pain of losing Serena and the fear of letting me go too far out of their sight.

"I'll be careful," I say, because it's easier just to agree.

He nods, pushes himself to standing, signaling the end of the conversation. "Gina and I were going to watch a movie. Want to stick around?"

Gina's got a taste for the classics, which my father patiently indulges. I'm sure it will be some old black-and-white with over-acting and a fluffy plot, but I'm not ready to go home yet. "Why not?" I say, and follow him into the living room.

CAROLINE
Chapter Twenty-Nine

After I've dropped Evvy at home, I make myself a cup of tea and sit on the couch. My stomach turns over, still empty despite the burgers we just ordered, though the idea of eating anything makes me sick. Before Evvy confronted me at the restaurant about Connor, I'd snuck into the kitchen to talk with him. He was bent over a stainless-steel table, tapping at the screen of his phone, and Scott Lambert was at the grill. The heavy smell of French fries emanated from the small hot space.

"Mom. What are you doing here?" Connor looked at me warily.

"Evvy and I are here for dinner. I just wanted to say hi."

"Hi." His eyes flicked back to his phone.

"Do you have a minute? Can we talk?" I heard the desperate note in my voice and he must have too.

"I guess." He headed in the direction of the dining room.

"Can we go outside?" I gestured to the heavy metal door that led to the alley.

"It's fucking freezing."

The swearing made the hair on the back of my neck stand up on end. This wasn't the way he talked to me. I didn't acknowledge it. "Grab a sweatshirt."

He shook his head in exasperation but grabbed his hoodie from a hook on the wall. He held the door open for me and I stepped out into the frigid night.

"Are you okay?" I asked after the door banged behind us.

"Yeah, I'm fine." He was anxious and twitchy, ready to be rid of me.

"You're not."

Our breath puffed out in white plumes, lighting up the sky between us. I'd left my own coat at the table with Evvy, and I crossed my arms across my chest in a futile attempt to stay warm.

"What did you want to talk about?" He didn't even try to hide his impatience.

I tried to find a way to ask him my question without further angering him. When I realized there was no way to do this, I plowed ahead. "Whose drugs were those?"

"Can you keep your voice down?" He looked around instinctively, but there was no one else out there, just us and the starry winter sky. I could see that Main Street was deserted. "It doesn't matter."

"Yes, it does. They belonged to someone, and if they weren't yours, then someone is going to be looking for them. Whose were they?" I wished Jack were there for this conversation. He has always held an authority with Connor that I don't. I am the gentle one, the friend, the confidante and comforter, while Jack is the heavy.

"I can't talk to you about this." He took a step back, shoulders hunched, his body folding in on itself.

"You need to," I said. He had always talked to me, until this past year at least. When he was upset or worried, when he was angry, when he was excited about something. It scared me to think we might have lost that too.

"Not now. Not here." He looked around again at the vacant alley and desolate street beyond.

"Fine. Tomorrow night you're coming over for dinner."

"Mom," he said in exasperation. He wiped his nose on the sleeve of his sweatshirt.

"I'm not asking, Connor. I haven't told your father yet, but if you don't come over tomorrow night and tell me the full story,

I'm telling him everything." I hated to threaten him like this, but I didn't see what choice I had. I needed him to talk to me.

"So Dad won't be at dinner?" There was something accusing in his voice that caught me off guard, and I was silent, formulating my answer. In my rush to get him to come over, I'd forgotten about Jack.

"I'm not sure. I think he has to work." It sounded weak even to me.

"I know, Mom," Connor said in a flat voice.

I pretended not to understand. "Know what?"

"I *know*, all right? About you and Dad. I know he moved out."

"How do you know?" It was the least important question, but it was the first to come to mind.

He let out a huff, something between a bitter laugh and a sigh. "It's a small island."

"I'm sorry." I had no other words to offer.

"God, were you ever going to tell me?" I saw the hurt in his eyes, and though I hated that I'd caused it, I was relieved to see some emotion on his face.

"We were. I didn't know how."

We stood in the cold for another moment, without talking. The weight of everything we weren't saying hovered between us, an extra body in the night.

"I've got to get back to work," Connor said.

"We'll talk about this more tomorrow night, okay? Six?" I reminded him.

"Yeah, whatever," Connor said, and turned back to go inside.

Then I made him come and say hello to Evvy, to pretend that things were fine, but she picked up the scent of despair and hopelessness immediately. Far faster than I have. She's right, of course. I need to call Jack. So even though I promised Connor that I wouldn't, not even a few hours earlier, I steel myself to tell Jack everything. I take a sip of tea and dial his number. He picks up on the first ring.

"Hi. Everything okay?" Jack asks.

"It's fine." The word is meaningless, since none of us is fine, but no one is bleeding from the head, so I guess in that sense it's true, I'm fine. "I need you to come over tomorrow night. Connor's coming for dinner."

I don't know if I expected an argument, but he doesn't question why or try to make up an excuse.

"Okay."

"He's coming at six, but be here earlier. We need to talk first." I pull a blanket over my lap, finger the wool tassels along its edge.

"All right." He's so amenable that I wonder whether, if I told him he needed to move back home, he'd agree just as easily.

"He knows. That you're not living here."

There's a pause. "How?"

"It's a small island," I remind him. How many times has one of us said this? It sometimes feels impossible to keep anything hidden in a place like Great Rock, yet I realize suddenly how many secrets we've all been keeping.

"How is he?" Jack asks.

"I don't know." I recall Connor's pinched features, the distance between us. "Angry."

I try to picture Jack at the Feldmans' house, but I can't. They are a summer family that he's known for years and whose house he's caretaken for, but I've never been there. I can't place him in a living room or kitchen or bedroom.

"What do you want to talk about tomorrow?" Jack asks.

"Connor."

"What about him? I thought you said he seemed okay the last time you saw him." There's a note of panic in his voice. Maybe Jack knows just as well as I do. Perhaps he's known all along.

"I lied. He's not okay, Jack. He's not okay at all." I reach for the mug, enjoy the small comfort of the heat against my palm.

"What do you mean? What's going on?"

I sigh. "I don't want to talk about it over the phone. Can we just talk tomorrow? Come at six."

"I'll come over now," Jack says.

It's nearly nine. I'm wrung out and exhausted, yet suddenly alert at the thought of Jack coming over.

"You don't need to do that," I tell him. "It's not an emergency. We can talk tomorrow." I realize how ridiculous this is. If this isn't an emergency, what is? Have I steadily gotten used to the idea of Connor doing drugs, so the truth doesn't shock me as much as it should?

"I'm coming now. I'll be over in fifteen minutes," Jack says.

We hang up and I hurry upstairs to the bedroom. I'm in the yoga pants and sweater I changed into after dinner, the same outfit Jack's seen me in a hundred times. I stand in front of my dresser, wanting to put on something nicer, but not wanting him to realize I bothered. We've been married more than twenty years and he's seen me in sweatpants and sweaters nearly every night for most of our marriage. For me to put on something nice now would be absurd, given the reason he's coming over, not to mention obvious. I finally peel off the oversized cardigan I wear around the house most days and exchange it for a soft purple turtleneck. I leave on the pants, aware that I've lost a few pounds since he's moved out and the yoga pants show it. Then I'm ashamed because this is supposed to be about Connor, not me and Jack.

I hear his car pull up outside, and Champ's nails scrabble around on the floor as he hurries to the door to stand at attention. I run my fingers through my hair and go down to let Jack in, but he's already unlocked the side door and is squatting down beside Champ, rubbing him around the ears.

"Glad you're locking the door," Jack says.

"It's night. I always lock it at night." I add more hot water to my mug and pour another for Jack without asking if he wants one. He gives Champ a final rub and then reaches for the cup. A day or two's worth of dark stubble prickles his chin and cheeks. "You growing a beard?"

Jack's always been clean-cut, hair trimmed neatly every few weeks, freshly shaven each morning. He's not the beard type. I don't know why I'm making jokes, but I'm not ready for the conversation we need to have. He brings his hand to his face and rubs his cheek. "It's vacation week. I took a few days off. Didn't bother to shave today."

"No trip this year?"

He shrugs. "Didn't really feel like going anywhere alone." He lets the thought hang there, and I wonder if he means anything by it. He takes another sip of tea and then gestures with his chin. "Your hair looks nice, by the way. I forgot to tell you the other night."

"Thanks." I bring my hand up and finger the short ends self-consciously. I keep forgetting that I've cut it until someone notices. He's looking at me in a way that he hasn't in ages, like he's actually seeing me. After so many years of marriage, it feels like we've lost track of each other. But now he's paying attention, and I blush under his gaze.

He shifts gears. "So what's up?"

"Come sit."

I lead him into the living room and we sink into the couch. I take a sip of tea, and then another, stalling the conversation we need to have. I blink back the tears that have come out of nowhere.

"I'm not sure where to begin," I say.

His face relaxes and he pulls my feet into his lap. How many nights have we sat on the couch in this same position? Totally ordinary moments until they suddenly disappeared. I don't know where the unexpected tenderness comes from and why I'm not resisting it, but the wall of anger between us may be thawing.

"Just tell me," he says.

So I do. I tell him everything. I start with the bag of drugs I found. His jaw tightens when I tell him what I did with them, and my body is flooded with shame and fear for Connor. I don't know what I should have done, but it wasn't that. I tell him about Connor coming by to find the drugs, the rabid look in his eyes, the absence of our son in them. I tell him about tonight, what Evvy said. That I know it's true. Jack is silent, listening carefully, his face intent.

"I'm afraid, Jack," I finally say once I've finished.

"Of what?"

"Everything. I'm afraid that whoever's drugs those were is going to come after Connor. I'm afraid that these drugs are going to kill him, or if they don't, that they'll turn him into someone he's not." I purse my lips together, unsure if I should tell Jack my most urgent fear. But Evvy's right. I need to do everything I can to save Connor, and everything is all mixed up. "I'm afraid he did something that night. That he had some part in that girl's death."

Not much surprises Jack. He's been a cop for twenty-three years, and though we live on a safe and relatively sheltered island, that doesn't mean he doesn't see ugly things on a daily basis. When I tell him I'm worried Connor had something to do with the murder on the beach, I see his surprise, and I have a feeling it's not because the thought hasn't already crossed his mind, but because he didn't think I'd ever believe such a thing.

"Why do you think that?" he asks.

"You should have seen him the other day when he came over here looking for those drugs. He was so angry. I've never seen him so mad. I actually thought he was going to hurt me." I swallow down the waiting tears.

"He didn't have anything to do with that, Carrie. I'm sure of it." He holds up his hand to stop the rising river of hysteria that threatens to pour forth. I'm not the type to cry and fret and fuss at every little thing. I'm not like Evvy, who's always been temperamental, but Jack is put off by any show of emotion, and any sign of tears or anger must be tamped down. It's always driven me nuts how quick he is to quell the storm, but right now I'm grateful. I need his clear head to be rational and think calmly.

"How do you know?" I ask.

"I just do," Jack says, and I'm not sure if it's because he wants to believe it as much as I do or because he has information about the case that he's not sharing. "He's coming over tomorrow night?"

I nod. "He doesn't know you're coming though. I told him I wouldn't tell you."

"So we'll talk to him. We'll find out what's going on. We'll make him tell us the truth," Jack says. He makes it sound so simple. As if the answer were waiting all this time.

"What if he won't tell us?"

Jack takes my hand in his. His skin is dry from the cold winter air. "He will."

"And then what?"

"Then we figure out how to help him."

Relief floods through me. He'll do what he must to save Connor after all. "Thank you," I whisper.

"It will be okay," Jack says and squeezes my hand.

I nod, wiping my eyes with the heel of my palm. It wasn't until Jack came over that I realized how alone I've felt, burdened down with my worry for Connor. After so many years of sharing the day-to-day fears and triumphs of parenting, I didn't realize how lonely it could be. I wonder if Jack has been lonely too, or if he's allowed himself company over the long few months.

"What about Deanna?" I ask.

His eyes crinkle in confusion. "What about her?"

"Are you seeing her? Is something going on with the two of you?" I swallow down my embarrassment, needing to know the answer.

"No," he says softly. "There's only you, Caroline."

I'm half lying on the couch with my legs in Jack's lap, and he carefully lifts and lowers them to the floor then leans closer to me, till his face is just inches away and his chest is pressing down on mine. He smells like himself, Old Spice deodorant and the metallic scent of winter in his hair. His lips find mine. It's only been a few months, but I feel like we haven't really kissed in years, so used to the quick peck on the cheek or a hurried goodbye in the morning.

He holds my face gently in his hands, such an intimate and tender gesture, like he's guarding something fragile. My face is damp with tears, partly still about my worry for Connor, but more because I've forgotten that I missed him, so focused on staying strong and keeping it together that I've only let myself feel anger toward Jack, all the while pushing down the sadness and loss.

His hands roam the length of my body, his strong familiar fingers working their way under my sweater and bra. The light is bright above us and though the curtains are drawn, I worry about one of our neighbors driving home and seeing us making out on the couch like teenagers. Besides, I don't just want sex. I want to feel the warmth and safety of our bed, the comfort of Jack's arms around me in the dark.

"Come upstairs," I whisper, pulling away. He hesitates, and I can't help but be hurt by this. The twinge of hurt is the reminder that despite this moment, the trouble between us isn't over, even if this may be the first step back toward each other. Yet there's still so much unsaid that aches just below the surface.

He pushes himself up and pulls me to standing. I follow him, my stockinged feet quiet as Jack's heavy boots thud against the stairs. Connor's bedroom door is open and I feel a pang, a tugging of despair that I push aside for the moment as I follow Jack into our bedroom. He closes the door behind us.

EVVY

Chapter Thirty

I awake from an Ambien-induced night that leaves me dry-mouthed and headachy. When I finally venture downstairs to make coffee, Daisy is in the kitchen bowed over a textbook. She looks up from her reading.

"Morning. Did you sleep okay? Do you feel better today?" she asks. I shrug, not wanting to tell her that the type of rest I had last night barely restores the body, much less the mind. "Do you want me to make you something? I was about to make some eggs." I'm not hungry, but she looks so hopeful.

"Thanks, honey," I manage to get out. I slump into the empty chair beside her and she rises to pull out eggs and toast. There are times when it feels like Daisy is the adult and I am the child. She pours me a cup of coffee and then adds just the right amount of cream. I sip it and think about what needs to be done today. Call the lawyer, though I'm not sure there's anything I can do. I have a dinner this weekend that I need to think about, a private party at a house in Egret. I've already planned the menu, but I'll need to buy the ingredients at some point. Visit Ian? I know I should, that I *must*, but the idea of venturing into the dank town jail makes my skin crawl. I'm not cut out for this.

"So, I was thinking of going away for the weekend." Daisy interrupts my train of thought, and it takes me a moment to process her words.

"What? Where are you going?"

She focuses intently on the bowl of eggs she's stirring. "Boston. With a friend."

"This weekend? With all that's going on?" I can't help but be hurt.

"Tomorrow's my birthday. My twenty-first," she adds, in case I've forgotten. Which I have. Not exactly forgotten, but it's slipped my mind with everything that's happened over the past few days.

"I know, I just didn't realize you were thinking about going away. You didn't say anything before. And the timing isn't exactly great."

She pauses, the fork still in the egg yolk. "I won't go if you don't want me to." She looks so disappointed, though I sense her withholding her sadness for my benefit.

"Who are you going with?" I ask.

She begins to stir the eggs again, too quickly, and some yolk spills over onto the counter. "This guy, Todd, that I've been hanging out with recently. You remember him. Molly Rankin's brother?" I recall our argument the other night when she tried to tell me about him.

"You've been seeing him?" I try to sound pleased. I am pleased, relieved that it's not Connor she's been spending her nights with. Yet working up enthusiasm for anything right now is more than I have energy for. I reach out to still her spinning hand. "I think you've whipped those eggs enough."

She drops the fork and pulls out a frying pan, depressing the button on the toaster. She's nothing if not efficient, this daughter of mine. "He lives in Boston and he invited me to come for the weekend. I was thinking of leaving this afternoon to avoid the storm."

"Today? It's short notice to get a ferry reservation for the car."

"I'm going to take the bus."

"Oh."

She's got it all figured out, and while this shouldn't bother me, it does. Is it wrong of me to want her here? This is not a good week for her to be away from me. The eggs sizzle in the pan and she scrapes them with a wooden spoon onto a plate in front of me. They turn my stomach, but I manage to swallow a forkful.

"I won't go if you don't want me to," she says again.

This time I hear the undercurrent of annoyance. I know she feels she's entitled to this, that living here with me and Ian is sucking her dry of opportunity. She thinks she deserves more, that better things are out there waiting for her, if only we could get out of her way, or at least clear the path for her. When I was Daisy's age my days were spent changing diapers and trying not to lose my mind. It didn't occur to me that anything more was an option. I know I should be proud of Daisy for how hard she's worked to carve out a future for herself, but I can't help but feel as if she's thumbing her nose at the choices I've made over the years. Choices I didn't even realize I was making.

Yet she's spent so much of her life in the shade of Serena's death. It's not fair of me to keep her from what she really wants because I'm afraid. If I don't let her go, one day she will run from me.

"You should go," I say.

"Really?" Her face lights up with such joy that I'm ashamed to have considered anything else. She sits down beside me and begins to eat, shoveling the eggs into her mouth.

"I'll be fine. Go, have fun. You deserve it." I hate that expression. What does it actually mean? What do any of us actually deserve? I take a bite of toast, trying not to choke on the bitterness inside me.

"Thanks, Mom." Her cheeks are pink and now she's all smiles. "Dad said he'd swing by to check on you."

"When did you see your father?"

"Yesterday. I stopped by his house. I'll probably take the noon boat." Daisy brings her empty plate to the sink and refills her coffee.

"Okay." The clock on the stove says it's almost nine.

"You and Paul have the dinner this weekend under control, right?" she asks.

"Sure." I try to take another bite of toast, but I'm certain my stomach won't tolerate it. I feel so weary at the prospect of having to do anything today. All I want to do is press my cheek against the soft fabric of my pillow and sleep. Daisy must see something in my eyes because she sits back down at the table.

"Mom. Are you okay? Really?"

I force a smile. "I'm fine, hon."

"You don't seem fine."

She's so pretty, this baby girl of mine. Shiny blond hair and blue eyes, a smattering of freckles across the bridge of her nose. Serena was pretty too, but it was a harder beauty. More angles and edges. She had the same blond hair but her eyes were gray, and her smile didn't come as easily as Daisy's does. I was not the best mother to either of them, but Serena bore the brunt of it. I often wonder what she would be like if she were still alive. On good days, I imagine her growing out of her tumultuous temperament, her moods smoothing as she got older, a typical teenager with a summer job at one of the boutiques in Osprey, standing behind the cash register in a flowy sundress and sandals. On bad days, I imagine her coming to a different end, at twenty, or twenty-two, or twenty-five, her ashen face staring at nothing. Serena inherited my demons. Who knows how she would have dealt with them as an adult?

I force myself to focus on Daisy, the daughter I still have, the child who does her best to look after me even when we rub each other raw. I reach for her hand, aware of how freckled and lined mine looks next to her pale smooth one.

"It's a difficult time. With Ian. I'm worried about him and what's going to happen. But I'm okay," I say. Daisy's worried I'm going down the rabbit hole again, like I did when Serena died, and while part of me wants to dive head first back into that bottomless black place where nothing else mattered, I know I can't. Not again. And not for Ian. I'm not willing to plumb those depths for him. I don't know what this says about our relationship, but I know it's true. And now, promising Daisy that I'll be okay, I know I will be because I won't do that to her again.

She gives me a cautious smile and leans in to hug me. I breathe in the smell of her perfume, something fruity and sweet that nearly brings me to my knees because Daisy's hugs are so rare and unexpected. When she pulls back, I blink quickly so she won't see the tears.

"I need to finish this chapter before I go." She tips her head at the textbook. "And then I need to pack. I have no idea what to bring." She runs her hand through her hair, likely envisioning how she'll look for Todd.

"You like him, don't you?" I say, taking a sip of coffee.

She bites her lip then gives a reluctant nod.

There are so many things I could say, about how he lives too far away, his age, his money, the world he comes from and how different it is from ours, all the reasons why it might not work. I don't say a single one of them. "I liked him the summer he worked for me. He was nice." Daisy beams. "So what are you going to do in Boston?"

"I don't know. Go to a bar, I guess. Isn't that what you do on your twenty-first birthday?"

I remember then the gift I have tucked away. I stand up quickly, nearly spilling my coffee. "I have a birthday present for you. Stay here." Daisy gives me a curious smile and I hurry upstairs to find the envelope in my nightstand drawer. I clutch it for a moment, uncertain suddenly if I want to give it to her, if I might need it now. But I've already told her about it, so there's no going back.

I return downstairs and hand her the envelope. "I'm sorry there's no card. I meant to get one this week and then…" I wave my hand, letting her fill in the gaps.

She opens the envelope and I feel a thrill of pleasure at her look of surprise. Her fingers flutter the hundred-dollar bills, all fifteen of them. "Oh my God. *Mom.*"

"It's for school. Or you can use it for the commute or textbooks. Whatever will help with the expenses. I know it probably won't go very far, but I hope it will at least help with a course or two." I realize I don't even know how much a class costs or how many more she has to take. I put those dollars away slowly, a little bit here and there, over the past six months. With two incomes, it wasn't as hard as I expected, though I wonder if it will be the last time I will have enough left over to be able to help her. I should have started earlier.

"Mom. Thank you." She's looking at me with an expression of tender disbelief. "Really. Thank you so much. This means a lot."

"You're welcome. I know how hard you've been working and how tough it's been on you. I'm proud of you, Daze. I'm really proud of you." I ruffle my fingers through her smooth blond hair, tuck a lock behind her ear. She lets me, though I sense she's holding herself in place for my benefit. I drop my hand. "You better go pack."

"Okay. Thank you, Mom. Really." She folds the envelope in half and tucks it into the back pocket of her jeans. I hope she has enough sense to deposit it soon or to at least put it somewhere safe till she has a chance to go to the bank, but I keep my mouth shut.

"Maybe we can have a little birthday dinner when I get back? We could go out or just cook here?" Daisy says.

"I'd love that, sweetheart." I give her a gentle push toward the stairs. "Now go. Get ready for your weekend away."

DAISY
Chapter Thirty-One

When the bus arrives in Boston, I trudge down the steps and into the bustle of South Station. For a moment, I scan the busy terminal, imagining Todd forgetting about me; maybe the whole thing is a mistake. Then I spot him, rising from a bench, a Starbucks cup in hand, which he drops in the trash. He wraps me in an embrace and I lean into the solid weight of his body.

"You made it," he murmurs into my hair. I close my eyes, feeling overwhelmed by how happy I am to see him. He bends to kiss me lightly on the mouth.

"Let's get out of here." He picks up my duffel bag, throwing it over his shoulder and taking my hand. The station smells like burnt coffee and fast food. I follow Todd down a set of escalators and out into the city night. The sky is fading to a purple dusk. People clutch briefcases and messenger bags, eager to get home after a long workday. City buses pull over to pick up waiting passengers, their faces lit by the bright glow of their phones. The T chugs along the tracks like a giant green caterpillar. The air smells sharp and clean, like snowflakes waiting to fall. The night holds a sense of expectation. Though I've been to Boston many times, I always feel like an interloper from another land. The women we pass wear nicely cut wool coats, their heels clicking along the pavement. I glance down at my clothing—a heavy white sweater, old jeans, worn boots. Standing before my mirror in Great Rock, I felt comfortably fashionable, but now I feel like a dowdy farmer's wife.

A few blocks away, we arrive at his car. He pulls out and we're quiet as he makes his way through the throng of downtown traffic, and I watch him expertly maneuver through the one-way streets, cars speeding past on either side of us. There are people on the sidewalks, darting out into the street to cross despite the green lights and flashing *Do Not Walk* signs. I can't imagine navigating these busy roads, but Todd drives with ease, unfazed by the traffic or pedestrians.

"I thought we could go back to my place for a little, get settled, and then go to the restaurant where I work for dinner. If that sounds okay to you?"

"That sounds great."

Todd turns down a street of brick brownstones and drives slowly. Bare trees line the cobblestone sidewalks and old-fashioned lamplights illuminate the evening. Wrought-iron gates protect tiny patches of manicured greenery not large enough to be called yards. I don't know much about Boston, but it's clear the neighborhood is expensive. We round the block and turn down another similar street as Todd hunts for a parking spot. After several minutes of searching, he finally parallel parks in a space that leaves just a few inches on either side. I have no idea how he manages to expertly slide his car into such a tiny spot, but he does it in one try.

We get out of the car and he takes my bag from the trunk, leading me away from the pretty street and back onto a main one.

"I'm a few streets over. Finding a spot in this neighborhood is a nightmare." We pass a coffee shop, an upscale restaurant, a small boutique that sells men's shaving products. Finally Todd stops in front of a dingy pizza place. He unlocks a small side door, and we climb the stairs to the second floor of the building. The dimly lit hallway smells of fresh bread and cheese. Todd opens the door to an apartment, and I follow him inside. He flips on the light switch, dropping my bag on the floor by the doorway. "Here we go. Home sweet home."

I've never been in a studio apartment before. On Great Rock most people live in houses, though they might have to move out every spring to make way for the summer people. There are apartments above the shops and restaurants in town, but most have at least a couple bedrooms. My own bedroom still looks like it did when I was in high school; pink walls plastered with the fraying posters of boy bands I no longer listen to. No one comes in my bedroom anyway, so it doesn't seem to matter that I keep forgetting to take them down.

Todd's apartment is not much bigger than my bedroom. Against the wall is a futon with an orange-and-red patterned quilt. There is a full bookcase, a television, a small table with two wooden chairs, and a spiky green plant in a large ceramic planter. I can see the entrance to a tiny kitchen and a closed door leading to what I assume is the bathroom. The clattering dishes and voices from the restaurant below can be heard, despite the heavy Oriental rug that covers the hardwood floors. There are a few decorations—a large painting of a porch overlooking the ocean, a delicate blue pitcher, and a few framed photos sitting atop the bookcase. It's spare and neat, each item purposeful and carefully chosen. I love it.

"Do you have a roommate?"

Todd laughs. "In here? Nah, just me." He pulls me to the futon, which is hard and low to the ground, and I sink down beside him. When he brings his face to mind, his cheek is cold against mine. "I missed you."

"You just saw me." I smile into his skin.

"I know." He tightens his arm around me. "I'm glad you're here."

"Me too."

"Your mom was okay with you coming?"

I feel a pang of guilt that I push away. "Yeah. It's fine. There's nothing I can do there anyway."

"So, twenty-one, huh? That's a big birthday. Are you planning on getting totally wasted on me tomorrow night?" His eyes crinkle at the corners with his grin.

"We'll see." I hear the steady thump of his heart through the thin material of his shirt. "How old are you, anyway?" I'm embarrassed that I don't already know.

"Me? Twenty-five."

I roll over so my head is on the pillow beside his. I stare up at the watermarked ceiling. "What were you doing at twenty-one?"

"Well, I was a junior in college. And I was pretty miserable."

"Why?"

"I hated school. Well, that's not true. I was a business major because my dad insisted on it and I hated that, but I was having way too much fun. Partying every night, hungover every morning. It was fun, but I felt like shit. And I was becoming a pretty big asshole."

"What do you mean?"

"I don't know. You go to a school like Dartmouth, and you're surrounded by a lot of people who see the world in a certain way. There's a sense of entitlement that comes with having so much at your disposal—all that money, all that opportunity. Don't get me wrong, there were a lot of nice people too, but I'd somehow become surrounded by guys who took it for granted that the world owed them more. Like they lived on a different planet from everyone else."

"Is that why you dropped out?"

"Pretty much. I didn't think I'd survive another year. And if I did, I wasn't sure who I would be by the end of it." He lets out a short laugh. "I don't want to be too grand here. It's not like I quit to join the Peace Corps or something. I know I have my parents' money to fall back on, and I work in an upscale restaurant where I serve guys like that every day. It's just different somehow."

I think about this. When he first told me about dropping out, I'd thought he was an idiot, but now I wonder if he may actually have been brave.

"Will you go back? To school?"

"Yeah. Not to Dartmouth, but I'll finish my degree. I took a couple of classes at UMass Boston last semester."

"So you'll have a degree from UMass, not Dartmouth." I think about all the doors a degree from Dartmouth could open. For the first time, it occurs to me that maybe some of the doors lead to places I wouldn't want to go.

"My dad's the only one who cares about that. I want to own a restaurant—you don't even need a degree for that." He rolls toward me and rests his hand along the length of my hip. "So you want to see where I work? It's not far from here. They'll serve you tonight even though you're a day away from twenty-one."

"Sure." I feel a flutter of nervousness at the idea of meeting his co-workers and friends. "Is it dressy?" I mentally scan through the clothes I brought and if there's anything in there that I can wear.

"Not really. You're fine. More than fine, actually. They serve till ten. So there's no hurry." He brings his mouth down upon mine and kisses me for a long moment. I feel it rush through my body, shooting its way down my arms and legs. There's no place I'd rather be.

CAROLINE
Chapter Thirty-Two

When I awaken, Jack is already up. I hear him in the kitchen and I lie in bed, hoping he'll come back upstairs. Then I worry he'll leave without saying goodbye, so I slip on my bathrobe and hurry downstairs. The hardwood floor is cold under my bare feet, and the sky is just lightening, the dusky crossroad between night and day.

Jack sits at the counter, staring into the steaming mug of tea before him. I wonder if he's already regretting last night. Champ dozes at his feet. He's brewed me a small pot of coffee, and even left a mug on the counter.

He looks up, a tight-lipped smile forming at his lips. "Morning."

"You're up early." Despite the many years between us, I'm shy in the fragile morning light.

"I couldn't sleep."

I awoke only once during the night, and though we'd shifted to different sides of the bed, I felt Jack's solid presence, and I drifted back into sleep with the familiar comfort of him beside me. I slept better than I have in months, and it pains me that he didn't too.

I pour myself a cup of coffee, add a splash of milk and then prop my arms on the counter, without sitting down. He's fully dressed, though not in the clothes he wore last night. He's found a pair of khakis and a white shirt from the closet, and his hair is still damp from the shower he must have taken while I slept.

"Do you want some breakfast?" I ask.

"No, thanks. I need to go home before I head to work." The word *home* must register on my face, because he adds quickly, "To the Feldmans' place.

"There's a storm coming. Do you have enough salt for the walkway?" he asks. I nod. "There's a good chance we'll lose power. Do you have new batteries for the flashlights? And extra candles and water? I'll bring some extra stuff by later." This is how Jack takes care of me. Not with words or affection but through simple acts that are easier to express.

"Thanks," I say. There are times I've watched Ian and Evvy together, the way he holds her hand or wraps his arm around her waist, fingers playing with her hair. Their relationship is obviously more flawed than my own, but it's those tiny moments of easy affection that I envy. It's something Jack and I lost long ago, sometime after Connor was born, and I don't know if we're past the point of getting it back.

"You're still coming over tonight, though, right? To talk with Connor."

"Of course." He swallows the last of his tea.

I clench the hot mug between my palms. It's cool in the kitchen, and I suspect he hasn't turned the heat up yet. I've gotten in the habit of cranking it high first thing in the morning. "Do we have a game plan?" I ask.

"We'll talk to him. Find out what's going on, and then we'll decide what to do." This morning, I find the simplicity of this more irritating than comforting. Jack rises and puts his empty mug in the sink. "I'll be by before six."

We stand a few feet apart, the heat from last night quickly cooled. "Jack," I begin, though I'm not sure what I want to say.

He cuts me off. "Let's not now, okay?" He takes a step closer and I smell the lemon-lime shaving cream he must have found in the medicine cabinet. "Let's deal with Connor first."

I nod, because I agree with him, but I'm also blinking back tears. I don't know what I'd expected or hoped for, but it wasn't this. He doesn't acknowledge the tears, but he bends his face to mine, kissing me lightly first on the cheek and then on the mouth. "It's going to be okay, Carrie. It will."

Jack is very good at saying what he wants to believe. It doesn't make it true, though.

After work I stop at the grocery store and pick up the ingredients for chicken parmesan, Connor's favorite, then I swing by the liquor store and buy two bottles of red wine, as if this is a festive family gathering. Both stores are busy, people stocking up for the storm that's coming. It's started to snow, tiny flecks of white dotting the dark sky. Nearly an inch has accumulated already, and I worry that Jack or Connor will call to cancel, not wanting to be out on the roads on a night like this. The wind howls like a wounded animal, high-pitched and woeful. Back home, I turn on the radio and prep the dinner, pounding the meat into submission with the very same mallet I used just a few days ago on the pills. I make the meal with the automaticity that comes with a dinner I've prepared hundreds of times. The kitchen soon fills with the savory aroma of roasting meat, the familiar smell of a normal happy home. I imagine tonight is just a regular dinner with my husband and son. Perhaps if I pretend hard enough, I can will it to be true.

Connor surprises me by showing up first. I've already poured myself a glass of wine, a futile attempt to relax. When Connor enters, he throws his coat on top of the washing machine rather than using one of the hangers in the closet. He looks a little better than yesterday, though he's as skinny and pale as ever.

"Smells good in here," he says.

"Chicken parm. Your favorite."

"You didn't need to bother. We could have just ordered pizza."

"I don't mind. I wanted to cook."

He opens the fridge and finds a bottle of beer in the door. He twists off the top and takes a long pull. "So what do you want to talk about?"

I'm not ready to do this without Jack. I top up my glass of wine. "Slow down, honey. Have your drink. I need to make the salad dressing." Impatience flickers across his face, but I turn away from him and pull out oil and vinegar. I'm mixing the dressing with a whisk and neither of us has spoken again when I hear the front door slam.

"You said Dad wasn't going to be here." Panic flits across Connor's face and then Jack joins us, still in the clothes he wore this morning, though he looks rumpled and tired now.

"Sit down, Connor," Jack says.

"What is this?" Connor looks back and forth between us, not sitting down. "What the hell is this?"

"Watch your language in this house," Jack says swiftly.

"You don't even live in this house. Don't tell me how to talk," Connor shoots back.

"Stop, both of you." I step between them, holding each by the arm. My frustration with Jack flares—this isn't the way to begin. It's not why I asked him to come. I wonder if this was a mistake after all. "Please. Let's sit down. Let's go in the living room." Connor eyes Jack warily but then slouches in with his beer. He plops down on the sofa and I follow him, sitting on the next cushion. A moment later Jack appears with a beer and sits in the easy chair on the other side of the room.

"I told your father," I say to Connor.

"What did you tell him?"

I purse my lips, wishing the answer were different. "Everything."

"Why, Mom?" Connors asks. He looks so hurt, and I can't help but feel guilty.

"I had to," I say, but I'm not sure this is true. When Evvy convinced me to call Jack, it made sense, but now all I can think about is how easy it would be for Jack to drive our son down to the station. For a moment I wish I hadn't told Jack a thing.

"You're going to tell us everything," Jack says.

"Or what?" Connor challenges. His eyes are empty, all of his anger directed at Jack.

"Or else we'll talk about this at the station."

"*Jack*," I say sharply.

My fists clench with unspent fury that after all this time, he's still not certain where his loyalties lie. Jack wanted a boy like himself, stolid and masculine, but Connor has always been gentle, with skin and feelings that bruise easily, his pale hair always in his face. Too often Connor has been the wedge between us as I cross sides to protect him from his father's disappointment, unintentionally alienating Jack. At his core, I know he loves Connor more than anything, but his praise is sparse and his attempts to connect often come off like judgment. Despite their fractured history, I was hoping that Jack would protect Connor above everything, and now I'm not certain he will.

Connor lets out a laugh of disgust and shakes his head. "Whatever."

"Honey, you need to tell us what happened," I plead. "No one thinks you had anything to do with hurting that girl. But you need to tell us where those drugs came from."

Connor lets out a harsh laugh. "Layla? This is still about Layla?" He shakes his head, a look of cruel disbelief lining his face. I feel a shiver of revulsion, as if I've stumbled upon something ugly; a black furred spider in the bed, a decomposing rodent in the attic.

"You still don't know, do you?" Connor turns to Jack. "You haven't told her?"

Something passes across Jack's face, but he doesn't speak. I turn to Connor in question. "Told me what?" I ask, but I don't want to know. Outside, the wind has picked up and the windows rattle in their frames.

Already I can feel the ground shifting, the rug unfurling and the floorboards giving way as the foundation falls out from under us.

EVVY

Chapter Thirty-Three

I pile a final bag of groceries into the back of my car and head toward Egret, to the assisted living facility where my father has lived for the past two years. Though he'll have heard about Ian, I know he won't say much about it, other than to check that I'm okay. He is a quiet man, more so with age, and any judgment will be gentle and kind. He has always been polite and friendly to Ian, yet I know he still considers Cyrus to be my husband.

I go see my father twice a week, and I always bring a few bags of food to get him through till my next visit. The items are always the same—a container of half-caffeinated coffee, a package of sliced cheese and a loaf of bread, a bunch of grapes, a box of pasta, a stick of butter, and a few other odds and ends that are part of his weekly meals. The food reminds me of what we used to eat when I was in high school, a weekly cycle of grilled cheese, spaghetti with frozen meatballs, and Hamburger Helper. Given the basic fare I grew up on, I can't help but laugh when I prepare Petunia's menus. A frisée and pine nut salad with local raspberries and fig vinaigrette is a far cry from the iceberg and ranch salads of my childhood.

I can't fault my father though, because he did the best he could. When my parents divorced my sophomore year in high school, my brother and I moved with my mother to her hometown of Pittsburgh. For a year we lived in a stuffy apartment across the street from a bus stop. At night I'd wake to the wheezing sound of the bus idling to let passengers off, the yellow streetlight flickering just outside the window. Even at midnight, the sky was a brownish gray, not a single star to be seen, so different from the view on Great Rock that it was hard to believe it was the same sky.

I went to the public high school in the district, a run-down building from the 1950s that had more children than desks or textbooks. There were some classes where we had to rotate who sat on the floor, drawing colored popsicle sticks to see who got a desk that day. It wasn't just the school that I hated, though I never fitted in and didn't have friends. It was the vast emptiness of the city, the anonymity of every interaction that was so startling. One afternoon, on my way home from school, a panhandler stretched his hand out to me. I'd never seen homeless people before, and to see them sleeping in the streets was terrifying and confusing. When I paused to put a few coins in the man's hand as I'd seen my mother do, he tugged on the sleeve of my shirt, pulling me closer. I yanked from his grasp and ran the whole way home, holding back tears. I don't know what he would have done if I hadn't escaped—maybe he only wanted to thank me for the spare quarters, but all I could see was the desperation that penetrated his skin.

At the end of the school year, I begged to return to Great Rock, and my mother finally relented, allowing me to move back to the island to live with my father, while my brother remained in Pittsburgh. The house was different without my mother. Quieter. Emptier. I missed her, but was relieved to be back home and to see faces I'd known my whole life. My mother never did return to Great Rock, not for more than a long weekend, and she still lives in Pennsylvania. It's been years since she's been back.

The one year away changed me, made me realize that I never again wanted to live among strangers. From then on, I understood what made Great Rock different, understood what made people move here after lives spent elsewhere.

Ian is from a little town in Western Massachusetts, similar in size and population to Great Rock. His parents still live there and he has a brother out there too, who comes to visit every Thanksgiving. Ian moved to the island fifteen years ago, when Cyrus and I were still together. If anyone asks, Ian says he moved to Great Rock because he loves the ocean and wanted to live in a place where he could spend every day on a boat. However, I know this is only part of the story.

I remember the Thanksgiving dinner when I first met Ian's brother, Troye. We'd only been together for a year or so. Ian drank too much that night, an afternoon of beer and wine finally catching up with him, and he passed out upstairs just after dinner. Troye stayed in the kitchen and helped me clean up. Between packing leftover mashed potatoes and scrubbing the roasting pan, Troye told me how Ian had been arrested for assault and battery before he moved to Great Rock. He broke the jaw of Tina Graham, a woman he never bothered to mention to me, his live-in girlfriend at the time. Supposedly it was an accident—he pushed her and she smashed her jaw on the brick floor surrounding the fireplace. He drove her to the hospital afterward, sat in the waiting room while she underwent surgery. She ultimately dropped the charges, claiming she fell down a set of stairs. But everyone knew—the police, Tina's family, every friend and acquaintance he had. It's a miracle Tina's father or brother didn't kill Ian, though he didn't stick around for very long before leaving town and eventually settling on Great Rock.

Troye claimed he told me as a warning of what Ian was capable of, as a measure to keep me safe. He loved his brother but knew the force of his anger, having been on the receiving end many times as a child. I assured him that Ian was different now, that I'd never seen any evidence of such violence in him before, which was true, at the time. I wanted to forget the story, to go back to a place where every squabble or petty argument didn't hold the potential for pain, a place where I felt safe. But there was no going back.

As far as I know, Ian never found out what Troye told me, but within a few months, I saw the cracks along the surface. The way Ian's fists clenched when he got angry, the twitch in his chin when he was trying to control himself. I wondered if the signs had been there all along or if Troye had unleashed a beast in my home. The incident at Joe and Christine's potluck happened just a few months later.

Sometimes, after an argument with Ian that either escalates or does not, hinging on just this side of normal, I think about Tina. I've googled her many times though I'm always careful to clear the browser history afterward. Tina is an insurance agent in the same little town where Ian is from, a place I've never visited. There's a picture of her on the agency's website, and she's pretty in a wholesome kind of way, with light brown hair that falls to her shoulders. She's smiling shyly in the photograph, no visible evidence of a broken jaw, no obvious scars from her years with Ian. Her bio says she's married with a son. Her picture is proof that life moves on.

More and more, I've been imagining how Tina must have felt when Ian left. Maybe she loved him, and maybe she missed him. Maybe she even pleaded with him and tried to convince him to stay, despite the threats from her family. But when Ian's car finally drove away and all that was visible was the distant red of his taillights, she must have been able to breathe deeply for the first time in years. She must have sat at her kitchen table and inhaled, every corner of her lungs filling with air she hadn't even realized was there all along.

DAISY

Chapter Thirty-Four

Todd and I take a cab to Avenue X, the restaurant where he works. It's on Newbury Street, where I've been a handful of times as a tourist, a few blocks away from Berklee College of Music. I came to this part of the city when Connor had his audition his senior year; the year he was rejected, the year that everything started to change for him.

That afternoon, while Connor was having his interview and audition, Caroline and I browsed the expensive boutiques. It was December, a few days before Christmas, and the streets were crowded with people doing last-minute holiday shopping. The stores were decorated with silver and gold tinsel, the trees bejeweled with twinkling white lights. People hurried past carrying their offerings in colorful bags, and the whole street had an otherworldly feeling, the people and shops sparkling like the inside of a snow globe.

Until Connor called to say he was ready for us to pick him up.

He sulked the whole drive home, answering Caroline's questions with one-word responses.

How was the interview?

Fine.

What about your audition?

Okay.

Are you all right? Did something happen?

No.

Nothing.

I'm fine.

But he wasn't. He plugged his earbuds in and ignored us for the rest of the drive home. Caroline kept meeting my eyes in the rearview mirror, asking me silent questions that I couldn't answer. I didn't know what had happened any more than she did.

He didn't tell me that day or the next, not till several weeks later, at the tail end of our winter break. We'd gone to a movie in Egret and afterward to a coffee shop. The crumbs of a muffin lay on a napkin between us, and Connor began to tell me the story.

"I choked," he said. "During the audition. I got on stage and I couldn't play a damn thing. It was like my fingers were sausages. Everything I tried to play came out terrible." His face was pink with the remembered humiliation. "I got it eventually, finally hit my stride. But you only get fifteen minutes. I wasted almost ten of mine. Didn't even get to the second song I'd planned."

"How was the interview?" I asked. The interview was after the audition.

"Not much better. They kept asking me about stage fright. How long I'd had it. But I've never had it before. You've seen me. I've played in front of audiences a bunch of times." He shook his head in frustration.

"So what happened?"

"I don't know. I guess I've never had a performance that mattered so much. It freaked me out, and I blew it." He pressed his lips together, and stared out the window at Main Street.

Already I was thinking about what this would mean for him. Deadlines for schools were less than two weeks away, and Berklee was still the only college he'd applied to. I don't know if it was false confidence or fear that had kept him from applying to other schools, but every time I pressed, he'd told me that Berklee was the only place he wanted to go. I assumed that now things had changed.

"You still have a week to apply to other schools."

"I can try again next year."

Irritation prickled at my neck—at his short-sightedness and his naive assumption that things would work themselves out as the universe intended.

"At least throw your application into UMass," I urged him.

"I don't want to go to UMass."

"Well, you don't want to go nowhere, either, do you? The last thing you want is to get stuck here. Like me." I already knew I wasn't going to college in the fall. My mother had said I could work for her and save money to take classes at Cape Cod Community College in the spring.

"That wouldn't be so bad, would it?" Connor met my eyes across the table and squeezed my fingers. As much as I wanted him to stay for selfish reasons, I didn't want him to do it like this.

"You're going to get stuck here," I said.

"I'll reapply next year. It won't be the end of the world."

We didn't talk about it anymore, and he didn't apply anywhere else. When the rejection letter rolled in a few months later, it wasn't even a surprise.

From the window of the cab, I see Berklee, its gray concrete pillars glowing in the dim light. I wonder what life would be like if Connor had a different audition that day, if instead of a rejection letter, a fat acceptance package arrived in the mail. Who would he be now?

Todd reaches for my hand and places it in his lap.

"You're quiet," he says.

"Just looking at the city."

"Different from Great Rock, huh?"

"It's another world."

And it is. I will myself to be here, not in the dusty memory of the past, or the long-gone possibility of a future that didn't come to be, not back on the island, but here. For at least this moment, only here.

A little while later we're sitting at the bar of Avenue X. Todd was wrong; I'm totally underdressed compared to the other girls in the swanky bistro who are wearing sparkly tank tops and fishnet stockings, despite the freezing night. After the first drink, I don't care. Todd orders for both of us in a way that's authoritative without being obnoxious. The bartender brings me a pale green drink in a martini glass with a cucumber floating in it. When I take a sip, it tastes like spring, a bright green possibility laid out before us. The server brings out plate after plate, each dish more delicious than the last. Todd introduces me to people, and we order more drinks and I'm caught up in the whole scene, the glittering orange lamps and loud chatter of customers, the prettiness of everyone here, the crowded warmth. I sip my drink and laugh as the rest of my life falls away, the lonely island of Great Rock sitting abandoned in the ocean. Outside, it starts to snow.

CAROLINE
Chapter Thirty-Five

"Told me what?" I ask again, turning from Connor to Jack. Neither of them looks at me, though something unspoken crackles in the air between them.

"I saw you," Connor says to Jack. "I *saw* you."

"What are you talking about?" Jack barks. His face is unreadable. I blink, my lips forming words I'm unable to speak, trying to make sense of what Connor is saying. I look to Jack but his eyes are on Connor.

"I saw you follow her to the beach. She ran down there to get away from you. I stayed by the sea wall." Though Connor hasn't identified the *she* that he's talking about, somehow we all know. Layla Dresser has been in this house since Jack came over to tell me the news of her murder.

"You saw nothing," Jack snaps, though his voice lacks some of its usual authority.

"Connor," I say sharply, and they both turn, surprised to find me still here. "You're confused. You don't know what you saw."

"Are you so stupid? Are you really so blind?" Connor asks, his voice rising in anger and frustration.

I look to Jack, waiting for him to clarify, to explain. He doesn't answer, but his eyes are hard and bright.

"It was dark. I couldn't see you, but I heard her scream." Connor's voice cracks, his face crumpling. He swallows hard, regaining control. "I waited by the sea wall, but you didn't come back. You must have kept walking down the beach, over the jetty and to the other side. I didn't realize you killed her. Not until the next day." Connor's eyes are wild—with rage, but there's fear there too. He's always been afraid of his father. Maybe all along he saw something that I didn't.

I shake my head silently back and forth. I won't believe it. It doesn't make sense. Over the years, Jack has made me angry with his silent stoicism in the face of my unrest. I've questioned my choice to marry him, to move to Great Rock, to raise our son here. But never, in all of the years I've been with Jack, have I ever been afraid of him.

I put the wine down too hard. It spills over the rim of the glass into a red pool on the table that begins to drip onto the rug. No one moves. There's a ringing in my ears, and my head feels full of water. I can hear the sound of that poor girl screaming, and I know I'll never be able to forget it. I reach out a hand, to Connor, to Jack, for someone to catch me before I fall, but neither of them even looks at me. I bring my trembling hand back into my lap and stay where I am, motionless, watching our life collapse around us. I focus on the steady drip of red wine onto the pale blue rug, unable to rise for a cloth. It will leave a stain.

"Jack?" My voice is barely a whisper.

"You don't know what you're talking about," Jack says, his eyes on Connor.

"Will you just tell her, Dad? Please, just tell her." The anger is gone from Connor's voice, and now he just sounds tired and desperate.

I already know it's true. I can tell by Jack's silence and by Connor's confusion and fear. I can tell because none of us in this room wants it to be true, yet it is. Jack rises from his chair and heads to the kitchen. I hear the refrigerator door open and the hiss of a bottle being opened. He returns to the living room, but doesn't sit down, draining nearly half the beer in one gulp. He sinks to his knees before the couch, rests his large hands on my lap. I've never seen him look so vulnerable, so broken.

"It was an accident," he begins, and I feel the bottom fall out. For a moment, I'd been hoping he'd deny it and we could pretend to start all over. "You have to believe that. I never meant for this to happen."

On his knees before me, he is a shattered man. How long has he looked like this, hair thinning, wrinkles deepening in the furrow of his brow and around his mouth? He didn't look like that when I met him, a fresh-faced cop on the harbor, eyes shiny with hope. Life has chipped away at us slowly, day by day, chink by chink, so incrementally that we didn't even notice what was lost along the way.

"Jack?" I catch his hand, and he squeezes it so tightly that I feel the fragile bones in my fingers. "What happened?"

He's crying now, and Connor and I watch, horrified, as Jack's face contorts in grief. I've never seen him cry before, in all our years of marriage, not even when his father passed away last year. I realize the strangeness of this as Jack buries his face in my lap. I rest my hand against the warm skin of his neck, the stubble of a recent cut prickling my palm. I smooth his cropped hair down, just as I once did to Connor's stubborn cowlick, though Jack's always kept his hair so short that there's never a strand out of place.

"I'm sorry. I'm so sorry." The words are muffled against my body. Connor watches us, frozen in place beside me on the couch.

I hold Jack's head firmly and force it up so I can see his face. His eyes are bloodshot and his skin a mottled red. "What happened?" I repeat, louder this time.

Jack takes a shaky breath that looks like it takes all the energy he has. He pushes himself up and sits down on the edge of the coffee table, hands on his knees, as if trying to steady himself. Running his fingers along his face, he begins.

"Do you think I don't know what you've been doing?" He waves his hand at Connor, then wipes at his eyes. "Do you think I don't know what drugs look like? I can see it all over you." Beside me, Connor looks dazed and stunned. Jack's right. I can see the drugs all over him too, now that I'm actually looking. Jack continues. "Twenty years I've watched drugs come to this island. I've watched them destroy good people, turn honest people into thieves. I've seen parents have to identify their kids at the morgue." Connor's eyes are wide, the empty look in them finally gone. "Do you remember Patty Larkin's daughter who died of a drug overdose last year? And the Sullivans' son—remember him?"

I remember Patty Larkin, a single mother who lost her younger daughter to heroin and is now raising her four-year-old grandson. And I remember the Sullivans' son. His friends dumped him outside the hospital after he overdosed and then drove away. It was twenty degrees out. He was almost dead by the time the hospital staff even knew he was there. Last I heard he was in and out of rehab places off-island. I've heard about these people and their stories, but I haven't seen it the way Jack has. Their stories haven't touched me; not really, not beyond a fleeting moment of sadness and pity.

"I saw her that night at Moby Dick's. I wasn't on duty and everyone was doing crowd control for the festival, but I saw her, and I knew why she was there. She'd been bringing drugs over since the summer. Hell, I almost arrested her a few months ago, but we didn't have enough on her. We knew what she was doing." His eyes are glassy.

"I wasn't trying to hurt her. I just wanted to catch her with the drugs. When she left the bar, I followed her. She was outside with Ian. They were arguing, and her lip was bleeding, though she claimed she slipped." Jack shakes his head in disgust. "I don't know what Evvy ever saw in him anyways. He's a mean little man."

"But it wasn't Ian," I say softly. Jack shakes his head.

"Ian left and I searched her. I wasn't even on duty and she hadn't done anything, but I knew why she was there. *I knew*." He looks up at me imploringly, as if begging me to understand. "But she didn't have anything. Not even a purse. She laughed at me. When she started to walk away, I grabbed her. I must have scared her because she started to run. I'd been drinking, I wasn't thinking clearly. I thought maybe I could get her to admit to bringing the drugs, but she ran down to the beach. I followed her." He slumps into the easy chair, the fight finally slipping away.

"I just wanted to get her to admit what she was doing. But when I caught up to her, I was so angry. Someone needed to stop her." There's a hard determination in his words. "I was thinking about Connor, about what could happen to him." Though Connor is inches away, Jack's talking to me. He's explaining this story to me.

"I grabbed her. Around the neck. And I just started to squeeze. It was dark and I couldn't see her face. I wouldn't have done it if I could see her face." His voice cracks, and I don't know why he says this, why it matters. "I left her there, and I ran down the beach. I didn't mean to kill her. I keep wondering if maybe she wasn't dead yet. If she'd still be alive if I'd called an ambulance." He leans forward on his knees, buries his face in his hands, and I watch his shoulders shake with silent sobs.

Connor gets up from the couch and paces the length of the living room, fists stuffed deep in the pockets of his sweatshirt, his whole body jangling. None of us speaks for what feels like minutes on end.

"What did you do?" I finally ask. My voice is barely a whisper. Jack speaks into the refuge of his hands.

"I'd seen her with Ian. I knew his history. It wasn't that hard to make sure he was a suspect."

"She was having an affair with Ian," I say.

Jack looks at me, his face folding into a frown. "I don't know about that. But Ian was the one who'd pick up the drugs. She'd leave them on the boat somewhere for him. Something must have gone wrong that day if she still had them on her at the end of the night."

I feel like I'm floating in the room, suspended midair. Everything I thought I knew, thought I understood, has fallen away.

"What now?" I ask.

Jack raises his head and his eyes are red, his face still flushed, but when he speaks, he sounds more like himself. "I turn myself in. I'll go in tomorrow and give a statement."

The words land in the air with a dull thud. There is no other possibility.

"Dad." Connor's voice holds a plea, though I don't know what he's asking for. There's nothing for Jack to give.

"It will be okay," Jack says.

"I shouldn't have said anything. I should have stayed quiet." It hits me then that Connor's been carrying this around by himself all week.

"No. It's not your fault."

I turn to Connor. Maybe it's not too late. Maybe we can still salvage the wreckage. "Did you tell anyone?" He shakes his head. "No one at all? Not Daisy? Not Keith?"

"No. No one."

I turn back to Jack. "We don't have to tell. We'll pretend Connor wasn't there. No one knows." Even as I say the words, I know I don't mean them. I can't stand by and let Ian go to prison for a crime he didn't commit. I can't do that to him, and I certainly can't do it to Evvy. I'm grasping, scrabbling at straws in the sand.

Jack leans forward from his spot on the coffee table and holds me gently by the forearms. "No, Carrie. I need to turn myself in." I nod and the tears begin to streak down my own face. The secret is too big for this room. Already it's pushing at the windows, the weight of it leaning against the doorframe.

Jack turns from me to Connor. "What happened that night?" Connor doesn't answer and Jack speaks louder, asserting the authority he's so comfortable with. "What happened, Connor?" Connor doesn't sit, but he begins to talk.

"I saw Layla at the bar. I knew her from the summer. She was wasted. She got up to go to the bathroom and left her purse on the chair. I took it." He lets out a short bitter laugh. "So stupid. I screwed everything up."

"How did you know she had drugs in there?" Jack asks.

"I didn't, but I knew she was dealing."

"How did you know that?" Jack asks.

Connor looks at him in confusion, as if he can't believe Jack doesn't have the whole picture straight by now. "Scott Lambert set the whole thing up. The drugs go to him. In the kitchen of Moby Dick's."

I think of the empty restaurant in the middle of February, how Connor's worked there since he was in high school.

"What did you do?" Jack asks.

"I stuck her purse under my coat. I was just looking for a few pills. I didn't realize how much would be in there."

"So what happened next?" Jack asks.

"I went into the bathroom with the bag and saw what was inside. I freaked. I didn't know what to do. When I got out of the bathroom, she wasn't at the bar anymore. I thought about dumping her bag somewhere, so I headed to the beach. I saw you going down the stairs. I thought you were meeting someone. I didn't even realize it was Layla until the next day."

Jack takes a long sip from his beer. "What about you? The drugs. What are you doing?"

Connor stands awkwardly in the doorway, his arms crossed, leaning on the open frame. "Nothing."

"Conner, out with it," Jack says, his voice rising. "We don't have time for this." From the other room I smell the rich scent of meat and garlic. It's time to take it from the oven, but I'm fixed to this spot on the couch, unable to move.

"At first it was just pills. Oxy mostly." Connor keeps his head down, and I see the top of his head, the pale blond hair that people would exclaim over when he was a toddler.

"Since when?" Jack asks.

"It started after I had surgery on my shoulder last spring. It hurt all the time. Every time I tried to stop taking them, the pain came back. I couldn't sleep, couldn't work. It was easier just to keep taking them."

I think of all those years Connor played hockey. He was good, but I don't think he loved the sport like some of the boys. He did it for Jack, all those early morning practices, Jack and Connor rising at dawn and heading out into the blackness of morning to get to the rink by six. All those Saturday away games, the long ferry ride and trips on the bus, duffel bags bulging with pounds full of gear, Jack's hand heavy on Connor's back. When Jack watched Connor on the ice, his eyes shone. And Connor saw it.

"Just the pills?" Jack asks, bringing me back to the room.

There's a long moment of silence. It seems to last forever and I can't believe that Jack doesn't bark at him again, but he lets Connor take his time answering the question. Finally, he speaks.

"After a few months, the doctor wouldn't refill my prescription. I bought the pills from Keith for a while, but it got too expensive. Keith said heroin was cheaper and it was a better high."

I raise my hand to my face, suddenly aware of the tears that are falling. I wipe them away. They're useless now. They won't help save Connor. They won't help anything. What we need is action. I turn to Jack, for he's the one who knows this unfamiliar landscape better than any of us.

"What now?" I ask, the first words I've spoken in several minutes. My voice comes out hoarse. "What happens now?"

Jack looks over, almost surprised to find me sitting here. I realize that as far as he's concerned, this is between him and Connor. I feel a flare of anger at Jack, my husband who always needs to be the rescuer, the fixer, quietly controlling all of us as if he's the puppeteer and we're just wooden dolls with strings. And yet, as always, I'm the one who's looking to him for the answer.

"Tomorrow I'm taking you off-island," Jack says to Connor. "I'll make some calls tonight. I might be able to get you into St. Theresa's. There's a guy at New Beginnings who owes me a favor, and I know someone at Hope Street." Drug rehab centers on the Cape and beyond. My heart constricts at the thought of sending Connor to one of these places, at the idea that he needs them. Connor shakes his head.

"No, I'll stop. I don't need that."

"Yes, you do." Jack squeezes his hands together, his only tell that he's near anger. The knuckles bulge. "I've watched kids like you ruin their whole lives in a matter of months. If they even survive it. This is the only way."

"I don't want to go to a place like that. I'm not like that." He looks close to tears.

"Honey, please. Listen to your father. He knows what he's talking about. He can help you," I plead.

"I don't need his help!" He's trembling with anger, a vicious sneer on his face, and then his body loosens as the fight drains away. He slides down the wall until he's sitting on the floor, his legs pulled in tight to his chest. He looks so small, a frightened child folded in on himself. He rests his cheek on his knee.

I get up from the sofa and walk past the drying wine stain, to where Connor is huddled on the ground. Jack watches without speaking, and I sink to the floor next to my son. When I lean into him, I smell his sour odor, unwashed skin, clothes that haven't been laundered recently. I hold his hands in mine. They're cold and chapped, the skin rough.

"Connor." I speak quietly, so softly that Jack would need to crane his neck to hear me. I speak only to Connor. For most of his life, it has been me and Connor against Jack. Was this the start of it all? The way I'd ally myself with Connor rather than presenting the united front we were supposed to maintain as parents? Connor was so soft and Jack was so hard on him. Over and over again, I'd come to Connor's rescue, turning my back on Jack while I rushed to protect Connor. Was I too gentle with him? Did I leave him unprepared for the reality of the world, incapable of fending off the darker side of life? I squeeze his hands, willing warmth into them.

Sitting beside Connor, I realize that I will do anything for him to be okay. We are a team and we always have been. All those days and nights when Jack was at work, it was just me and Connor. I think back on all the meals we've eaten together, the TV shows we've watched, the tests I helped him study for, the songs he played on his guitar. Maybe it's because he was an only child, but I didn't resent everything that was required of me as a mother. I embraced it, all of the ways that he made me feel necessary. In those moments, I didn't need Jack. Neither of us did.

"Sweetheart, please. Do this for me," I say. Connor looks up, and I see the unspilled tears in his red-rimmed eyes, and I know he understands what I'm asking. He may not be cataloging all of the ways I've loved him over the years, but he knows that my love for him is bottomless, that I need him to be okay in a way that is both selfless and selfish. The moment stretches between us for what feels like forever, and in that space my mind reels with what I'll do if he refuses to go. The scenarios play out across my mind—how long can he go on like this before some real harm comes to him?

Finally, he gives a single nod. Something inside me cracks, the relief rushing forth, the fear for him and what is to come, but also the palest glimmer of hope. I rest my cheek against the knot of our hands, and the hot and cold life beats against my face.

Finally I turn to Jack. "He'll go."

Jack gives a nod, stoic and distant, and I want to beat my fists upon his chest. *Show him you love him*, I want to yell. *He needs to see you care.* But I don't, and maybe I'm wrong. Maybe Connor has known all along that Jack loves him. Maybe he long ago came to terms with his father's way of expressing love. Maybe it's just me who's still searching for something more.

Jack pushes himself to standing and I do too. Connor clumsily gets up, and we stand awkwardly in the living room.

"I'll drive you home," Jack says.

Connor rubs the heel of his hand against his cheek. "My car's here."

"Leave it. I'll pick you up tomorrow at seven. We'll get the eight o'clock boat. Pack a small suitcase."

"What about dinner?" I ask. Such a foolish question, to think that we could all sit around for the rest of the night and play happy family, knowing what the morning will bring. But I can't bear the thought of them leaving like this.

"He needs to get some sleep," Jack says. "Besides, the roads are going to be bad if we wait too long."

Connor and I follow Jack to the kitchen and toward the door. They shrug on heavy winter coats. Champ has risen from his bed and he trails us, nosing Jack's hand for attention. I realize that after today, I don't know when I'll see either of them again. This is all happening too fast, and though just moments earlier I begged Connor to go, for a moment I want to take it all back. Instead, I grab my boy in a fierce hug and bury my face into his dirty winter parka, my arms circling his slight frame. He hugs me back, his arms finding my shoulders, his hand upon my head, stroking my hair in a grown-up gesture of comfort.

"I'll be okay, Mom," he says quietly.

"I'll call you tomorrow." Jack opens the door. "I'll come over before I turn myself in."

Outside the snow continues to fall. There must be several inches at least, and the tree branches shake in the wind. I watch the two of them make their way to Jack's car. Just before they get inside, Jack rests his hand on Connor's shoulder for a second, pulling him close. I swallow the thick lump in my throat and close the door behind them.

I turn the latch, putting on the deadbolt. In the kitchen I turn off the oven and pull out the dinner. The chicken is overcooked, browning toward black, a dry crunchy waste. I scrape it into the trash and leave the oily casserole dish on the stove. Slowly I walk through the house, turning off lights as I go. Champ follows me, his nails skittering across the floor and up the stairs behind me as I head toward my bedroom.

It will be a long time before sleep comes.

EVVY

Chapter Thirty-Six

In the afternoon I get dressed to go see Ian at the jail. I fix my hair and spend the extra five minutes putting on makeup and picking out a shirt I know Ian likes. In my jewelry box I select a pair of earrings he gave me for a birthday, a bracelet from Christmas. He's been good to me over the years, showering me with gifts and attention, helping me to find a focus in my life. Yet I can't help but feel a relief he's not here, as if a burden has been lifted that I didn't realize I'd been carrying for so long.

I drive to the jail and park my car in the lot behind the building. And then I sit in my car. Visiting hours are from two till four, yet I can't make myself go inside. It's what a good wife or girlfriend would do. It's what I would have done if it was Cyrus locked up here. But something keeps me rooted to the vinyl seat of my car, a gray dread that I'm making the first of years of these visits, coupled with guilt that I haven't done more to get him freed. Most of all there is a sickening fear—not that Ian is guilty, but of the spiraling rage that will consume us if he's released.

I sit in the car until the cold has seeped into my bones, and even then I don't go inside. I merely start the engine and turn on the heat, leaving the car parked where it is. There are a few windows on the back of the building with blinds and bars on them. I imagine Ian inside, peering out at me through a space in the slats, waiting for me to come in, waiting for me to show him I'll stand by him through this. Snow falls across my windshield, blocking out the sun and leaving the inside of the car a dark blue cave.

I've stumbled upon an ugly truth in the days that Ian's been gone. I don't believe he killed that girl, but I don't want him to come home. I blink in the blue-gray quiet of the empty car, alert to the possibility that has suddenly presented itself.

Even if Ian is found not guilty, I can leave him.

We've never married, despite multiple proposals on Ian's part. Yet something has kept me from saying yes. For years I've managed to evade him, telling him I didn't want to marry again, that things were good the way they were and there was no reason to complicate things. In some dim corner of my brain I always knew I didn't want to marry Ian because then I'd forever shut the door on the possibility that someday Cyrus might come home. The other reason I never said yes, I realize now, was because I don't want to tether myself to Ian for the rest of my life. I don't love him enough. When Serena died and Cyrus left, I was lost. Ian found me again, that much is true, but I no longer believe this is enough to forgive everything else.

After two hours, when visiting hours have ended, I pull out of the lot. My windshield wipers clear the fluffy snow off the glass, revealing the surprising brightness of late afternoon. The sun is an orange flame across the trees, the late day suddenly full of promise. The heat pours from the vents, thawing me slowly, and I grip the wheel as the warmth finds my fingers. I back out slowly from the spot, hoping Ian hasn't seen me here, grateful that if he has, he cannot unleash his rage upon me tonight. Or perhaps ever again.

I stop for groceries, wishing I'd picked up food the other day when I'd gone for my father. It's impossible to go to the grocery store without bumping into a handful of people, and I haven't had the energy to face anyone I don't have to. Ian usually does the shopping, stopping to socialize and then taking his time in the gourmet section, returning home with jars of olives and blocks of expensive cheese, which he presents to me like gifts. I feel a tug of love for him that I can't quite reconcile with my inaction just minutes earlier.

The store is packed, everyone running around stocking up on things for the storm—a blizzard I barely knew was coming.

"Eight inches, at least ten, maybe even a foot!" I hear the predictions buzz around me as the other shoppers fill their carts with bottled water and batteries, candles and lighters. Everyone is in a hurry to get their shopping finished before the roads get too bad. I fill my cart with enough food to get me through the weekend and then throw in a few packs of batteries and bottles of water, just in case. I remind myself to dig out the flashlights and candles when I get home. The woman at the cash register tells me they're predicting eight to twelve inches with high winds overnight. The boats will likely be cancelled by evening. By the time I pack the groceries in my car, the sun has set and the wind whips my hair around my face. The snow falls heavier, tiny white flakes that crowd together so the road is nearly invisible.

In the kitchen I unpack my groceries and crank up the heat. The house is quiet without Daisy. It's not as if she's home often anyway, but knowing both she and Ian are gone gives the house an empty feeling. The weather app on my phone shows it's snowing in Boston too. She sent me a quick text to tell me she arrived, but it's all I can do not to check in every hour. Having the ocean between us makes me clingier than usual.

I eat some leftover pasta, then I take a long hot shower and change into pajamas, though it's only seven. I comb out my hair, and stare at my reflection in the mirror of the bathroom. The glass is foggy from the steam of the shower, giving my face a softness it doesn't actually have. I see Daisy and Serena in my reflection and turn away from the mirror.

I'm searching for a weather report on TV when I hear the crunch of tires in the driveway. For a moment I think it's Ian, and the physical sensation of my heart dropping into my stomach takes me by surprise, especially when I know he's still in jail. When I pull back the curtain I see it's not Ian but Cyrus, and relief floods over me like a warm bath, followed by a flutter of excitement that I wish his presence didn't still bring. He knocks on the door with three heavy raps. Snow swirls around him, and his black ski hat is covered in flakes of white. There must be at least four inches covering the railing of the porch.

"Hi, Cy. Here to check on me?" He gives me a wry smile. "Come on in."

The wind whistles and the trees sway back and forth in the night. I hold the door open wide and he comes inside. Across the road I notice Mary Porter peering through her pulled-back curtain, likely tucking Cyrus's presence into her bag of gossip for later. I shut the door tight.

"You know there's a blizzard watch, right?"

"Yeah, I know. Boats are cancelled. Gina was at a conference, and she's stuck off-island." He takes his hat and coat off and drops them on one of the easy chairs. "I wanted to make sure you had everything to get you through this storm. And I promised Daisy."

"So I heard."

"She was worried about you. She felt bad leaving you alone, with everything that's going on. She asked if I'd check on you." He shrugs sheepishly.

I'm touched that this occurred to Daisy when she was so obviously excited about going away with Todd. "That was nice of her. But I'm fine. Really."

Cyrus raises an eyebrow. "Heard you spent two hours not visiting Ian today."

I feel my face flush and let out a sigh. "This island."

He shrugs. "What happened?"

I sink onto the couch and Cyrus joins me. "I don't know. I wanted to go in, or I *wanted* to want to go in, if that makes sense. But I couldn't."

"Are you going to stand by him through this?" His voice is gentle, and I want to smooth down his hair where his hat has mussed it.

My resolve from earlier this afternoon has seeped away after coming home to the empty house I share with Ian. There are reminders of him everywhere—his muddy boots by the front door, piles of change on the dresser, his sweater thrown over the arm of a chair. Extricating myself from the life we share seems harder now.

"I don't know," I answer.

"You don't have to," he says, and I press my lips together to stop the tears.

"Don't I?"

When Cyrus and I were in high school, we used to skip our second period study hall and spend the hour in Cyrus's twin bed, our clothes in a heap on the floor. I remember returning to school and the secret warmth that would stay with me for the rest of the day. I'd try to focus in math class, but Cyrus's hands would still be on my skin.

"You're not even married. He's hurt you before. Whether he's guilty or not, no one will hold it against you," Cyrus says. I hang my head, ashamed that he's right, that the public opinion of Great Rock means so much to me. How can it not? This is my home. These are the people I've known all my life. "You can leave him. Just walk away. Pack his things. You don't need him. I'll help you, if you're afraid."

Those days when we were in high school, I'd go home and take off my clothes, stand in front of the mirror naked. I wanted to see what Cyrus saw. I was always surprised that there wasn't some evidence of him left upon me, the pink imprint of his palms along my waist, golden circles along my chest. From the inside, I was glowing. On the outside, I looked just the same.

Despite the love I've felt for Ian over the years, it's never come close to what Cyrus made me feel. All this time I've tried to chalk it up to the way love changes with age, but now I wonder if maybe it's just been Cyrus all along.

"If it were you, it would be different," I say.

"It wouldn't be me," Cyrus says, holding my gaze.

Outside the wind tears at the sky, threatening to rip it in half. The lights flicker off, then back on, then off again and the room stays black. Neither of us moves to get candles or a flashlight, but Cyrus's hand finds my face in the darkness. He reaches out and wipes the tears that have fallen. "I can't stand him, Evvy. It kills me to think about you with him. What he could have done to you."

He's the one to reach for me tonight. His lips, his tongue, his fingers on my neck, he's been waiting for me all along. He pulls me to him hard, his hands sliding under my pajama top, the same hands that held me so long ago when I was just a girl. He graduated and I waited for him, stuck around because I knew he would come home and I'd be here waiting. I gave up the chance to go to college or travel or live somewhere else, and as he strips off my clothes just as he did in the secret cave of his childhood bedroom, I feel so happy I could sing, because I would give it all up again if it meant that he was mine.

DAISY
Chapter Thirty-Seven

I wake to the dinging sound of an incoming text. Todd breathes softly beside me, lying on his stomach, an arm thrown across the pillow. My head aches from whatever I was drinking last night, and I know I'll be fuzzy for the rest of the morning. I don't care, though. Last night I felt like I stepped out of my own life and into another possible version.

I reach for the phone where I left it on the nightstand. The text is from Connor. My clothes are on the floor by the bed and I pull on a tee shirt and tiptoe into the bathroom to pee, grabbing the phone as I go. I close the door softly behind me, not wanting to wake Todd.

going away for a while. Prob wont have phone. wanted to say happy birthday. miss you.

I sit on the terrycloth bathmat and stare at the cryptic message. It's not even eight. I fumble with the phone for a moment and dial Connor's number. He picks up after the first ring, his phone likely still in his hands after sending the text.

"Hey." His voice is soft and hoarse. For some reason I wonder if he's been crying, though this doesn't make any sense.

"Where are you going?" I ask.

"I'm with my dad right now. We're on the boat. Hang on." There's a shuffle and a long pause and then he comes back on. "Happy birthday."

"Connor, where are you going? Why are you on the boat?"

"I'm going away for a bit."

"What does that mean? Where are you going?" I ask in frustration.

There's another silence before he answers. "My dad's taking me to a place on the Cape. To get clean. Like rehab, I guess."

"Oh." I feel such a rush of emotions that I don't know how to sort through them. Relief that his parents finally know and are doing something. Fear for what will happen to him next. Sadness for what he'll have to endure over the next few weeks. "For how long?"

"I'm not sure. About a month, I think. I don't really know." I imagine him on one of the upholstered blue seats of the boat, staring out at the gray ocean churning under the giant weight of the ferry.

"Are you okay?"

"Not really. But I guess that's why I'm going." His voice is shaky, and I wish I could hold him in my arms and comfort him. From the other side of the bathroom door there's a knock.

"Daisy? Are you okay?" Todd asks.

"I'm fine. Just on the phone. I'll be off in a minute," I say without opening the door. I hear Todd pad back to the bed.

"You're with him." Connor's voice is flat.

I lower my voice, not wanting Todd to hear the conversation. "I'm sorry."

"No, it's cool. I'm kind of a mess right now. I get it."

"I think it's a good thing," I say, wishing we weren't having this conversation over the phone. I wipe away the tears that suddenly course down my cheeks. "You need some help with this."

"Yeah." Over the line I hear the low bleating of the foghorn. "I should go. We're going to leave in a minute."

"Okay." I want to say something to him, something encouraging or meaningful. I know I'll see him again, but it feels like an important moment, like after today nothing will ever be the same for him or between us. There's no going back. I wish I had something to offer him, something he could hold on to in the coming days. But I'm empty-handed. "Good luck." The words are so worthless I wish I could snatch them back.

"Yeah, thanks."

"Connor," I say, not ready for him to hang up.

"What?"

"It's going to be okay. We're all going to be all right."

He lets out a hollow laugh. "Yeah, sure. Happy birthday, Daze." The line goes dead.

I hold the phone in my hand, wishing the conversation hadn't felt so much like a goodbye.

"Daisy?" Todd calls again. "Everything okay?"

"Fine. I'll be right out." I force myself up from the floor, flushing the toilet and catching sight of myself in the mirror. I wash my face and run my fingers through my hair, staring one last time at the phone, contemplating calling Connor back. Deciding there's nothing more to say.

I open the door and emerge from the bathroom. Todd's in bed, an extra pillow propped behind his head.

"Sorry about that."

"Who was it?"

"Just a friend calling to wish me happy birthday." I swallow the rest down. I see him waiting, wondering if I'm going to say more, but I can't. Even if I wanted to explain, I'm not sure I could.

"Happy birthday. It snowed." He pulls back the curtain and I peer out the window. There is only white. There must be close to a foot of snow. "I don't see any reason to leave the house anytime soon." Todd reaches for my hand. I hesitate, the conversation with Connor still so fresh, the defeat in his voice still ringing in my ears. Maybe I should have fought harder for him, but the boy I once knew isn't coming back, and it's time for both of us to grow up. I take Todd's hand and climb back into the safe space of his bed.

CAROLINE
Chapter Thirty-Eight

When I wake up the next morning, the island is bathed in white. Icicles drip from the trees as I drive to work, their glassy fingers dangling like Christmas ornaments. I drive slowly, navigating the unplowed streets, marveling at the untouched beauty of the morning despite the pallor of sadness that colors my mood.

The library is quiet, few people motivated enough to venture out on such a day. The children's room is empty, families choosing to spend the day watching movies or building snowmen in the backyard. I try to busy myself with tasks, but my mind wanders to Connor and Jack. Moments from our life together flash through my mind like a slideshow. Connor and Daisy playing igloo in a plastic playhouse, lying flat on their bellies in the dark hollow cave, then coming inside to drink steaming mugs of hot chocolate; Connor and Jack coming off the boat after a hockey game, Connor hauling his massive duffel behind him, Jack smiling proudly after a day's win. Connor as a toddler perched on Jack's shoulders at the Fourth of July fireworks display, resting his sleepy cheek upon Jack's head, holding a red, white, and blue pinwheel that sparkled in the midday sun.

While I'm shelving books, I linger in the section dedicated to addiction. I slide several titles from the shelf and manage to get them back into the office without running into anyone. I spend my lunch hour flipping through the books, learning about heroin and opioid addiction, the symptoms of withdrawal, the likelihood of relapse. After half an hour, my turkey sandwich sits untouched, and I feel sick to my stomach. I'd gone into the day hopeful that Connor will emerge from the treatment center like the young man I once knew. Yet the books make it clear that this may just be the first step in a long and possibly endless road. I'm tempted to re-shelve the books, but I can't look away any longer. I check them out and then put them into my bag.

I don't hear from Jack. After work I let Champ outside and he bounds into the snow, full of energy after being cooped up all day. I'm standing on the back deck watching him, when Jack appears behind me. He pulls me into a tight embrace.

"Did you find a place for him?" I murmur into the cold fabric of his jacket.

"I did. It took a few hours and some favors, but I got him a bed at St. Theresa's in Hyannis." Jack's voice is solid and reassuring, and it quickly calms me. Despite our months apart, it terrifies me to think of being away from him. I push the idea from my mind. I'm not ready to think about that yet. I need to focus on Connor.

"How was he when you left?"

"He was okay." Jack lets out a breath, and I know he's lying to me, but I'm grateful.

"He'll be there for thirty days, if all goes well. There's paperwork in the car with all of the information. No visitors for the first two weeks." He releases me and I look into his face. He looks tired, but more than that. He looks defeated, something I've never seen in him before. "I'm so sorry, Carrie. I didn't mean for this to happen. I'm just so sorry," he says again.

"Shh. It will be okay." I hold up my hand to quiet him. "We'll get you a lawyer. Someone good. She was bringing drugs to the island, drugs that were killing people here. A jury will understand." Even as I say it, I'm not sure it's true. Would I understand? Jack murdered a woman with his own hands. The idea is so outlandish that I still haven't wrapped my head around it. I cannot allow myself to fully grasp what he's done.

Jack shakes his head. "No jury will understand." He holds my hands in his, squeezes them tightly. He has large hands, capable and strong. I have always felt safe when he's holding me. "I need you to realize that there's no way out of this. I need you to understand that." There is an urgency in his voice. I don't understand why he needs me to believe in the hopelessness of it all. Even unreasonable hope is something to hold on to. I nod anyway. He brings his hands to my face and cups them around my cheeks. Often, I've wished Jack were more capable of showing affection, but now the tenderness of his gesture jars me. It's an indication of how certain he is of the future, the finality of it. "I've always loved you," he tells me. "I'm sorry if I haven't always been good at showing it. I know you haven't always been happy. I hope that you'll have a chance to be happy again. You don't need to stay here if you don't want to."

I shake my head. "We don't need to talk about all that now. We don't need to figure anything out. Not this very minute."

Jack pulls me to him again and I sense the desperation in his body, in the strength of his grip. His hands clutch me tightly and maybe I should be afraid, these same hands that squeezed the air from Layla Dresser's body, but I feel only a profound premonition of loss, though I can't quite absorb it yet. It hangs in the air between us, suspended.

"I love you, Carrie. And I love Connor. Please always remember that." He lifts my face to his and kisses me, a soft slow kiss that feels like an ending. When he lets me go, I'm enveloped by the cold. Jack calls to Champ and he comes bounding over, his tail wagging, happily oblivious.

"I'm going to take him for a walk before I go to the station."

"I'll come," I offer.

Jack shakes his head. "I need a few minutes on my own. To clear my head. I'll take him to the dog park. I'll be back soon."

"Are you sure you don't want some company?" I'm starting to feel frantic at the idea of him leaving. There are only minutes remaining until our life is turned upside down.

"I just want to be by myself for a little while. When I get back, we'll drive to the station together." He turns and goes into the house, calling for Champ over his shoulder. There's nothing to do but follow them inside and wait for the end to begin.

He's gone over an hour before I start to worry. When he left, the sky was a watery gray, but it's quickly darkening to night. I call Jack's phone, but he doesn't answer, and I wonder if he decided to drive straight to the station, wishing to spare me the pain. I pace the length of the kitchen until seven o'clock and then grab my coat and keys and head for the dog park.

It's only a five-minute drive away, and I don't find an accident along the way; Jack's pickup truck flipped over, or an ambulance on the side of the road. When I turn into the dirt lot by the park, Jack's truck is there, and I pull up beside him, leaving my headlights on. It's fully dark now, winter dark. Somewhere in the distance I hear the dry incessant bark of a dog. No one's in the car when I peer inside, not Jack or Champ. The wind lifts up snow and tosses it in the air, and tiny leftover flakes sting my face. In my rush I forgot a hat, and my hair whips around my head, sticking to my cheeks. It will be even colder in the open unprotected field of the dog park, but I don't venture out of the lot. I get back in the car and lock it, though other than Jack, there's no one else here. My fingers shake as I pull my phone from my pocket and dial Jack's number again. No one answers, but on the dashboard of Jack's truck, I see the blue glow of his cell phone as it lights up. I rest my head on the steering wheel and try to breathe.

I've just lifted my head when I see the dark shape. Shadowed by the trees, something glints in the blackness, and for a moment

I think it might be Jack. I register the endless bark at the same moment I recognize Champ as he darts frantically in front of my car. In the yellow flood of headlights, I see the tension in his body as he spins in circles, jumping on the side of the car, letting out an endless raspy bark.

I open the door and Champ buries his face in my lap, whining and nuzzling into me, then barking again. He runs back to the thin dirt path that leads to the center of the dog park then runs back, nosing me with his snout, emitting a heartbreaking whine between barks. I get out of the car and stand at the end of the path, but I can't bear to walk it, despite Champ's pleas. Instead, I return to the car and call Cyrus. He answers on the second ring.

"It's Caroline. I'm at the dog park in Osprey. I need you to come." My voice cracks as I speak.

When I hang up the phone, I turn off the headlights and sit in the dark. I clench the steering wheel between my palms until my fingers ache. I bite my lower lip until I taste the tang of blood. Beside me, Champ's barks have turned to a steady whine. Finally, there is the sound of the siren.

Evvy arrives with Cyrus. She gets in the front seat with me while Cyrus and the other police officers follow Champ into the dog park with flashlights. She doesn't try to talk, only holds my hand. I expect it to take hours for them to find him in the night, but less than thirty minutes later they emerge. Cyrus approaches the car and his expression is grim.

"He's dead, isn't he?" I ask.

"I'm so sorry, Caroline," he says. Beside me Evvy inhales sharply.

"How?" I ask.

"He shot himself. It would have been over in an instant. He didn't suffer."

I swallow down the rage I'm choking on. He didn't suffer, Cyrus said. What about the pain that's accumulated over the years, this job that broke him down bit by bit, the daily toll of seeing people on the worst day of their lives? What about the suffering Jack has caused, for Layla Dresser and the people who loved her, but also for me and Connor, the suffering that is only just beginning?

I wait for the weight of what Cyrus has told me to descend, a pile of bricks hovering just above my head, but it doesn't fall, just hangs there suspended, swinging in the breeze. All I can think about is that I know he did it this way for me. He could have done it anywhere, but he did it out here, in an empty park at night, where I wouldn't have to find him when I got home. There will be no stains on the carpet for me to stumble upon each day.

"Why?" Evvy whispers. I shake my head, unable to explain. I hear their words, but can't react. I've gone numb, my whole body tingling with pins and needles. The truth will trickle out in the next hours and days. For the moment, I cannot bear to try to unravel this tragedy and figure out where it all went wrong. "You need to call Connor."

It is the name of our child that snaps the cord and brings the bricks down, pitching me forward into the grief. The sob escapes my throat like a bubble of air, followed by another and another. Evvy grips me tightly. I press my face into her shoulder and let her hold me as the tears finally come.

EVVY

Chapter Thirty-Nine

Cyrus and I drive Caroline home and we both go into the house with her. She looks like she's aged ten years. Her face is drawn, and her hair hangs limply around her face. She goes up to her bedroom while I put on water for tea.

I feel empty, drained by the events of the past few hours, by the way Caroline clutched at me as she sobbed. I stayed with her at the station where she gave a full report that Jack killed Layla Dresser. I am sick—with the knowledge of what Jack did, and how Ian almost took the blame for it. She spoke of Ian's connection to the woman, not an affair as I'd suspected, but an accomplice in bringing drugs to Great Rock. I don't know if I'm relieved that he's not cheating on me or horrified at what he's been doing. I haven't yet wrapped my mind around it, the cold and calculated way that Jack let Ian take the blame. Yet there's a part of me that suspects Jack did it for me as well, that he was offering me a chance at freedom that he knew I was unable to take on my own. More likely Jack let Ian take the fall because it was convenient, because he valued his own life, Caroline, and Connor more than me and my family, but it must say something that I feel no pleasure knowing that Ian will be released.

"Do you want to stay for a while?" I ask Cyrus. I want him to come home with me tonight, before Ian returns, but Gina is back and I can't leave Caroline anyway, much as I might want to. Not tonight.

"You need to be with Caroline," Cyrus says, and he's right, of course. "I'll call you tomorrow, okay?" He bends to kiss me, soft and gentle on the lips, and I know that Gina won't know about that kiss.

"When will Ian get out?"

"Tomorrow morning. Though there will probably be other charges filed." I should be happy. Ian is not a murderer. Only a batterer. And a drug dealer. "You don't have to stay with him, Evvy."

I give him a weak smile. "What about us?" If I knew Cyrus would take me back, I'd leave Ian in a breath.

Cyrus lets out a sigh. "I don't know. I love you, Ev, but there's just so much between us."

He's right. Even before Serena died, I swallowed him whole with my insatiable needs, my endless unhappiness. It rubbed off on everyone. But I'm different now, or at least I think I am. I don't know if it's age or medication or having a job I care about, but I feel stronger. Or maybe it has nothing to do with any of those things. Maybe it's because Cyrus and I are no longer together. Maybe we weakened each other with our love and our grief, too consumed by it to see anything else, picking at each other with our teeth, tearing each other apart bit by bit.

"It's okay," I say, even though it's not.

"It's not going to get any better. With Ian." The kettle starts to whistle and I go to turn off the burner.

"I can take care of myself," I say.

"Can you?"

Something inside me snaps. "Fuck you, Cyrus. I've been taking care of myself since you left. You might not like the way I do it, but I'll be just fine."

Cyrus nods unhappily, unfazed by my outburst. "Sure, Ev."

My hand shakes as I pour water into the cups. I'm furious with him, but I'm not sure why. "You left. You *left* me. I know I fell apart after Serena died, but I needed you, and you just walked out the door." I feel the sadness inside me all over again, but this isn't the depression that the pills keep at bay, this is a sadness so deep it will never be fixed. More than sadness though, I'm angry. He stands with his arms crossed over his chest, his eternal posture of self-defense. I shove him, and he sways slightly but doesn't even drop his arms. "After sixteen years of marriage, you just left. You didn't fight for me at all."

"God, Evvy, she died. Our baby girl died. You wouldn't even talk to me. You just shut down." He blinks back tears.

The secret presses at my throat, the dull ache that is always there. I don't know if I can go on living with it. "I took my eyes off the road," I say, so softly he has to tip his head to hear.

"What?"

"She was having one of her tantrums. She wanted me to stop for chips. You know what she was like when she got going. She was screaming and crying and kicking at me, and I turned around and I yelled at her. I *yelled* at her, Cyrus. And then the car hit us."

My legs buckle beneath me as if I've been kicked in the stomach, and I crouch on the floor, my body curled in on itself. Cyrus sits down beside me, his hand lightly on my back. I force myself to look at him. "It was my fault," I say.

"No, it wasn't."

"Don't you hear what I'm saying?" I wail. "I wasn't watching the road. The last time I ever spoke to her I was yelling at her. It was my fault."

I bury my face in the cloth of his coat and I cry; for everything we've lost—not just today, but all those years ago—for the child I loved imperfectly, whose absence looms so large that I can feel it in every corner of my body, a damp coldness in the center of my chest.

"It wasn't your fault, Evvy."

"Yes, it was!" I look at him, furious that he's not understanding, after all this time, after all these years of carrying this alone. "It was my fault."

"Then I forgive you," he says, and pulls me back against him. I sob into his coat and he clutches me as I shudder in his arms, but he doesn't let me go.

Ian is released the next morning. I drive to the jail to pick him up, parking the car and going inside this time. I wait on a hard, wooden bench and then he is there, wearing the same clothes he wore the day they brought him in. He looks different, though it's only been a few days. His hair is unruly, his skin pasty. When he sees me, he gives me a tight smile. I force myself to hug him and he smells different too, like hospital soap and sweat.

"Let's go home," I say, and take his hand. In the car he's quiet, and I'm glad for the prattle of the radio. He doesn't ask why I haven't been to visit, and while I don't know what I'll say, part of me wants to get the conversation out of the way. Instead I ask him if he wants anything special for dinner.

"I don't care. I just want to take a shower and go to bed," he says.

When we get home he does just that. I try calling Daisy to tell her what's happened, but her phone goes straight to voicemail and she hasn't responded to any of my texts. I keep myself busy preparing a dinner Ian will like, a pork loin and a nice bottle of wine. Over dinner I try to keep the conversation light, but it's nearly impossible given the events of the last few days. Ian finishes the last few bites of his potatoes and takes another sip of wine. I've only had one glass but he must be on his third by now. He pushes his plate away.

"So, did you actually think I killed her?" he asks. His voice is quiet, as if he's not sure he wants to hear my answer.

"Of course not. I knew you never would have done something like that."

"So why didn't you come?" He sounds like a little boy whose feelings have been hurt. I feel a wave of love for him and wish I could explain without making him feel worse. He looks better after his nap, the color back in his cheeks, more like himself.

"I'm sorry. I tried but I was scared."

"Scared of what?"

"Scared to see you there."

"I thought you were leaving me," he says softly.

"Oh, honey." I rise from my seat and go to sit in his lap. He buries his face in my chest. "I'm so sorry." I can't tell him I've wondered the same thing over the past few days.

"What have you been doing?" I ask after a moment.

He looks down at his empty plate, shamefaced. "I didn't think it was a big deal. Once or twice a month, Layla would take the boat over. She'd buy a sandwich, take the carton into the bathroom and fill it up, then leave the takeout container under a seat. I'd pick it up and bring it to Scott."

"But why? Why would you do that?" I ask. I think of Connor, wasted and hopeless, using drugs that Ian was supplying.

"We needed the money. Do you think Petunia's is paying the bills? Paying your mortgage?" He waves his hand at the house, the food, the electricity and heat, all of which I've let him take care of. I realize how complacent I've let myself get since Serena died, barely opening my eyes enough to see what I've let happen. "It seemed like easy money."

I nod, wanting to understand, even though I don't. "Why were you fighting with her?" I ask. I don't ask if he hit her—why he hit her—though this is what I'm wondering.

"She didn't want to do it anymore. She said this was her last trip. She was going to move down to Florida." Florida, a pink and green paradise made of plastic and concrete, a world away from Great Rock. I vaguely remember reading that this is where her mother lived, and I think about her, maybe for the first time, so excited that her daughter would be living nearby.

"Shh." I rest my hand against his cheek, trying to soothe him. "It doesn't matter now. Everyone knows you're innocent."

"They're going to arrest me again."

"But not for murder," I say, wondering how long the sentence is for what Ian has done.

"Those two, always thinking they're better than everyone else." I can taste the bitterness in his voice and feel the shift in his mood, from remorse and self-pity to anger and resentment. "They pinned it on me because I was an easy target."

"It was Jack. Cyrus had nothing to do with it."

"Why are you defending him?" Ian's grip around my upper arm tightens. "Why are you always on his side? Can't you ever just be on my side?" His breath smells like wine, only inches from my face.

"I am on your side. Of course I am."

"You're not though." He sounds so hurt, and I know he's right. I can never be only on his side, not if Cyrus is on the opposing one. "Was he here while I was gone? Were the two of you playing happy family while I was sitting in jail for something I didn't do?" His face darkens in anger, and he teeters just on this side of in control. I should lie, tell him I haven't seen Cyrus in weeks. That would be the smart thing to do, but I'm feeling reckless. I need to know what will happen, just how far he's willing to go. I don't need to tell him everything, just enough to test him.

"He came over to check on me. He was worried." Ian's face contorts into an ugly sneer.

"You slept with him, didn't you?" The disgust is all over his face. Just moments ago, I loved him, and already it's fading into fear and revulsion. I wonder if it's ever been love or just relief at not being alone. Somehow that doesn't seem so bad anymore. "You stupid slut."

Ian gets up from the table abruptly, and I scramble not to fall onto the floor. His hands are clenched in fists by his sides. I know I should be scared, and I am, but I feel free. I can't do this anymore. I won't.

"You need to leave." Try as I might, my voice still shakes.

"I'm not going anywhere, Evvy. Not until you tell me what the hell happened while I was gone." I shake my head and start to back out of the room. Ian lunges at me, grabbing me by the arm. His fingers sink into the thin skin. Tomorrow there will be a purple-tinged bracelet of bruises around my bicep. "Where do you think you're going?"

Something flares in me. For once the anger is stronger than the fear. "Let me go," I yell at him, louder than I've ever dared. He flinches, but still doesn't loosen his grasp.

Cyrus is right; Ian will never change. It is so little effort to take a life. You squeeze too tight, until there's no more air. A click of metal into your mouth. You take your eyes from the road for a second. *Poof.* How much longer till Ian kills me? It won't be tonight or tomorrow, but what about next month or next year?

"Let me go," I say again, yanking away, and this time he doesn't hold on.

"Calm down." He can see the change in me and now he's backpedalling. There's nowhere for him to go.

"You need to leave this house right now. You need to pack a bag and go to a hotel and then find another place to live. Because *this* is over." I tremble as I speak, but my voice is strong.

"Evvy, relax." He tries to smile, but I can see the fear and fury lurking at the corners. "Let's just both calm down."

I shake my head. "You want to hit me, don't you?"

"Stop it," he hisses.

"You do. I know you do. But I'm not going to stay quiet about it anymore. If you hit me now, I will drive myself to the police station. I'll show them the marks. I'll tell them about every single time you've ever laid a hand on me. If you hit me now, I will testify against you, pull up all of our bills and the financial statements for Petunia's." Ian swallows but doesn't speak. I'm not even sure if I'm bluffing, if this may be something I'm subpoenaed to do anyway, but I'm electric with adrenaline. I have never spoken to him like this. He's only had a few drinks, not enough to dull his judgment completely, and I see him calculating; how many times he's raised his hand to me, the other time the police already know about, what will happen if he dares to hit me now. He may have trouble controlling his temper, but he's not an idiot either.

His fists unfurl and he shoves his hands into his pockets, suddenly the picture of calm. "I get it, you're upset. I haven't always treated you the way you deserve. But that's over. I'm going to be better from now on. I promise." He tries to smile, but I see the falseness in it, the way his mouth doesn't open all the way.

I shake my head. "I'm done, Ian. I'm done." He gets it then. It registers in his eyes, that this is actually the end. His face crumples and his eyes grow damp.

"I'm sorry, Evvy. I'm so sorry. Please don't do this. I need you." He takes a step forward and reaches for my hand. The forgiveness rises up and I know how easy it would be to take it all back. We could go upstairs and make up, wash the whole week away in the safety of our bed. But this black cloud would always be between us, its cold fingers just waiting to grab me when I least expect it.

"It's over, Ian," I say again, and his fury is back with such a force that I wonder if the sadness was just an act.

"Like hell it's over," Ian snaps and grabs me again, his fingers clenching at my neck. I feel my throat closing in, the muscles contracting, my windpipe shrinking. He doesn't squeeze hard enough to completely cut off the flow of air, just enough to cause pain. Is this how Layla Dresser felt in the final moments before Jack snuffed out her life? I try to speak, and my voice comes out in a dry rasp.

"You could have killed her," I whisper. "You didn't, but you could have. You have it in you. And we both know it." He releases me abruptly. I've touched something, some secret knowledge about who he is, who he could be, at the soft and tender center. "Get out."

He backs away, his hands in front of him as if warding off an attack. "Okay, okay. I'll go, for tonight. We can talk tomorrow."

"Leave your key," I order.

His face contracts as if I've slapped him, but after a moment he reaches into his pants pocket and fishes out his keychain, removing the house key. He lays it flat on the counter. Tonight I'll remove the spare from where it rests under a beam on the front steps. Tomorrow I will pack his things and have him pick everything up while I'm at Caroline's. He has no claim to this house. The mortgage is in my name and Cyrus's. Ian writes me a check each month to cover his part, like a tenant. For a moment I think ahead to next month, the payment that I'll have to make on my own. March is still a slow month for catering, but I'll figure out a way to pay the bills alone. I have to, otherwise it will be me lying dead in the middle of the night—but instead of finding me on a beach, Daisy will find me on my own kitchen floor or in a tangle of bedsheets upstairs.

I stand with my back against the wall while Ian gathers his things. He gets a change of clothes from upstairs and I hold my phone in my hand, 911 already dialed, just waiting to press *send* in case his mood shifts again in his few minutes upstairs. He returns, shamefaced and subdued, carrying an overnight bag.

"I'll call you tomorrow, okay? We can't leave things like this." There is a desperate note in his voice that I ignore.

"Please go."

I lock the door behind him and watch his headlights until they reach the end of our street and then round the corner. I slip out into the cold black night and slide the spare key out of its hiding spot. It sits in my palm like a sliver of ice, and I hurry back inside and re-latch the door, sliding the deadbolt in place. I want to call Caroline to tell her what I've done, but it's not fair to burden her with my own drama right now. Tomorrow I have to go with her to the treatment center on the Cape and sit with her while she tells Connor his father is dead. She doesn't need my chaos on top of her own grief.

I call Cyrus instead. He answers on the second ring and I wonder if Gina is sitting beside him, both of them tucked in cozy on the couch before the glow of the wood stove.

"I kicked Ian out," I say without any preamble.

"Are you okay? Did he hurt you?"

It's the tenderness in his voice that brings forth the tears. I take a shaky breath and wipe them away with the palm of my hand. "I'm okay."

"Do you want me to come over?"

Yes. More than anything. But I know that my dependence on Cyrus is part of the problem, that as much as I love him and want him back, I can't make him or Ian the center of my life anymore. "I'm okay, but can you do me a favor? Can you send a patrol car to our street? Just to make sure he doesn't come back later. I don't think he will, but I won't sleep otherwise."

"Yeah, sure. I'll call the station right now. You're sure you don't want me to come over?" He lowers his voice, and I'm sure Gina's nearby. I wish I could hate her, but I know living with her is probably a lot easier than living with me. Though that doesn't mean Cyrus loves her.

"It's okay. Just send a car." I peer through the kitchen curtains to make sure Ian hasn't returned, but the street is empty, only my car in the driveway.

"You did the right thing, Ev. You don't need him." I wish I believed this, but I haven't lived alone for most of my life. It occurs to me that Caroline will be facing the same steep learning curve. "Call me if you need anything."

When I hang up, I go into the living room and sit by the window that looks down the street. After only fifteen minutes, I see a black cruiser slow and pass my house, then park on the corner, just a few houses down. I let out the breath I hadn't realized I was holding and go into the kitchen to try calling Daisy one more time.

DAISY
Chapter Forty

I hang up the phone and lean against the brick exterior of the restaurant. Todd is inside, eating his rare steak, pommes frites, and fried Brussels sprouts. The city is still covered in a thick layer of white, though the restaurant is full and the street bustles with people. My head spins—from the wine and the news from my mother. For a moment I think I might be sick, and I close my eyes and force myself to take deep breaths.

"Are you okay?"

I'd turned my phone on for the first time all day. I forgot my charger at home and Todd's didn't fit. To conserve the battery, I left the phone off, not checking texts or scanning social media every few minutes as I usually do. I didn't even miss it, too absorbed in being with Todd to want the rest of the world to intrude. Until I turned on my phone at dinner and saw the frantic calls and texts from my mother.

I open my eyes and Todd is there, his face furrowed in concern. I shiver in my thin sweater. "No. Not really."

"Who was that? What's wrong?"

I shake my head without speaking. How do I explain that Jack was a second father to me, that when my parents were going through their divorce, he'd pick me and Connor up every day after school, sometimes in his police cruiser? Jack taught me to make chili and cornbread, and for the months that I lived with them, I spent every Sunday watching football with him, something I didn't even do with my own father. When I turned twelve, Jack gave me a necklace with a silver starfish, and I still have it in my jewelry box. How do I tell him that the same man who brought home half a gallon of mint Oreo ice cream every Friday murdered a girl and let Ian take the blame, then stuck a gun in his mouth and blew his brains out? I can't tell Todd any of this, not yet, so I don't.

"Someone died. A good friend of our family." And then my legs give out, and I feel myself falling, down toward the icy sidewalk.

"Hey, hey, easy." Todd catches me before I hit the concrete. I press my face against his sweater as the sobs overtake me. I cling to him and he lets me, smoothing my hair with his hand. I think of Connor, detoxing alone in some treatment center, still unaware that the worst is yet to come. I think of Caroline, her husband dead and her son's future suspended in no man's land. My own mother, finally strong enough to kick Ian out, always terrified of being alone. I look through the picture window of the restaurant. Candles glitter on the tables and beautiful young people eat their grass-fed beef and organic roasted vegetables. It's another world, sparkly and full of promise. I want to go back, but I can't.

"I need to go home," I tell Todd.

CAROLINE
Chapter Forty-One
April

Spring on Great Rock is a thing to behold. Cautious flowers poke their heads through the ground, sniffing to see if winter is finally gone. The air smells of damp earth and sun. Purple crocuses line driveways, and daffodils fill front yards. Walking Champ one morning I pass a bush of forsythia, the yellow stalks so bright they nearly hurt my eyes. The leaves are back on the Japanese maple in our front yard, and I remember how Daisy and Connor used to sit in it when they were children, dangling from the spindly branches like monkeys.

In the springtime, the island wakes up. On Main Street in downtown Osprey, businesses reopen one by one, their walls repainted, their interiors redone. The carousel is open again, and on weekend nights the music echoes on the street, the twangy notes of the organ carrying out onto the water. Children tug their mothers' hands, eager to climb onto their favorite horse and try to catch the brass ring. Their pockets bulge with quarters. There will always be another chance.

I sit on the open deck of the Great Rock Ferry and tilt my face to the sky, feeling the sun on my skin. Jack has been dead for six weeks. Since that bleak February night, my kitchen has been filled with a steady stream of women bearing food. Lasagna, pots of chicken soup, enchiladas, green bean casseroles, spinach quiches, and baskets of muffins cover the counters and fill the freezer, an endless supply of food and goodwill. Women I hardly know volunteer their husbands for home repair. The postmaster leaves yellow pickup slips in my box, and each week I retrieve an armful of condolence cards. I read the words of the women on this island, platitudes written in careful script. *Time will heal. May God be with you. We're thinking of you in your time of need.* The newspaper has been filled with letters to the editor about what Jack did, but also about the opioid crisis on Great Rock. I read them all and think of Connor and Layla.

I have heard people speak of the strength of this community, but the kindness is unexpected. This desolate strip of land I've wanted to escape for so long is suddenly a place filled with people who care about my loss, who clutch my hands and say the right things and the wrong things, but *they try*, they try to show that they care. Their caring has nearly knocked me over, and though it is not enough, will never be enough, I'm surprised to realize that it has brought some comfort.

It doesn't surprise Evvy. She just shrugs her shoulders and nods when I point at the day's offering, a blueberry pie or loaf of homemade bread. "That's just Great Rock," she says. "That's the island." Evvy has lived here her whole life and the strength of ordinary people coming together to offer support is just as much a part of the island as the papery beach grass or the lady-slipper shells that cover Osprey Beach. It's just the way Great Rock is.

Evvy comes over nearly every day and picks at whatever dish has been brought by. I don't eat much myself, but she fixes me a plate anyway and makes me have a few bites. We're like two old widows shuffling around my kitchen, talking occasionally, mostly just sitting in a companionable silence or watching TV. Though I'm the only one who's actually a widow. She doesn't talk about him often, but I know she's seeing Cyrus again. He moved out of

Gina's house and took over the Feldmans' sublet. I have a feeling it's only a matter of months before he moves back in with her. Then again, Evvy is full of surprises.

Charges have been brought against Ian, but he's out on bail, waiting for the slow grind of the legal system to determine his fate. Through some miraculous feat of the ferry union, he's still working in the ticketing office. I saw him this morning when I bought my ferry ticket, and though I stepped into another line, we met eyes and nodded at each other.

Daisy is still at home, but she's transferring her credits to UMass Boston after the summer. Todd has said she can move in with him, and though I worry about her becoming financially dependent on a boy she's known for such a short period of time, I can't deny the look of love on both their faces when they're together.

The foghorn lets out its deep blare, and I sip my coffee. It's the first boat of the day, the six-fifteen, and I could have taken a later one, but I chose this one because I knew it would be the least crowded. Less chance of bumping into anyone. Old habits die hard, and I'll never be fully comfortable with the way the most personal moments can be made public on an island as small as ours. Today I will pick Connor up at rehab, and I don't feel like telling anyone where I'm going or mustering up the energy to lie. He's been there for the recommended thirty days, plus the two more weeks they added after I told him his father was dead. As if two weeks will be enough for him to recover from that. The moment comes back to me in the dark hours of the night, the cataclysmic anguish that altered his face and tore his body down, the sound of his cries like nothing I'd ever heard before. Deep body-shaking sobs filled with rage and guilt and the physical pain of Jack's absence. I know that pain. It's a dull ache behind my breastbone, something rotten in the center of my belly that causes my intestines to twist upon each other, coiling together like a restless snake.

Scott Lambert is in the island jail awaiting his trial for drug dealing. Moby Dick's has closed, and I hear a sushi restaurant will be opening up this summer. Life on Great Rock marches on.

Connor and I will miss spring on the island this year. When I pick him up from the rehab center, we'll drive south to Alexandria, Virginia to where my sister Shana lives. She has already found an outpatient center where Connor will go for the next few months while I figure out where to go from here. Cyrus will look after the house while I'm gone and perhaps I'll decide to sell it. I've always loved the redbrick downtown of Alexandria, with its vibrant shops and restaurants and cobblestone streets. Maybe I'll stay, find an apartment of my own and a job in a library, or maybe doing something else entirely.

And yet.

And yet I know Great Rock will call me back. Evvy and Cyrus, the gaggle of retirees with their morning coffee and newspapers, the circle of women with pressed hands and words of comfort, the acquaintances I bump into at the grocery store, the people I've known for over twenty years whose presence I've taken for granted. The purple sky at sunset on the beach, the ever-present smell of salt and fish in the air. Somehow, without my even realizing it, Great Rock has seeped into my skin and taken root in my heart.

I'm afraid to see Connor. I'm afraid of his grief and his chances of relapse. In my purse I have a prescription for Narcan, the drug that will reverse an overdose, though I pray I'll never have to use it. I pray this is a new beginning for Connor, not a stop along the long path of addiction, but I'm no fool, not anymore. I've read enough to know how many people use again as soon as they get out.

And yet.

And yet I can't wait to see him. I want to hold Connor in my arms and take him away from all of the bad things in our lives, even if just for a few months. I want to imagine that we can find our way through the mire that has pulled us down, the tangled vines of death and disease that keep us struggling in place. I want to believe that we can find the other side and emerge, if not whole, if not healthy, not completely broken, either. I want to believe that life is possible for us both.

The foghorn bleats again and the announcement comes over the loudspeaker, reminding passengers to make their way to their cars. The sun is up now and the sky is a pale yellow. Boats bob in the harbor. Across the sound, Great Rock is just a spit of land, a scrap of green and tan. No one would know the life that beats inside. No one would know how full such an empty place can be.

I head downstairs and wait my turn to disembark. I wave to the ferry attendant as I creep from the belly of the boat and out into the bright morning. I feel Great Rock pulsing behind me, but I keep my eyes on the road and don't look back.

A LETTER FROM EMILY

Dear Reader,

I want to say a huge thank you for choosing to read *Everybody Lies*. If you did enjoy it, and want to keep up to date with all my latest releases, just sign up at the following link. Your email address will never be shared and you can unsubscribe at any time.

www.bookouture.com/emily-cavanagh

I hope you loved *Everybody Lies* and if you did I would be very grateful if you could write a review. I'd love to hear what you think, and it makes such a difference helping new readers to discover one of my books for the first time.

I love hearing from my readers—you can get in touch on my Facebook page, through Twitter, Goodreads or my website.

Thanks,
Emily Cavanagh

emilymcavanagh77

@emilymcavanagh

emilycavanaghauthor

emilycavanaghauthor.com

ACKNOWLEDGMENTS

This novel was started at a time when people were just beginning to talk about opioid abuse. During this period, there were several fatal overdoses on the small island where I live, a few of them by people I'd once known, though none of them close to me. Suddenly, everywhere I looked—in the local and national papers, on the news, in movies and books—people were talking about addiction and pulling the curtain back on an issue that hadn't been so openly discussed before. I wanted to write a story about the ripple effects of addiction and the shame and denial that is so often associated with it, particularly within the context of a small community. Any time a writer takes on a project with which they don't have first-hand experience, there is always the worry of not getting it right. This is a work of fiction, but I hope I have done justice to the real people, mothers and fathers, sons and daughters, whose lives have been impacted by addiction and its far-reaching effects. Many books, films, and podcasts informed my writing, most notably *Heroin: Cape Cod, USA* and *Dopesick*.

Thank you to my early readers: Mathea Morais and Sarah Smith for astute editorial guidance, insights into character development and island life, and our much loved if sporadic writing group; an extra shout-out to Sarah for our ongoing writing retreats, including the last few in your Fairhaven home which provided further inspiration; to my parents, Pam and Tom Cavanagh, for reading both eagerly and critically; to my aunt, Lynda Bernard, for her boundless generosity and support; to Scott Ogden, for reading from the perspective of an island police officer; to Hilary, Isadora, and Ciarda Fitzgerald, my family in Ireland, for their generosity and long-distance encouragement, and for always keeping me supplied with Boost bars and Taytos.

A huge thank you to my editor, Cara Chimirri, for her strong editorial guidance, her excitement over this novel, and her steady hand in shaping it; to the brilliant team at Bookouture for embracing me into the fold and making me feel welcome from day one. To my agent, Marlene Stringer, for being a champion of my writing, for her unflagging wisdom and professionalism, and for encouraging me to take a leap of faith.

Thank you to my group of Vineyard ladies: Holly Thomas, Anna Cotton, Moira Silva, and Skye Sonneborn, for making our real-life Great Rock such a wonderful place to live, even in the middle of winter.

To Marya Cohen, for over thirty years of friendship and support and for always making me laugh, even when nothing is funny.

To Amelia Angella, for a lifetime of friendship and support.

To Reuben Fitzgerald: for the idea that became the first seed of this book and for believing that I could write this story. And to Oliva and Nevah, for everything, always.